SON OF THE ROCK

BY

VIOLETTE L. MEIER

Sequel to Angel Crush

VIORI PUBLISHING
vioripublishing.com
Atlanta, GA

ISBN: 978-0-9887805-9-0

Printed in the United States of America

Cover Designed by En El Publishing

Dedicated to:

...my wonderful husband, Ari. Thank you for always supporting, encouraging, and believing in me. I love you more than you can ever imagine.

...my children. God has blessed me with you all and I am forever grateful to have all of you in my life. I love each and every one of you so very much. You allow me to be a perpetual optimist because the look in your eyes inspire me to dream bigger each day. I dream so that you will never ever forget to dream. Keep pushing forward and promise me you will never stop.

...my family. I have the greatest mother, aunt, and siblings in the entire universe. Thank you for all that you are and all that you do.

...my friends. Thanks for all your support and reassurance! You guys are great!

Acknowledgements:

A special thank you to my cousin Charles Tucker for your generosity and support; you are a blessing.

A special thank you to all who support my books and believe in my dreams!

1

Babies are such wonderful creatures. They seem to love unconditionally as soon as their eyes open to the world. Sadie thought as she forced herself to smile. She looked down at her six month old son who smiled gleefully up at her. Khalid's smile was a stinging balm to her grieving heart. Her best friend and father, Mr. Covington, dropped dead suddenly months before, and it seemed as if the world was still in a strange melancholy place. So many changes had taken place; so many changes good and bad. She had been able to deal with many of them, but the death of her father weighed on her heavily. Looking down at her smiling baby boy, anxiety seized her chest. She couldn't help but to think her father's death was Khalid's fault. Sadie felt horrible for feeling that way, but there was something ominous about the baby she held in her arms. Every time Khalid smiled at her, an aching chill traveled down her back.

Sometimes the smell of myrrh would wake her up in the middle of the night and Khalid would be standing up in his crib, holding on to nothing, and needing absolutely no support, giggling at the corner of the wall. Standing! *What six month old stands?* Sadie asked herself. Not only could he stand on his own, but sometimes when she readied him for his morning feeding, the bottom of his feet would be dirty as if he had been walking around outside. The soles of his little feet would be black as tar and sometimes smudged with soil. Little footprints decorated the sheets in dusty patterns. Frightened and frantic, Sadie would question her husband James and her mother, Mrs. Covington, about it, and she was answered with perplexed eyes and lifted shoulders.

The dirty feet were only one of many strange things. Khalid seemed to be perpetually enveloped in an eerie energy. There were countless times when Sadie woke up in the middle of the night because she heard conversation in the baby's room. One of the voices unmistakably matched the sounds of Khalid's coos but the language was mature and articulate as if Khalid was already a master of the English language. The other voice was horribly familiar. It had the sound of many waters; echoing with a quiet roar laced within each syllable. Sadie would jump out of her bed and rush into Khalid's room only to find Khalid standing in his bed smiling so wide that his face stretched beyond human proportion. His dark eyes reflected the nightlight and the juiciness of his teething gums glimmered wet and dangerous.

Sadie assumed that post-partum stress mixed with her imagination was the culprit not her child and not the creature that spawned him. All of her ill feelings were suppressed within a tiny little box in her mind, and she tried hard to make life normal but there was no pretending that Khalid's origins were not supernatural. The child was angelic; literally. Sadie looked down into Khalid's eyes and the fiery eyes of his true father shined through his newborn sockets. Memories of terror and seduction racked her mind. She placed the baby in his crib and fled the room.

TWO YEARS LATER

It was noon when Sadie felt the first labor pain. She was awakened from her nap by a jolt of pain shooting from her lower back to her pelvis. She opened her eyes and her mouth at the same time letting out a deep moan. Her child was not due for another two weeks. Sadie assumed she was having false labor until the next pain hit so hard that she felt her backbone vibrate. Her eyes spied her cell phone on the nightstand. As soon as she sat up, her water broke; soaking the mattress beneath her. At first she thought she had urinated, but the liquid splashed out like a bucket was being emptied.

"James," Sadie called, squeezing her eyes tight; trying to control the pain. The pain came again quickly, snatching her breath from her lungs. "Jame…" she began but stopped mid-pronunciation; remembering that James was at work, and that her mother was at the grocery store. Khalid was down for his nap. She was alone and the pains were coming so fast that she could hardly catch her breath. Sadie pulled herself upon her knees and removed her soiled undergarments. She tossed them to the side and kicked the wet duvet off of the bed.

"Ahhhhhh," she moaned, gripping the sheets and breathing deeply. Pressure from within her pressed hard against her lower pelvis. The pain came again harder and faster; harder and faster; harder and faster until she felt her body open beneath her.

"Ahhhh," she wailed, tears falling fast. Sadie got on all fours. The pressure pressed harder. She leaned backwards and placed her hands between her legs in time to grip the head of a human emerging into the world. Sadie pulled the slimy head down and allowed the rest of the child's body to fall onto the bed. Sadie rolled onto her side, and pulled the blood speckled baby close to her chest, patting his back until he coughed. She stuck her finger in his mouth to clean away any excess goop. Sadie reached for a gift box sitting on her nightstand. James had given her a pair of amethyst earrings in a beautifully wrapped box just last week. The occasion was that he loved her. Sadie pulled the ribbon off of the box and tied it around the umbilical cord. With her crying baby cuddled in one arm, the other armed fished in her nightstand drawer for scissors. She found them and cut the cord. She laid her baby on her belly as she leaned back and pushed the afterbirth out of her body onto the bed. When the bloody mess was expelled, Sadie scrambled to her feet. She balled the sheet up on the bed, and staggered to the bathroom; blood covering her hands and blood running down her legs leaving footprints on her white carpet. Dragging one foot before the other, she turned on the bathroom sink. Sadie placed her baby boy into the sink and began to bathe him.

"You shall be called Uriel," she cried as she washed him. He looked up at her with eyes that looked like they housed an old soul; eyes that looked like they understood the mysteries of the universe; eyes that had beheld the divine.

"Mommy," Sadie heard a small voice call from behind her. She turned around to see her two year old son Khalid staring at her with a blank face; his small body as stiff as a board. She wondered how much he had seen; if he had been traumatized. All of a sudden she was aware of her bloody gown; her gooey legs; her teary eyes.

Khalid pointed to the newborn as if he was oblivious to his mother's appearance. His eyes were darker than usual; his face more serious than a child his age should ever look. He whispered, "Don't let him kill me."

"Kill you?" Sadie asked dumbfounded. "Why would you say that?"

"Say what?" Mrs. Covington asked as she walked into Sadie's open bedroom door. She picked up Khalid and put him on her hip. The bloody carpet alarmed her.

"Where are you Sadie?" she asked before she looked up and saw Sadie standing in her bathroom doorway with a newborn in her hand. Mrs. Covington was taken aback. She put Khalid down and rushed over to Sadie.

"What happened here?" Mrs. Covington asked rhetorically. "Are you okay?"

"Yes," Sadie responded weakly. She tottered out of the bathroom. Her mother grabbed her arm and escorted her to the bed. Mrs. Covington went into the bathroom and gathered warm wash cloths and towels. She wrapped the newborn and laid him on the bed, then she gave her daughter a sponge bath from head to toe. Mrs. Covington dressed Sadie.

"Where is your hospital bag?" Mrs. Covington asked.

"In the closet," Sadie said, pointing to her closet door.

Mrs. Covington grabbed the bag and opened it. She pulled out baby clothes and clothed her grandson.

"I'll clean up this mess when I get back. I have to get you and the baby to the hospital," Mrs. Covington said as she pulled Sadie up, strapped the newborn in his car seat and picked it up with one hand, and picked Khalid up with the other. "Let's go!" Mrs. Covington yelled. "Call James on the way to the hospital. Right now, I have to make sure all of my babies are okay."

SIX YEARS LATER

"Great job Khalid! You are such a smart boy," Mrs. Anderson gushed over her star student. It seemed as if the boy's intellect was unlimited. He was only eight years old and he was the star of the fifth grade. Gifted was too simple of a word to call him. It seemed that he was beyond genius; a mastermind and the boy knew it. His test scores indicated that he was on a ninth grade level, but his parents did not want him to miss being around children his age; so they only allowed him to be moved two grade levels up and allowed him to participate in academically advanced extracurricular programs.

"Thank you Mrs. Anderson. I do my best," Khalid smiled as he walked away from the large classroom computer screen and made his way back to his desk with his head held high, and a confident grin on his face.

Khalid Tucker was tall for his age. He was already four feet ten inches tall and he seemed wise beyond his years. Very handsome he was, caramel skin, thick hair, heavily lashed eyes, and an intoxicating smile. It was difficult to believe that an eight year old could possess such confidence and knowledge.

Khalid was a people magnet. Everyone who knew him loved him. Wit and charm adorned him like fine jewelry. It seemed as if he could talk anyone into anything. Persuasion was as natural to him as breathing. Once he talked a bully into letting a girl slap him in front of the whole cafeteria. The boy stumped away angry and confused because he could not understand how he let a nerdy eight year old talk him out of taking a girl's lunch money, and into allowing her to slap him silly. That was the power of Khalid. Kids and adults alike were often bewildered at how Khalid convinced them to do things they would not normally consider doing. He made offers that were hard to refuse. Every word he spoke was laced with temptation. Like the serpent in Eden, Khalid was the craftiest among creatures.

Mrs. Anderson smiled a great toothy smile as she folded her wrinkled pink hands, and admired Khalid through her smudged cat eye glasses.

"The class could learn a lot from Khalid. He always knows the correct answers unlike many of you," she scolded. "Hard work and dedication is very rewarding."

Evadne Reid frowned and mumbled something under her breath. It irked her how Mrs. Anderson always fawned over Khalid. No one cared about his science awards or reading achievements or math prowess. Evadne liked Khalid, but she, like all the other fifth graders she knew, recognized him as nothing more than a baby nerd. Although he was just as tall or taller as everyone two years his senior, he was still just an eight year old. The only thing that kept him from being known as a complete infantile geek was his popularity. Evadne often wondered why everyone was so enthralled by him. To her, Khalid was simply sufferable.

"Is there something that you want to share with the class Evadne?" Mrs. Anderson frowned as she eyeballed Evadne. The sight of the child made her head hurt.

Evadne ran her fingers through her wild kinky hair, and shook her head answering no.

"I am positive that I heard you mumble," Mrs. Anderson crossed her arms and peered over her outdated eyewear; her beady blue eyes fierce. Her eyewear wasn't the only thing that was outdated. She wore an awful knitted sweater that looked like it had survived two world wars, and silly black and white saddle shoes.

Evadne rolled her eyes, and let them fall upon Khalid's smiling face. It was obvious he was smitten by her onyx skin and untamable hair. Often she caught him staring at her with a cheesy smile on his face. She had to admit that he was pretty cute, but eating a bug seemed more flattering to Evadne than entertaining the pining of a pre-tween twerp.

"Are you sure you have nothing to say?" Mrs. Anderson prodded. Her eyes could not hide her aversion for Evadne. Everything about the girl caused Mrs. Anderson alarm. She could not stand the opinionated wild child, and she wanted nothing more than to send her out of her classroom. Evadne had been a thorn in Mrs. Anderson's side since the first day of school. Evadne was always difficult and controversial. For Black history month, her hero was Nat Turner. Evadne talked about the slaying of slave masters as a holy cleansing while looking directly into Mrs. Anderson's eyes the entire time. Around Columbus Day, Evadne reminded Mrs. Anderson how Africans discovered America hundreds of years before Columbus was even born. Around Thanksgiving time, Evadne insisted that the Native Americans should've killed all the English settlers as soon as their feet touched the shore.

Mrs. Anderson frequently imagined taking her knitting needles and driving holes through the girl's mouth, so Mrs. Anderson could lace it shut with the thickest yarn she could find. Mrs. Anderson would even imagine tying the yarn into a neat little bow at the end of Evadne's mouth just to show she had no hard feelings.

"No! If I had something to say, I would say it!" Evadne snapped and crossed her arms. "Why can't you just leave me alone? I'm not starting with you today."

Mrs. Anderson bolted over to Evadne's desk like a giant spring atop her chair popped her across the room, and pulled the girl up by her arm.

"I will not tolerate your disrespectful tone!" The howling teacher scolded as she shook the dangling child. "You will not talk to me that way!"

"Let me go!" Evadne squirmed. "I didn't do nothin'!"

"You're always doing something!" Mrs. Anderson croaked as her grip grew tighter around the girl's arm. "I want you out of my classroom right..." Mrs. Anderson's words died midsentence as Khalid got up from his seat and locked eyes with her.

Mrs. Anderson dropped the struggling Evadne causing the child to plop hard on the floor. Khalid's gaze paralyzed Mrs. Anderson as the whites of his eyes turned the deepest pitch. His pupils spun like endless black holes sucking the life force out of the wrinkled pink teacher. Mrs. Anderson fell to the floor clutching her chest like a purse holding a million dollars.

"Hit the call button!" Khalid yelled as he rushed to his teacher's side. "I think she's having a heart attack!" He grabbed Mrs. Anderson's hand. Tears rolled down the sides of her wrinkled face as her lipless mouth ripped back in terror.

"Hurry!" Khalid yelled as he looked down at the teacher. His eyes again flashed black causing the old woman to gasp for her last breath. "Hold on Mrs. Anderson, we will get you help," he said unconvincingly. "Everything will be okay."

A student quickly hit the call button and alerted the office to the emergency. The class sat quietly in awe of their befallen instructor as Khalid held her limp hand.

Evadne remained on the floor, full of fear and confusion, trying hard to gather her discombobulated thoughts and reconcile with her overactive imagination. She looked at Khalid's innocent face; his big brown eyes; his concerned crinkled brow. Moments before, his face was sinister; his eyes were bottomless pits; his brows were pointing arrows. *How could this be?*

It had been a long day. Sadie was very glad that it was over. She drove slowly down the quiet suburban street, and turned into a driveway where it read "Tucker" on the bright purple mailbox just above the house number. When the car came to a stop, she slowly climbed out and managed to drag her tired bones to the front door and open it.

Sometimes it seemed strange how much her life had changed. Sadie and James had been happily married for a little over eight years, and they were blessed with two healthy boys. Her metallic silver hair had dulled into a sparkling gray which was unable to be dyed; yet it didn't add much age to her youthful face. She left her downtown Atlanta apartment for the quiet comforts of the suburbs. She and James bought a large family home to accommodate her mother. Sadie felt that there was no reason for Mrs. Covington, Mama C, to remain in Florida all alone. Sadie's father and her best friend, whom her family and friends affectionately called Pappa C with two p's because he said that it was pronounced like *pop pa* and object of her adoration, was deceased.

The thought of Carlos Covington instantly made her heart hurt. His death haunted her day and night. Although he died of a heart attack, somehow she felt that her choosing to bring Khalid into the world had aided in her father's death. The last time thoughts of him came frequently was when she was carrying her youngest son. Her father came to her in her dreams several times telling her to name her second son Uriel Harvir. Sadie loved the first name but struggled with the middle name.

Sadie was not a religious woman, and frankly had a bone to pick with God for allowing Turiel to come into her life, so it was very irritating that the Uriel Harvir meant "my light is YWYH (God)" and "warrior of God." Nonetheless, in order to keep her father from haunting her sleep, she named the child as she was instructed.

Lately thoughts of her father permeated her mind on a constant basis. Sometimes she would wake up in the middle of the night sensing him near her, and sometimes the smell of his cologne would linger in the air when she was alone. Sadie ignored these frequent reminders of him, and chalked them up to missing her father. However, with every feeling of her father's presence, uncomfortable memories of Khalid would surface.

Years had passed since she had heard from her best friend Sky. The last time Sadie talked to Sky, Sky and Forrest were married and enjoying life in New York. Sadie heard through the grapevine that they had three gorgeous children all named after planets: Jupiter, Venus, and Earth. Sadie smiled at the thought. It wasn't at all surprising that Sky's children would be higher than the heavens.

"So many changes," Sadie mumbled and continued to reflect. Her recreational therapy job with nuns escalated into her own business which managed recreational therapy for three convents, and three employees of her own. She was the mother of two children: a child prodigy who was the manifestation of earthly flesh and celestial lust, and an abnormally strong little boy with the sweetest disposition she had ever encountered.

It had been eight years since Turiel had visited her. The thought of the ungodly angel, whose name ironically means rock of God, made her stomach queasy. Vomit threatened to reach her lips but it receded back into her churning belly.

Sadie had not thought of Turiel in ages. She had been able to lock him into the dim corners of her memories; but, for the past few days, the demon seemed to have broken through her chains of forgetfulness. The thought of his burning lips made her lips sting as if a hundred bees were perched upon them. Memories of piercing light invading her sacred parts, and the potent funk of myrrh filled her with desire and dread. Just a day ago, Sadie awoke to the slight smell of myrrh and almost had an aneurism.

Sadie often wondered why the angel chose her. What was it about her? Why her out of all the billions of women in the world? Was she the only one or was she one among many who fell victim to the angel's passion?

"Hey baby," James said as his wife walked through the front door. Mrs. Covington sat on the couch next to him, and watched Sadie as she shuffled through the door. He put down the TV remote and hurried over to his wife. Quickly, James grabbed her attaché case and closed the door behind her.

"How was your day?" James asked.

"Long," Sadie whined. "I'm just glad it's over." She was thankful that James interrupted her thoughts of Turiel. Her memories were just on the brink of taking her into a state of panic.

"Well, you're home now. Relax yo'self and take yo' shoes off," James said as he kissed her gently on the mouth, and gave her three quick pecks on the neck. "Khalid! Uriel!" James called to the back of the house.

"Yes Dad," Khalid answered quickly, his voice echoing from upstairs.

"I'm coming Daddy," Uriel announced as he ran into the living room. He held out his arms to hug his mother and gave her a juicy kiss on the lips. Sadie smiled and pinched his chubby cheeks. He was a beautiful child; the spitting image of his father, with beautiful black skin and a knee weakening smile.

"Khalid, come kiss yo' mama and bring her a glass of sweet tea mixed wit' lemonade," James requested as his other son ran into the living room and threw his arms around his mother.

Sadie relished Khalid's tender kiss on her cheek and took a seat next to her mother. The boy hurried into the kitchen to retrieve his mother's sweet drink. He brought it to her and plopped between her and his brother. Uriel frowned and began to pout. Sadie gently sat him on her other side and kissed his cheek. James sat on the other side of Uriel and picked the TV remote back up.

"How was your day at school boys?" Sadie asked as she sipped her tea-monade. It was sweet just like she liked it. It was so sweet that it should give instant diabetes with each sip. She put the glass down and placed her nylon covered legs on the table.

"School was okay. We did math and painted in art class," Uriel answered. "I made a picture for you, Mommy. We'll be able to bring them home tomorrow."

"That's so sweet Uriel. I can't wait to see it. I'm going to frame it and take it to work." Sadie was very proud of her first grader. Uriel was always so thoughtful, and took pride in doing his best in school because he knew it pleased her. Bringing his mother his progress reports was a source of great joy to him; although, his grades were not always the highest.

Uriel smiled a great big smile and said, "God told me to paint it."

Discomfort filled Sadie. It unnerved her how much Uriel talked about God. She and Mrs. Covington were not staunch unbelievers, but they had no dealings with the divine. James, while not as annoyed by God as they were, never talked about spiritual matters. Nevertheless, Uriel said his prayers every night. He blessed every meal before he ate it. Ironically, he recited scripture as easy as the alphabet, although they family did not own a Bible. Uriel spoke often about God speaking to him through vivid dreams. Sometimes he claimed that he heard the voice of God as clear and crisp as any other voice. Sadie sometimes worried about his lucidity, but she took heart in knowing that he was a happy and healthy child. As long as he behaved normally, she wouldn't worry about it. Who was she to discount his visions? Stranger things had happened to her. As long as Turiel wasn't communicating with Uriel, she was just fine. Sadie had questioned the boy several times and Uriel confirmed that he had never had an encounter with the rogue angel.

"How about your day Khalid?" Sadie asked as she took another sip of her tea-monade and kicked her shoes off. Uriel helped pull the heels from her feet. She smiled at his sweetness.

"Today was a cool day at school. So much happened! I made an A on my math test. The posters for the 5th grade dance got plastered all over the hallways. I want to ask this pretty girl in my class to the dance. I hope she'll say yes." Khalid paused and smiled. "Oh yeah, Mrs. Anderson died. I made the soccer team and there was a fight on the school bus," Khalid answered. "You should have seen the fight Mom. I laughed so hard. A boy named Dreek tried to look under a girl's skirt and she kicked him in the face!" Khalid laughed as he leaned back, and kissed his grandmother on the cheek causing her to blush, and then looked back over to his mother. "Other than that, it was the same old thing." He lifted his mother's arm and cuddled up beneath it.

"Mrs. Anderson died?" Sadie asked in complete shock. "James, did you know about this?" She turned to him; wrinkling her forehead.

"Not 'til now," James answered; turning down the TV and furrowing his brow. The shows on his DVR would have to wait.

"Did you know Mom?" Sadie asked as she turned to face her mother.

Mrs. Covington shook her head no, and lifted her shoulders. She rubbed Khalid's back and ran her hand over his head. She asked him, "Are you okay baby?"

"Yes grandma," he replied.

"How did she die?" Sadie inquired, a bit disturbed by Khalid's calm. Mrs. Anderson was supposed to be his favorite teacher, and Khalid didn't seem the least bit bothered. He sat between Sadie and her mother as happy as a picnic basket. "How did you hear about her death?"

"I didn't hear about it. I saw her die," Khalid said. He grabbed Sadie's glass off of the table and asked, "Ma, can I have a sip?"

"Sure baby," Sadie's brows wrinkled. "Tell me what happened."

"Mrs. Anderson was fussing at my friend Evadne. She's the one I want to take to the dance." Khalid said with a smile. "She's so pretty Mom. I can't wait…"

"Khalid, get back on subject!" Sadie warned.

Khalid sighed. Talking about Evadne was way more interesting than talking about Mrs. Anderson. Too bad his mother didn't second that notion.

"Mrs. Anderson was fussing and then she dropped to the floor. She hit the ground quick and hard. I think she had a heart attack. Everyone was all scared, so I took charge and told the class to notify the front office. Then, an ambulance came and got her," Khalid said nonchalantly as he turned to watch TV. "Dad, did you record any of my shows?"

James looked at Sadie speechless.

"Aren't you a little sad?" Sadie asked. The coldness of her son was disconcerting. Maybe he didn't understand death, but that was hard for her to believe because he was so intellectually advanced that he seemed to understand a multitude of complex issues. Why would death not be one of them?

"Not really. She was being really mean to Evadne and I didn't like it, so Mrs. Anderson got what she deserved," Khalid retorted.

Sadie grabbed Khalid's arm and spun him around to face her. A look of surprise and confusion filled Khalid's eyes. Sadie pulled him close and scolded, "No one has the right to say who deserves to live and who deserves to die! That is cruel and disrespectful. I taught you better. Where is your compassion? I thought Mrs. Anderson was your favorite teacher?"

"She was. Now she's not," Khalid yanked away. His eyes darkened for a millisecond.

Sadie's heart pounded within her chest. She was unsure of what she saw.

James stood up and grabbed the boy. James yelled, "Apologize to yo' mama and go straight to yo' room. I'll talk to you later!"

Khalid frowned at his father and turned to his mother. Anger filled him. He didn't like to be grabbed, but he disliked a spanking from James even more.

"I'm sorry Mama," he mumbled and slowly left the living room.

Sadie watched him disappear from the room. Her heart pounded within her. A feeling of dread slowly eased its way into her bones. Her son's inky eyes confirmed that somehow Mrs. Anderson's death wasn't just fate.

Dinner was delicious. Mrs. Covington cooked an old fashion southern supper. She made fried chicken, cream potatoes, green beans, fried okra, buttered rolls, and sweet tea. Mrs. Covington cooked every Monday and Thursday night and this Thursday, the dinner was as delectable as usual. The family loved when Mrs. Covington cooked because on the other nights Sadie only cooked healthy meals. Although they were good too, the family liked the nights when they could eat fried foods and plenty of bread.

The family ate their fill and sat around the dinner table engaged in conversation.

"Are you ready for graduation?" Mrs. Covington asked her grandson.

Khalid nodded yes. He couldn't wait to go to middle school. Elementary children were a supreme bore to him. The simple mindedness of children annoyed him. What he really desired was to go straight into the world, but Khalid knew that timing was everything and the proper thing to do was to let things run their course. His time would come soon enough. Khalid leaned back in his chair and drank the rest of his sweet tea.

"You're turning into such little a man right before my eyes," Mrs. Covington cooed as she tickled her grandson's chin. "Are you sure you're going to be okay in a sea of big kids?"

Khalid nodded and smiled nonchalantly.

Sadie watched him carefully, still perturbed by his lack of compassion concerning his teacher's death. To her, it was odd for a child to be so cold hearted and unsympathetic, but if she had to be honest with herself; Khalid had always been that way. He never showed very much compassion. Last year, when his dog got hit by a car, Khalid watched quietly from the sidewalk as Uriel cried like a baby. Later, Khalid talked endlessly about how the dog's blood made interesting patterns on the asphalt. He didn't seem at all saddened by his best friend's death.

When Sadie talked about her father, Khalid always seemed very disinterested. He was awfully indifferent to his grandfather's memory, and often tried to change the subject when Mr. Covington's name came up. Khalid once even replied, "Let the dead worry about the dead!" after over hearing Sadie and her mother reminiscing about how Mr. Covington was always so protective and attentive.

Sadie also recalled Khalid telling her of his reoccurring dreams about being a great warrior, and how he celebrated being bathed in the blood of his enemies. These dreams made him so excited that he would not come off of his power high for days. Khalid would go on for hours at a time acting out gruesome victories. Chills ran down Sadie's spine every time Khalid reenacted these fight scenes with his brother and reveled in being blood drunk. When she brought her concerns to James, he dismissed it as boys being boys and told her maybe they should monitor more closely what Khalid watched on TV and the internet.

"You okay?" James squeezed Sadie's knee under the table. "You seem distant."

"I'm good," Sadie lied. How could she possibly be good when her son could be a budding sociopath? She continued, "Just a little tired. Believe it or not, nuns can wear you out." She mustered a smiled for her husband.

James smiled back and turned to Uriel and asked him about his day. He did the same to Mrs. Covington. The three of them chit chatted randomly between chewing food and listening with smiling eyes.

Sadie turned her attention to Khalid.

"Sweetheart," she called her son. She looked into his eyes; his beautiful devious eyes. They looked wise beyond their years and slightly malevolent. The thought of raising a monster unnerved her. What if he grew up to have the character of Charles Manson with the fashion sense of Marilyn Manson? Sadie shivered at the thought.

"Yes Mama," Khalid answered with a mouth full of food.

"I want you to know that it's okay to admit when you're sad or hurting. A real man isn't afraid to be honest with his feelings. Are you sure you're okay with Mrs. Anderson's death? She was your favorite teacher and I'm sure seeing her die had to scare you. What an unpleasant surprise," Sadie said as she caressed her son's cheek. Sadie searched his eyes for some sign of emotion. There was none. Her heart dropped.

"It wasn't a surprise," Khalid said. He picked up a buttered roll and put some jelly on it. He leaned in closer to his mother and whispered, "I told her to die. She was simply following directions." Khalid smiled, his unblinking eyes burning right through his mother's, and took a big bite of his roll.

Sadie dropped her fork on her plate and quickly excused herself from the table. Claiming to be tired from work, they let her leave without query. Her family, unaware of Khalid's admittance to murder, continued to enjoy their Thursday night meal.

Sadie felt sick to her stomach. Maybe her father was right! Maybe Khalid was the monster Mr. Covington had tried to force her to abort. Regret for birthing him trickled through her thoughts. She instantly felt guilty. *No good mother should regret giving birth; even if the child was strange. Right?* Sadie shook away those thoughts and focused on her father. Before he died, Mr. Covington told her that nothing good could come out of birthing a Nephilim. In Mr. Covington's eyes, Khalid was a demon: son of Turiel the fallen one; son of the rock! The hall spun around her as she desperately tried to place one foot in front of the other. Her bedroom seemed so far away. Tears clouded her vision. She moved like a drunken sailor dancing in the dim moonlight. Finally, she reached her bedroom door and stumbled through it haphazardly. The bed caught her trembling body and enveloped her within its plushy comfort.

Sadie tossed and turned all night. Thoughts of Khalid's teacher would not leave her. Her firstborn's voice rang in her head. *I told her to die. She was simply following directions.* Those words kept repeating over and over in her mind. How could that be possible? Did Khalid have such power? Did he tell her father to die also? Sadie finally threw the covers from her body and got out of bed.

James opened one of his eyes and spotted his wife in the dark; moonbeams lighting the side of her woeful face. The warmth of her body leaving him had taken him from his sleep. He sat up in bed and looked at the clock. It read 3:03am.

"What's wrong baby?" he asked in a groggy voice. "Why are you pacin' the floor in the dark? It's late. Come back to bed," he said as he lifted up the bed covers as an invitation. A crooked smile accented his sleepy eyes.

"I can't sleep," Sadie snapped. "I don't understand how you can." Sadie crossed her arms. She looked at her husband as if he was committing a great sin.

"I don't follow," James said. "Am I missin' something? Did I do somethin' to you?" He swung his legs off the side of the bed. James felt that Sadie had been having so many mood swings lately, and he was really getting annoyed with her; but he knew that articulating his annoyance would not get him back to sleep so he decided to be proactive by calmly soothing his wife. He stood up and walked across the room.

"No James. You didn't do anything. That's the problem!" Sadie snapped, as she grabbed the sides of her head. A low growl escaped her mouth as she began to pace once again. She couldn't believe that Khalid's coldness didn't unnerve James. His silence on the matter was driving her nuts. Her mother didn't seem at all bothered either. Was she the only one in their family who was not oblivious to the situation?

Calm, James was no longer. A tinge of anger bent his brows. James flicked on the light hard; real hard.

"What's your problem Sadie? You wanna fight? You bored 'cause we haven't fought in a long time?" He grabbed her hand and pulled her on the bed. "You need me to put it on you? Is that why you so wound up? Big Daddy ain't givin' it to you enough?" James laughed sarcastically as he grabbed his wife's butt.

Sadie threw his hand away. Despite her feelings, a giggle seeped from her lips. A surprising tingle flickered through her sacred parts; but, there was no way she was going to drop the subject. She pushed him away and stood up.

"This is serious James. How can you think of sex at a time like this? I'm genuinely bothered!"

James sat up and swallowed his smirk. "What's goin' on?" he asked.

"You didn't see how Khalid was so unaffected by his teacher's death?" Sadie inquired. She folded her arms and looked James in the eye.

"He just a kid Sadie?"

"You and I both know he is *not* just a kid!" Sadie snapped.

"What you want him to do Sadie? Cry? Fall on the floor and scream?" James asked. "He a boy. Maybe he ain't overly emotional. I'm sure he'll miss her. Maybe he still in shock and it ain't registered yet."

Sadie leaned forward and said slowly, lingering on every syllable, "He told me that he told her to die and that she was simply following directions."

"When he say that?" Worry creased James' brow. Now he clearly understood Sadie's fear. A chill ran down his spine. James subconsciously knew that the boy was potentially dangerous, but James couldn't understand what the death of Khalid's teacher had to do with Khalid.

"At the dinner table James. I'm scared," Sadie whined.

"Sadie, Khalid can't make someone die just by tellin' them to die." James scratched his bald head after he heard the words come out of his mouth. He wasn't sure if he believed them.

"How do you know? She dropped dead just like Daddy dropped dead. Maybe he told him to die too!" Sadie cried. Tears ran down her light brown cheeks and moistened her shoulders.

"Baby you takin' this too far. Khalid was a baby when Mr. C died. A baby can't kill nobody. I know the boy is special but he ain't that special."

"I don't know James. I just don't know." Sadie shook her head.

"Just come back to bed. You thinkin' too much. Our son is arrogant and insensitive. That's about all the power he has. I'll talk to him about it tomorrow. For now baby, come to bed. Everything will be alright. I promise. Okay?"

"Okay," Sadie sniffed.

James held out his hand and Sadie accepted it. Sadie kissed him gently, and James took the peck as an okay to undress his sniffling wife. He knew she would feel better in his arms. He would make her forget about her worries if only for a moment. They made love quickly and James drifted off to sleep. Sadie lay staring at the wall for she knew that everything was not okay and would probably never be okay again.

7

Saturdays were always relaxing at the Tucker house. The adults slept late, and the kids played video games and wrestled as much as they liked. This Saturday began like many of the ones before. Uriel woke up first. Uriel always was the first to awake. It seemed as he had his own private rooster crowing in his head at the break of dawn. He opened his little eyes and sat up. Stretching and yawning, he climbed down from the top bunk bed and stood over his sleeping brother.

"Khalid, wake up." Uriel shook Khalid's shoulder. "Wake up," he said again as he popped his brother lightly on the forehead.

"What!" Khalid snapped. "Stop touching me before I slap you!" Khalid pulled his blanket over his head.

"Let's go downstairs and play video games after we eat our cereal," Uriel laughed as he slapped his brother across the chest and jumped backwards.

"I know you didn't just wake me up for video games," Khalid huffed as he jumped out of bed and pushed his little brother to the floor. Although they were only two years apart, Khalid towered over Uriel like a giant but Uriel was strangely just as strong as his older brother.

Uriel jumped up and pushed Khalid back. He loved to wrestle his brother. It made him feel powerful.

Khalid grabbed Uriel and slammed him down. Like a spring was attached to his back, Uriel popped back up and punched Khalid in the hip then took him down with a leg sweep. Khalid fell hard. A quiet growl left his lips. His body stiffened like a board and he levitated off the floor.

Uriel backed up; his eyes stretched wide and his heart beating fast. He felt like he would pee himself but decided against it. His young mind fought to process his floating brother. Uriel's breath started to quicken. The pee came, regardless of his decision, soiling his superhero pajama pants.

"H...h...how you do that?" Uriel stammered as he witnessed his brother hovering in the air like a ghost.

"Do what?" Khalid answered as he floated upward, his entire eyes black as car tires.

"Stop it!" Uriel screamed! Khalid's eyes showed no white at all. Fear snaked through Uriel's body. He fell to the floor and covered his head with his hands and continued to scream, "Stop it! Stop it! Stop it!"

"Say you're sorry!" Khalid demanded as he levitated towards his trembling brother.

"I'm sorry! I'm sorry! I'm sorry!" Uriel screamed. "Please don't get me! Please don't get me!"

The door flew open and Khalid dropped to the floor.

"What's going on here?" Mrs. Covington asked as she walked into the room.

Uriel was crying uncontrollably and Khalid was laughing.

"What did you do to your little brother?" she questioned. Mrs. Covington pulled Uriel up from the floor and hugged him tight. "It's okay baby. Stop crying."

"I didn't touch him," Khalid laughed.

"Did he hit you Uriel?" Mrs. Covington asked her sobbing grandbaby.

"No but he scared me," Uriel whined, clinging to his grandmother. He wrapped his arms around her legs and buried his head into the side of her thigh. She rubbed the top of his head and begged him to stop crying.

Mrs. Covington glared at Khalid and told him to stop laughing. She looked back at Uriel and asked, "What did he do?"

"He turned to a monster and was flying," he sobbed.

"Foolishness!" Mrs. Covington barked. "You better stop watching junk on TV Uriel, and Khalid you better stop scaring your brother. I don't know what you did but cut it out! I'm going back to bed!" She pushed Uriel's clinging arms away and stormed out of the room mumbling something about them disturbing her beauty sleep.

"I'm sorry Uriel," Khalid apologized. "I was just trying to get you back for waking me up. I won't scare you anymore."

Tears streamed down Uriel's chocolate cheeks.

"But how did you do that?" Uriel whined. He stepped backwards as he stared at his brother. His small body was still trembling.

"I don't know, but I can do lots of things," Khalid said as he grabbed his brother and pushed him into the bathroom. "Take a shower pissy pants!"

Uriel began to bawl.

"I'm sorry," Khalid said. "Get in the shower before Grandma comes back and Mom and Dad wake up." Khalid went back into the bedroom and grabbed a fresh pair of underwear and a pair of shorts for Uriel. "Here." He handed them to his brother.

Uriel took a quick shower and slowly emerged from the bathroom. Khalid was waiting in the hallway for him. Khalid put his arm around his brother's shoulder and whispered, "I'm sorry I scared you."

Uriel sheepishly nodded and they began to walk down the stairs to play video games. He was still trembling. To be in close proximity to Khalid at the moment was the most frightening point of Uriel's young life, but his curiosity was as strong as his fear and he asked Khalid, "Are you evil?"

"That's stupid! Was Jesus evil?" Khalid snapped. Jesus was Uriel's favorite person in the world to talk about. If there was a Jesus comic book, Uriel would have every issue.

"You're not Jesus," Uriel snapped back.

"Jesus did tricks. I do tricks. It was just a trick," Khalid responded, holding his brother's shoulder tight.

Uriel felt uneasy. He didn't think Khalid was anything like Jesus. Jesus did do miracles and he said that whoever believed in him would be able to do even greater works than he did. But, Uriel wasn't sure that Khalid believed in Jesus. If Khalid did, he didn't seem to like Jesus very much. Khalid treated Jesus' name like a curse word most of the time.

Uriel asked, "Show me how you did that?"

"In time," Khalid answered. "You will see things you won't believe. But for now, it's our little secret."

The boys plopped down in front of the giant flat screen TV and the games began.

Sadie opened her eyes and turned her head towards the clock. It was noon already. James opened his eyes moments later and kissed his wife on the shoulder. The room was mildly dark. Slivers of sunshine seeped through the blinds.

"How did you sleep," James asked. He sat up and fluffed his pillows then propped them behind his back.

"Not well," Sadie confessed. "I'm still worried about Khalid. I'm afraid that Daddy may have been right."

"Right about what?" James asked.

"Right about Khalid. Right about the dangers of me having him," Sadie whispered. "What if he's bad James? What if he hurts us or others?"

"Where's all this comin' from? You got all this from a teacher havin' a heart attack?" James' voice was rough and his face seemed to fold in. "You talkin' 'bout our son Sadie! He's here. Ain't nothin' we can do 'bout all yo' what ifs, but love him and raise him right!"

"My son," she mumbled.

There were no words that James could form to express the pain and power her last statement hit him with. James knew the boy was not biologically his son, but Khalid was his from the moment he opened his eyes. James was the one who caught him in the delivery room. It was James' name that Khalid carried. James was the one who taught Khalid how to pee standing up. James was the one who helped Khalid with his homework, and James was the one who Khalid mimicked from the tone of his voice to his smooth walk. Khalid was his son in every way except biologically.

James tried not to think of the fiend that violated his wife. To preserve his sanity, he chose to lock those thoughts away. James shook his head. His head thundered as his temper rose. Sweat formed on his furrowed brow. All they had been through and Sadie had the audacity to say that to him. He just looked at her; his brown eyes piercing like needles. For a moment he wished that she was a man so he could tackle her to the floor.

"I'm sorry," Sadie whispered. She reached out and touched his hand. He pulled away and got up from the bed. He left the room, the door slamming hard behind him.

"I'm sorry," she whispered again into the empty air.

"Khalid," James called as he walked through the hallway, chewing gum like a cow, his mouth alternating between smacking and frowning. He wore basketball shorts and a tank top.

Khalid appeared beside James, and began to walk side by side with him.

Uriel saw the two of them and joined in step.

"Come ride wit' me to the store. I need to holla at you," James commanded.

"Okay Dad," Khalid said as he followed his father out of the house and into the car.

Uriel followed them out of the house and approached the car.

"Uriel, go back in the house. It's just gone be me and Khalid this time. Next time it will be just you and me," said James.

"Okay Daddy," Uriel pouted. He turned on his heels and ran back in the house.

James pulled out of the driveway quickly; soon he was on the main road.

"What's up?" Khalid asked. "What store are we going to?"

"The shoe store in the mall. I gotta get some new basketball shoes," James answered, his face still twisted from hearing Sadie's words earlier.

"You gonna get me some too?" Khalid's voiced echoed with excitement. Thoughts of the new Jordans made his heart skip. He knew that his parents were against buying overly expensive shoes, especially for children because they believed that it bred materialistic people who did not appreciate the power of earning things. But, James promised to get them for Khalid if he got all A's. Khalid had a hundred average in all of his classes. Those shoes were as good as his.

"Maybe," said James, turning down the radio and pulling the car over on the side of the road. He turned the car off and turned to face his son. James' eyes looked wild and angry.

"What's this I hear about you tellin' yo mama that you killed your teacher?" James placed his hand on Khalid's shoulder and squeezed lightly. Khalid frowned under the pressure. "What did you say and don't lie to me boy? I ain't in the mood for no BS today!"

Khalid looked out of the car window and sighed. He answered in a voiced laced with supreme annoyance but utmost respect, "I didn't tell Mom that I killed Mrs. Anderson. I told Mom that I thought Mrs. Anderson deserved to die because of the way she was treating my friend," Khalid lied. "Mrs. Anderson was always mean to her and I don't like people picking on my friends,"

"Look me in my eyes boy," James roared.

Khalid turned to face his father.

"You tellin' me the truth?" James asked between his teeth.

"Yes sir."

James searched Khalid's eyes. The boy seemed sincere. James shook his head in annoyance with Sadie's overreaction and said, "Watch what you say to yo mama. You really upset her."

"Okay Dad. I'll apologize when I get home."

"Good," said James as he cranked up the car and pulled back into traffic. "Now let's get us some shoes."

It was obvious that something was wrong in the Tucker house. Usually it was full of chatter, laughter, hugs, and kisses. Now it was stoic. Silence echoed through the room in invisible waves of discomfort. Shadowy eyes and downward curved lips painted the faces of discontent lovers.

Sadie and James passed by each other without speaking a word. Sadie tried to catch her husband's eye but he avoided her face at every turn.

Mrs. Covington was still grouchy about being awakened earlier. She was not a morning person and when her sleep was disturbed, it made her grouchy the whole day.

The boys played games silently. Uriel kept a small distance from his brother; periodically glancing at him in terrific curiosity. He was still perplexed about what happened earlier that morning; but, the new Spiderman shoes that James and Khalid brought back from the mall made him feel better. Spiderman was his new favorite superhero since Miles Morales became the new Spiderman in the comic. Uriel was proud to have a cool superhero that looked like him: young, powerful, and black.

The phone rang, breaking the uncomfortable atmosphere of the home.

"Hello," Sadie answered the kitchen phone. She sat next to her mother, and across from James at the kitchen table. She stared right at him. He lifted his newspaper to block her gaze.

"Hey girl! How are you?" an extremely familiar voice squealed through the receiver.

A smile crossed Sadie's face. She could not believe her ears. It had been so long since she heard that voice.

"Sky?" Sadie asked in complete wonderment.

"Yours truly!" Sky answered. "How are you?"

"I'm good. I can't complain. I'm blessed. How are you?" Sadie asked.

"I'm okay. The kids are a handful and Forrest is doing wonderful things at the hospital. I've gotten hotter than ever. I can't believe I finally grew a booty!" She laughed. "I guess kids will bless you like that. I've been a pencil all my life now I got mo' stuff than you!"

Sadie laughed. "I doubt it."

"Can a girl dream?" Sky chuckled. "Forrest and the kids are great. They're getting so big. Forrest is doing really well here. He works so much now that he's the Chief of Medicine. I feel like I'm a single parent. The kids miss him too, but I know he tries to see us as much as he can. We have lots of lunches at the hospital, and he really takes advantage of his vacation time. Who would have thought being married to a doctor would be so stressful? I take solace in the fact that he saves lives and loves us. He still treats me like I'm the greatest thing since sliced bread, so I guess I betta stop complaining. I just miss him. That's all. How's James?"

"James is doing fine," Sadie looked over at her husband.

James pretended that he didn't hear her and flipped the page of his newspaper.

"Tell him I said hi," Sky requested.

"Sky said hi James," Sadie said to her husband. She touched his hand, but he moved it from beneath hers. James said nothing. Sadie lied into the phone, "James said hi."

"Cool. I've finished two books, and I'm working with an artist who wants to turn a few of my novels into comics. These kids of mine are a handful. All they do is text each other in the same house! Crazy little things! They all love to shop too. The oldest one, Jupiter, watched a PBS special about the Black Panther Party and decided that he wanted to be a militant revolutionary. I asked that fool, 'how you gone have a Jewish daddy and a biracial mama and just be about Black power?' I told him that he was too much of a mutt to pick a side. He needs to embrace all sides of himself. He agreed but said he was keeping his big red afro." Sky laughed. "You should see how big his hair is girl. He looks like a strawberry lollipop!" Sky paused to giggle then continued. "My youngest, Earth, is so sweet and well-mannered that I can't believe that she belongs to me! You know I've always been a hell raiser. Now Venus got some of my hell in her."

Sadie held the phone and smiled. It was nice to hear Sky run her mouth one hundred miles a minute. Sadie missed her friend. The anger Sadie felt for Sky conspiring with Mr. Covington to get rid of Khalid before he was born had subsided. Almost a decade had passed. That was all in the past. Sadie had long forgiven her. She wanted her BFF back.

"I've started going to church," Sky said.

"To church?" Sadie asked in shock.

Sky was not a religious woman. She believed strongly in God and considered herself a follower of Christ but Sky abhorred organized religion. She was too free for that. She always said that she didn't need people to tell her how to talk to the God that created her. That was like someone telling her that she had to go through them to talk to her own parents. Sky felt that the church had too many people in bondage with their various doctrines. It made her think about how Jesus talked about how the Pharisees tied a yoke on people they could not carry themselves. That was one of the reasons it was so easy for her to marry a Jew. Religion meant nothing to her. Sky was more concerned with a person's relationship with God. Sky saw more God in Forrest than any other man she had ever met, Christian or non-Christian. If that made her a heathen, so be it. She lived her truth and the truth set her free.

"Yeah but you know that didn't last but a month. I got bored and started worshiping with my kids in my own house on Sundays and we celebrate the Sabbath with Forrest on Saturday when he's not working. He's such a hypocrite!" Sky giggled. "As you can see, our weekends are busy!" Sky laughed.

"Yes it is," Sadie agreed. "Tell me about the kids."

"Venus is strikingly beautiful," Sky paused, "like her mama!" she squealed. "And Earth is the sweetest girl in the universe. She curtsies when she leaves the room. She saw it on a movie and have been doing it ever since."

"How old are they?" Sadie interrupted.

"Jupiter is eight. Venus is seven and Earth is six," Sky answered.

"Wow. You didn't waste any time!" Sadie laughed.

"Nope. I'm pregnant now with another baby and after I spit this one out, I'm going to get my tubes tied, fried, and laid to the side!" Sky joked. "I think I'm going to name him Mars or Saturn if it's a boy. If it's a girl, I'll name her Moon or Star. I haven't decided yet, but I'm leaning towards Mars or Star."

Sadie laughed and said, "Congratulations. I can't wait for them to meet their play cousins Uriel and Khalid. It's a shame they have not met yet. I miss you so much. Too much time has passed."

Miraculously Sky was speechless. Hearing Sadie say that she missed her brought her to tears. So many years had passed since she had talked to her friend. Guilt and shame crippled her from calling Sadie sooner. Sadie's forgiveness is all Sky yearned for.

"Are you there?" Sadie asked; discomforted by Sky's silence.

"I'm here." Sky sniffed. "I missed you too girl! I missed you so much," Sky cried. "I've prayed that you had forgiven me..." her voice cracked and faded into faint sobs. "I'm so sorry Sadie. I never meant to hurt you. Pappa C thought it was for the best and..."

"The past is the past. What you did, you did out of love. I understand that now. My father loved me, and he knew you loved me enough to try to save me. There is nothing to forgive," Sadie replied. Tears came slow and then fast. Memories of crimson liquid flowing from her body in torrents of pain made her chest rumble. She closed her eyes and shook her head forcing the painful thoughts away. Forgiveness required forgetfulness. Sadie prayed to stay in the moment and to cast away all recollection of pain, fear, and angst. Her very best friend was back and that's all that mattered now.

"How are your boys?" Sky sniffed. She hated to cry. She hated to think of the night she gave Sadie abortion pills without her knowledge trying to force her to abort the angel's baby. That night she thought Sadie would bleed to death. Sky would never forget the blood. All the blood! Scarlet was everywhere, covering the floor like a strawberry river, inking it with liquid life. The images were a symphony of insanity playing over and over in her mind. All these years she wondered what had become of the baby boy she tried to destroy.

"The boys are great. Khalid..." Sadie's voice trembled when saying his name. "Khalid is smart and handsome; looks just like my dad. When you see Khalid, you are gonna freak! He is doing very well in school. He will be graduating from fifth grade at eight years old, and will be heading to middle school next school year. A nine year old in middle school; I hope he makes it out alive." She uncomfortably giggled. "Uriel is a sweetheart. He is very kind hearted and such a good boy. He's six years old. He looks just like his daddy. Girl, he is as strong as an ox! James can barely beat him in arm wrestling!"

"Aww. How sweet!" Sky squealed. "I'm..." she got cut off. The sound of children running and screaming pulled the words out of her mouth. "Girl, I gotta go. These freakin' kids gone make me kill them! They're running through this house like they're at the playground. Jupiter has one of my scarves tied around his waist like a Kung Fu belt, and Earth and Venus look like they are wearing my new earrings and lip gloss! They think I can't catch them because I'm pregnant, but I'm going to skin their tails when I hang up this phone. Girl, let me go for I give you a reason to call social services," Sky ranted in jest.

"Okay," Sadie responded. "Call me soon."

"I will. You've been heavy on my heart. I have been dreaming about you a lot lately. About you and your dad," said Sky. "I gotta go! Love you! Talk to you soon."

"Love you too," Sadie said and hung up the phone. A strange feeling circled around in her stomach. She had been dreaming a lot too; about her dad and Sky.

10

Evadne seemed like the only one who was angry that the school did not close in reverence of Mrs. Anderson's death on last Friday. It was Monday and everyone moved through the hallways like nothing ever happened. The world kept on spinning. Life lived on. Mrs. Anderson was not her favorite person, far from it, but she was hoping that the school would show some sympathy and close for a few days. There had been no snow days that school year. She needed a break! Evadne thought that she should have gone to the counselor and pretended to be traumatized by Mrs. Anderson's death just so that she could stay home an extra day. After all, it was true that Evadne was traumatized, but not by Mrs. Anderson. It was Khalid's blackened out eyes that haunted her dreams and thoughts without ceasing. Evadne was afraid to come back to school because she was afraid to see him. She walked down the hall with her arms wrapped tightly around her books. Her big ball of hair cast a shadow upon the floor in front of her. Mrs. Anderson's class room was only steps away, but every step felt like the hall was getting longer. With very step, Evadne imagined that the lights were flickering and dimming, every child was vaporizing, and she was left alone to face the boy monster sitting in their math class.

A hand touched Evadne's shoulder. She screamed and dropped her books. She looked up; happy to discover she was staring into the chocolate eyes of her friend Zahyir.

"What's wrong with you?" he asked; his voice deep for his age.

Zahyir Aniwodi-El was a handsome child with hair so thick that it looked impossible to penetrate, and sparkling brown eyes that had the power to make the hardest heart swoon. His skin was the color of Georgia red clay stirred with dark coffee. Zahyir was a beautiful boy, not a feminine kind beauty but the kind of beauty that would grow into powerful manhood and inspired women to dream poetry.

"You scared me!" Evadne yelled.

"I just touched you apple head!" Zahyir snapped back as he adjusted his backpack. "You look like something is wrong."

"I'm okay.   Sorry for yelling at you," Evadne apologized. She picked up her books and walked with Zahyir into the classroom. The two sat side by side; two chairs behind Khalid. Evadne tried fruitlessly to keep her eyes from drifting over to Khalid but it was to no avail. Her eyes were burning a hole in the back of his head until finally he turned around and smiled. Evadne's chest became tight and her breath froze within her. She raised her hand.

"Yes," said the substitute teacher as he pointed at Evadne.

"May I go to the bathroom? I...I...I don't feel very well," Evadne whined.

"Sure hun," he answered as he handed her a wooden hall pass with a red cord hanging from it.

Evadne took the pass and trotted out of the class. When she hit the hallway, she ran full speed into the nearest restroom. Once inside, she caught her breath and tried to determine how long she could hide before the substitute sent another student after her.

Children swarmed the school bus stop like a swarm of ants nibbling on a dead cockroach. Evadne stood among the crowd hoping that the bus would hurry and come. The school day was finally over and all she wanted to do was go home. She put her backpack on the ground and sat on it.

"Hi Evadne," a voice from behind her greeted.

She turned around slowly and looked directly into the eyes of Khalid. Her breath quickened. *This is was what an asthma attack must feel like.* She thought.

"Hi," she answered then swallowed hard. Her knees knocked softly.

"How was your weekend?" Khalid asked with a wide confident smile plastered across his face. "Can I sit next to you?" he asked; as he sat without waiting for an answer. Khalid dropped his backpack on the ground and sat down next to Evadne.

"It was okay," she answered with a horrified look in her eyes. She looked down at her legs and began to fiddle with her knee high socks. With each moment of eye to eye avoidance, her pulse started to normalize.

"What's wrong?" Khalid questioned. "Why are you acting so scared?"

Evadne's thoughts raced within her head. She struggled to decide if she should explain to him what she thought she saw on the day Mrs. Anderson died and ask for an explanation or should she just lie and say nothing. Evadne opened her mouth but nothing came out. She tried again then words poured from her throat like vomit.

"I thought I saw your eyes turn black," Evadne belched. "When Mrs. Anderson died, you were looking at her with spooky black eyes!"

"Turn black?" Khalid laughed. "My eyes can look black I guess." He flashed a devious smile that brought the look of horror back into Evadne's eyes. "My eyes are dark brown. What color did you think they were?"

"No! I saw your *whole* eyes turn black. No white was visible!" Evadne squealed. "They were black like those monsters on scary movies!"

"That's silly Evadne. Mrs. Anderson falling to the floor must have scared you. You let your imagination run wild," Khalid responded, shaking his head, the tone of his voice like a patronizing elder.

Evadne frowned.

"I know what I saw! I ain't crazy and my imagination ain't wild!" Evadne jumped to her feet.

The school bus pulled in front of her. Kids rushed to the bus doors from every direction.

"I gotta go," she said as she ran to the bus. "I know what I saw."

Khalid picked up his backpack and headed towards his bus. Disappointment contorted his face. He hoped that Evadne would get over what she saw because she was going to the dance with him; or else.

11

Sky plopped down on her living room couch. Her wild red hair draped the sofa like a throw blanket. The children were finally asleep and now she could rest. It had been a long and tiring day. All the children had various practices and afterschool activities. Afterwards, they all went to the hospital to have dinner with Forrest. After they returned home, Sky made sure the children were showered, and that their clothes were ready for school the next morning. She finished two chapters on one of her books. Now it was midnight, and she was too tired to crawl into her bedroom.

Sky opened her mouth and let out a loud, hot yawn. Her round belly popped from under her top as she stretched her arms and legs wide and purred with pleasure. Stretching felt simply orgasmic! Sky allowed her eyes to close for a moment. Sleep came to her quickly, wrapping her tightly in its arms as it stole away her consciousness.

"Sky."

Sky opened one heavy eye. The light reflected off of her scarlet lashes as she fought to keep the lone eye open. The room was empty so she attributed the call of her name to a remnant of dreamland. She closed her eye again and let her soul drift back into sleep.

"Sky."

Sky turned her body on the sofa and unconsciously murmured.

"Sky."

"Huh?" she answered, her eyes still closed and her neck cradling the armrest.

"I need your help again."

"Huh?" she grumbled. The grasp of sleep was too tight. Her eyes refused to open. They felt as if they were held in place by two heavy golden coins waiting for the hand of Charon to confiscate them.

"Listen to me. I need your help."

Sky sat up and slowly forced her eyes open. The dim room danced in shadow. Chairs faded into tables and tables faded into walls. The sandman held onto her with an iron fist.

"Sky!" the voice echoed through the room loud and firm.

Sky snapped to attention. The shapes in the room became distinctive. Her eyes stretched wide as the formation of a bear of a man appeared within arm's length of her. He was a tall, handsome, older gentleman with paper sack brown skin and curly hair. Sky blinked her eyes rapidly as her heart pounded against her ribcage.

"Pappa C?" Sky whispered as she focused on his face. She pushed back against the sofa as chills snaked through her system. She closed and reopened her eyes. He was still there.

Mr. Covington stood before her; a flesh and blood human being. His freckled cheeks were glowing with good health. His eyes sparkled in the dim light. The small wrinkles that used to decorate his eyes were gone. He looked like a younger version of his living self; even more handsome, if possible, in death than in life. He wore a polo shirt and knee length shorts that mirrored his clothes that he wore in his former home of Miami.

Sky couldn't believe her eyes. She pulled her legs up on the couch as if some part of the spirit standing before her was going to attack her feet. Sky slapped her cheeks to ensure her consciousness. She closed her eyes tight and opened them again. He was still standing there. *How could this be?* She thought to herself. She had never seen a ghost before. Her mother was the one who could see spirits. Her mother saw them so clearly that she had to make sure that they were really there by seeing if anyone else could see them before she engaged in conversation.

Seeing spirits was never Sky's gift. Sky was a dreamer of dreams. Her dreams told a little of the future and brought her clarity in times of confusion. It was true that Mr. Covington had been visiting her a lot in her dreams. A matter of fact, it was him who prompted her to call Sadie. He had been haunting her dreams for months, and now he was standing before her as real as she was.

"Sky," Mr. Covington called.

"P...P...Pappa C? What are you doin' here?" Sky stammered.

"Sadie needs our help," he answered. His voice was crisp with concern.

"How are you here?" Sky asked, still uncomfortable with his presence. She felt nothing malevolent about his presence, but she was still in a state of unease knowing that the veil to the spiritual world had been pierced.

"I don't know," he answered honestly. "I have been coming to you in your dreams, but you did not seem to understand what I was telling you so I kept focusing on you and here I am."

"Just like that?" Sky asked.

"Just like that," Mr. Covington answered.

Sky unfolded her legs and leaned forward. She took a deep breath and forced herself to relax. Memories of her mother speaking to spirits and memories of her mother ensuring her that there was nothing to fear, permeated her mind. Sky knew that she was truly the one in control of this encounter. Her mother taught her how to cast out unwanted spirits if need be. Mr. Covington was not an unwanted spirit. Mr. Covington was almost as close to her heart as her own father was. Then and there, Sky decided to relax and listen to what he had to say.

"What is it Pappa C?"

"It's Khalid," Mr. Covington answered, his mouth twisting in displeasure. "He is beginning to use his powers against others."

"What do you mean?" Sky asked. She didn't like the direction in which this conversation was going. The last time Mr. Covington enlisted her help, she put her best friend in the hospital by trying to cause her to miscarry her baby.

"Khalid has killed," Mr. Covington said, his voice trailing off.

"Killed?" Sky questioned. "He's only eight years old. How can he kill anyone?"

"The same way he killed me!" Mr. Covington barked as he faded into nothingness.

Sky bolted from the sofa and looked around the room. He was gone. She ran into her bedroom and fell to her knees in prayer.

12

Mrs. Ebbie Covington stood at the edge of the street waiting for the school bus to appear. Walking the boys to and from home was a part of her daily routine. She timed her afternoon walks perfectly so that she would end up at the bus stop around 2:30pm every day. As she waited, she marched in place, her nylon, hot pink sweat suit sounding like a shower curtain each time she lifted a leg. Her knees pointed in ninety degree angles. She still took pride in maintaining her figure although the love of her life had passed away nearly a decade ago. Remarrying never entered her mind. There would never be another man who could fill the shoes of Carlos Covington so to even entertain such an idea would be merciless and unconscionable to any poor fool who showed a romantic interest. Ebbie's love for Carlos was perpetual. To pretend that it wasn't was not only delusional; it was an exercise of cruelty.

Mrs. Covington marched in a small circle to break the monotony when she saw the big yellow bus turn the corner. The bus came to a stop right in front of her, and her two grandsons ran off the bus into her arms.

"Hey grandma!" Uriel yelled as he squeezed her tight. She kissed his cheek, and turned to Khalid.

"How was your day?" Mrs. Covington asked him before she kissed his cheek.

"It was okay..." Khalid answered. His face was solemn; not his usual cheerful self. He took off his jacket and balled it up, and placed it in his backpack.

Mrs. Covington placed one hand on each of the boy's shoulders, and they began to walk home.

"Why just okay?" Mrs. Covington asked. She rubbed the top of Khalid's head. She loved the softness of his hair. He had thick curls like her late husband. Khalid was handsome like him also. The resemblance was uncanny. Looking at Khalid was like looking at her late husband in his youth. This made her feel as if Mr. Covington defied death, and found a way to remain by her side.

Uriel wiggled out of her grasp and started doing flips on the sidewalk.

"Be careful," she warned as he flipped and flipped. Every time she looked at him, she saw a miniature version of James. They both had smooth dark skin the color of midnight, and regal facial features. Uriel was just as handsome and intriguing as his father and brother. Mrs. Covington felt proud to be surrounded by such divine males. A smile curled her lips at the thought then she refocused on Khalid.

"Tell me what's going on sweetheart. I'm sure talking about it will make it better," said Mrs. Covington.

"This girl named Evadne is giving me a hard time," Khalid shook his head. "She's vexing me!" He kicked pine cones as he walked down the sidewalk. Slowly he too wiggled out of his grandmother's grasp.

Mrs. Covington tried hard not to smile. Children were so amusing. *Boys and their pride*, she thought. *They're getting too big for grandma to hold them.* She smirked and asked, "What did she do?"

"She's being difficult!"

"How?" Mrs. Covington inquired.

"I want to ask her to the dance but I think she may not want to go with me," Khalid growled. He kicked a pinecone so hard that it flew all the way across the street.

"How do you know?" Mrs. Covington asked. "Did you ask her?"

"No, but I asked to sit next to her at the bus stop and she acted like she was afraid of me," Khalid whined.

"Why would she be afraid of you Khalid? What did you do?" asked his grandmother.

"I didn't do anything! She said that I freaked her out when Mrs. Anderson died," Khalid snapped. "She's confused."

"How is that?" Mrs. Covington asked.

"I don't know," he lied. "Girls are crazy!"

Mrs. Covington let out a loud and hearty laugh.

"Yes, we women can be a handful." She chuckled. "I'm sure she'll come around. Who can resist someone so handsome?"

"She better!" Khalid barked and ran down the sidewalk and into the house.

"Baby you have to speak to me," Sadie purred as she grabbed her husband's charcoal hand, and kissed each finger gently. "I hate you being mad at me. I'm so sorry I hurt you. That was not my intention. Please forgive me sweetheart. I was so wrong saying that to you."

Sadie sat next to James on the sofa and wrapped her arms around his neck. She kissed his face, then his neck, then the collar of his shirt by mistake. The burgundy lipstick stain made her wince because she knew James would have an adventure getting it off of his white shirt.

James looked at Sadie. Traces of hurt still lingered in his eyes, but he forced a sickly looking smile to his face.

"I'm sorry baby," he uttered. "It was wrong for me to hold a grudge for two days. We both know what you said is true but if you want our family to work, we gotta forget about that. I am his father as far as he and I are concerned. I'm the only father he will ever have. Could you imagine tryin' to explain otherwise Sadie?"

"I know," she admitted. "But, you need to see that our son is different. I am afraid of what he has done and what he might do. We can't ignore his potential danger baby. As hard as it is to admit, we're not a normal family. Khalid..." Sadie stopped mid-sentence as her two sons burst through the front door.

"Ma, what are you doing home?" Uriel asked as he ran to Sadie and gave her a big hug and a kiss. "You're supposed to be at work."

"I left work early," Sadie replied. "I wanted to spend some time with Daddy. He left work early too so that we could spend time together and be here when you guys got home from school."

"Yay!" Uriel danced around. He dropped his book bag to the floor and plopped right between his mother and father.

Khalid walked in slowly. He went to James first to give him a hug then to his mother. Sadie hugged him with slight reservation, then hugged him tight after she caught herself withholding. She kissed his cheek and rubbed his head.

Khalid wasn't fooled by the overcompensation. He moved outside of her grasp in fear that she might pick him up and spin him around like a baby.

"How was your day boys?" she asked.

"It was good Ma!" Uriel squealed. "I'm hungry!"

"It was okay," Khalid mumbled with his bottom lip poked out.

"Just okay?" James asked. He put his arm around the boy and walked him to the kitchen table.

Sadie prepared lunch for the boys. She fixed turkey sandwiches, sliced apples, carrot sticks, and two glasses of milk.

"Do you want something baby?" she asked James.

"Sure sweetie."

She prepared him the same thing as the boys but instead of milk, she gave James apple juice. Sadie sat the food before her sons and husband, and sat down across from the boys. James sat next to her.

"Why was your day just okay Khalid?" James asked, his onyx hands folded on the table like two cast iron vice grips.

Khalid answered with a mouth overflowing with food, "This girl is giving me a hard time."

Sadie and James both burst out laughing.

"How so?" James asked. He took a bite of his sandwich and waited on his son to answer.

"She acts funny around me like she's scared of me or something. I don't' like that because I want her to go to the dance with me," Khalid uttered while chewing.

"Why would she be afraid of you?" Sadie asked.

"Because she can see who I really am."

After lunch, Khalid rushed into his bedroom and slammed the door, locking his brother out.

"Open the door!" Uriel yelled.

"Go away!" Khalid growled.

The sound of Khalid's voice crawled down Uriel's back like a millipede. Uriel, still full of trepidation from the levitation trick Khalid did the previous weekend, decided to let his brother have his peace and went to play in the den.

Khalid sat upon his bed; his arms crossed and his face twisted in frustration. Thoughts of Evadne made his head hurt. He didn't understand why she wasn't in the least bit swayed by his persuasive personality. She seemed to be immune to his charms. Khalid always got what he wanted one way or another but this girl was being difficult. If only he could undo what she saw, she would like him and be overjoyed to accompany him to the dance.

"Arrrggggg!" Khalid growled. He dropped his head in his hands and gripped his hair tight. "Father! Where are you when I need you? Why have you forsaken me?" he yelled aloud.

The smell of myrrh filled the room. Khalid coughed uncontrollably. The temperature dropped at least twenty degrees. Out of nothingness stepped Turiel; wings folded behind his back and his face shining like the sun.

"Mercy!" Khalid yelled, covering his face. He buried his head in his trembling arms trying desperately not to be blinded. "Mercy!"

Turiel's countenance dimmed and his beautiful face appeared. He opened his mouth and his words floated from his lips like the sound of ocean waves.

"Yes my son," the angel answered.

13

"Baby, what movie do you want to watch?" Sky asked as she flipped through the selections on the TV. She balled her feet beneath her and cuddled close to her husband. It was rare for Forrest to be home for a full day. The hospital always had him on call, but today she had him all to herself. They ate breakfast in bed, took the children to the movies, cooked dinner as a family, and now they settled in together on the couch.

Sky lifted his arm and allowed the heavy limb to fall around her shoulders. He kissed her forehead and laid his head against the sofa pillow. His hair brushed past her face. She could smell the sweetness of his conditioner, and the freshness of his neck. Sky kissed his shoulder blade softly then turned her attention back to the TV.

"Baby," Sky called. "What are you in the mood for?"

"I don't care," Forrest mumbled. "I'll probably be asleep before the credits roll."

Sky turned the TV off and laid the remote on the table. Without warning, she pounced upon her husband, straddling him like a war horse. She kissed him deeply; until sleep was the last thing on Forrest's mind.

Forrest grabbed her waist, careful not to press too hard against her swollen belly, and began to grind against her. He squeezed her bottom and nibbled her neck.

Sky pulled away. "I thought you were sleepy?" she laughed.

Forrest pulled her close and started to kiss her cheeks and down the side of her neck. He pulled her shirt over her head, exposing a bright green lace bra.

"Nice," he mumbled with a mouth full of her lips. He grabbed a fist full of her rosy hair and pulled her head backwards. "I missed you so much baby," Forrest whispered in her ear. "I'm so sorry that I work so much. Please know that I think about you all the time."

Forrest pulled away from Sky and stood up. He unpinned the yarmulke from his hair and tossed it upon the table. He had forgotten to take it off when they returned home from the movies. Forrest pulled his shirt over his head; his beautiful olive skin glistening in the lamp light. Firm muscles covered every inch of his torso.

"I want you so bad," he growled as he dropped his pants to the floor.

"Daddy," a small voice called from the hallway. "Why are your pants down?"

Sky busted out laughing as Forrest pulled his pants up; a deep frustrated pout on his face.

"What are you doing up Earth?" Sky asked, laughing at Forrest trying to hide his erection under a sofa pillow.

"I was thirsty," Earth answered, her red hair crowning her head like a halo. Her suspicious green eyes darted back and forth between her mother and father.

"Get your water and go to bed sweetheart," Forrest told his daughter. "And hurry up!"

"Okay Daddy," Earth walked slowly into the kitchen and poured the water so slowly that it seemed that minutes passed between each drop.

"Girl, if you don't pour that water and take your butt to bed, I'm gonna wear your tail out!" Sky scolded with a smirk on her face.

Earth filled the glass halfway and gulped her water down quickly. She put the glass into the sink and ran over to her parents. She gave each of them goodnight hugs and kisses and disappeared back into the hallway.

Forrest turned towards Sky and pulled her near.

"We have to wait a second Forrest. She may not be in her room yet." Sky laughed. "I promise you that you will get *everything* you want!"

Forrest smiled. "I better." He lifted the pillow on his lap and looked down. They both laughed loud and hard.

Sky picked up the remote again. "Movie?"

"No baby. All I want is you," Forrest purred as he dropped to the floor and started kissing her feet.

"See, that's how I got this belly and the other three kids!" Sky giggled.

"You love me giving you bellies full of love," Forrest mumbled with a mouth full of toes.

"The hell you say," Sky snatched her foot from his mouth. "No more!" she laughed.

"Well, we can just practice," Forrest said as he started singing *Yummy Yummy Yummy* while rolling his hips and pulling his pants down.

Sky lifted his chin. "Sit next to me. I want to talk to you about something." Her face was suddenly serious.

"Is everything okay baby?" Forrest asked as he got up from the floor and sat next to his wife.

"I'm not sure. I talked to Sadie the other day," Sky responded. She put the remote on the table, leaned against the sofa, and stretched her legs across Forrest's lap. He began to massage her feet.

Forrest asked, "How is she? I haven't talked to James in a minute. How are the children?"

"Everyone is doing just fine. I was so happy to hear her voice. It made me realize how much I missed my best friend." A tear traveled down Sky's cheek. "We let way too many years pass by. Our children have never met. I haven't visited Atlanta and she hasn't visited New York in almost a decade. You and James don't talk as much either."

"All that matters is that you called her. Now you two can make up for lost time. James and I are as right as rain. I'm always working in the hospital, and he's running a business," said Forrest, his face red as a beet and his breathing labored.

Sky realized that her husband's desire for her and his love for her was battling within him. Talking about Sadie could wait until later. Her husband needed her in the worse way and she needed him. She stood up and grabbed his hand and pulled him up from the sofa.

"Baby…" Forrest's words were silenced by a deep penetrating kiss. She let her hands drop to his waist and pulled his hips close to hers.

"It can wait baby. I want you just as much as you want me," Sky whispered in Forrest's ear.

14

"Yes, my son," the angel said. "Why have you summoned me?"

Khalid looked into Turiel's eyes with fear and trembling. "This girl..."

"A girl?" Turiel questioned. "You summoned me concerning a girl?" Turiel's wings stretched from wall to wall casting Khalid in darkness.

"Y...y...yes," Khalid answered. "Her name is Evadne. She goes to my school," his voice trembled.

"The children at your school are so inconsequential!" The angel's eyes flashed like tongues of fire. "My time on the earth is limited. You must not summon me for such minute things." His wings folded behind him swallowing the darkness.

Khalid wept, wheezing like an asthmatic. Tears flowed without ceasing. He looked into the angel's eyes and cried, "Father, you promised me that I would want for nothing!"

"You will forget her soon. The girl will be nothing more than a distant memory in a month or so," Turiel responded, disturbed by the boys frailty.

"But I love her," Khalid wept. "And she doesn't even like me."

A look of confusion crossed Turiel's face. Love? Within the body of the beast, still beat the heart of a child.

"If you want her, you shall have her," Turiel uttered. The room filled with light and he was gone.

Khalid wiped away his tears and allowed a smile to transform his forlorn face. He stood up from the bed when his door swung open.

"Khalid..." Sadie's words dropped from her mouth like rotten food. Her face went from joy to unquestionable repulsion. "What is that smell?" she screeched, knowing full well what that smell was. She could never forget the stench of Turiel. The smell of myrrh was the source of petrifying perversions that stalked the soul of her nightmares. The thought of that demon consorting with her son made her want to cast it into the bowels of hell.

"What smell?" Khalid asked with mendacious intent. He sat down on his bed and conjured up the most innocent expression he could muster.

"Don't play with me boy!" Sadie bolted towards him and grabbed him up by the arms; her fingertips digging deep within his flesh.

"Mom!" Khalid screamed. "Stop it!" He struggled but her grip was tight. Submission was the wisest option.

Sadie shook him violently.

"What is that smell?" she screamed. "What is that smell?"

Khalid began to cry. He sobbed, "I don't know!"

"Don't lie to me!" Her grip felt like thorns digging in his arms.

"It is the scent of my father," he whispered.

Sadie pulled him close to her and hugged him tight. Tears flowed from her eyes as she kissed the top of his head. Her heart pounded against his cheek.

"What did he do to you?" she wailed. Mucus and tears mingled with her words.

"He didn't do anything to me," Khalid cried. He buried his face in his mother's bosom. "He didn't do anything," Khalid sniffed.

"What did he say to you? Why was he here?" Sadie asked. She pushed him backwards so she could see his face.

"I called him," Khalid cried.

"Why?"

"Because he will make Evadne like me!" Khalid yelled; his eyes dark and full of the hurt of rejection.

Sadie looked into her son's eyes and saw dreadful determination. She knew that she must protect the girl from him at all costs.

15

Forrest fell sideways after his breathless release of passion. The room stopped spinning after his head hit the pillow. Sky's thin body glistened in the lamp light as the currents of ecstasy subsided.

"I missed you so much baby. We shouldn't wait so long," Forrest sighed.

"You shouldn't work so much!" Sky quipped. "If you came home more often, we could be like this every night."

"Waiting makes it more intense," Forrest said, kissing her forearm then licking her armpit.

Sky jumped to the side in ticklish laughter.

"Stop it you fool!" she giggled.

"You know you love it!" Forrest laughed as he fell back on his pillow. "What were you trying to tell me earlier about Sadie?"

"Well." Sky faced him. "It's more about her father."

"What do you mean?" Forrest asked, propping himself up on his elbow.

"Remember how I've been telling you that he has been visiting me in my dreams?" Sky asked.

"Yes."

"Well," Sky swallowed hard. Her cheeks reddened as she rubbed her fingers across her husband's chest. "Mr. Covington visited me again."

"So...," Forrest urged her on.

"This time I wasn't sleep," she replied. Sky looked into Forrest's dark eyes and tried to anticipate his reaction. He stared at her calmly so she continued, "Pappa C was here in the house."

Forrest face crinkled. He asked, "What are you talking about Sky?"

"He was here," Sky said.

"Are you telling me that you saw Mr. Covington's ghost?" Forrest questioned. Suddenly, all residual sensuality went out of the door.

Sky rested her head on his chest and said, "Yes, that's exactly what I'm trying to tell you."

"Are you sure you weren't dreaming Sky?" Forrest asked. His wife had a very vivid imagination. A matter of fact, the untamable fantasies that swam around in her head made her a fortune from writing. Maybe seeing Mr. Covington was a lucid dream she was having.

Sky sat up in bed. She kicked the covers to the floor and pulled her legs into the Indian Style position.

"I wasn't dreaming," she whispered. "At first I thought I was dreaming, but I woke up and we talked."

"Sometimes the mind may trick you into thinking that you're in a conscious state when in fact you are still dreaming. You see…"

"Forrest, I know what I saw," Sky retorted. "He was right in front of me as clear and as solid as you are."

"But…" Forrest took a deep breath. He started to say something but decided against it. Although he was skeptical, this was a time to just listen to his wife, and that was what he intended to do. Forrest was a scientist but he was also a devout Jew, so spiritual matters weren't foreign to his belief system. He wasn't sure if he believed in ghosts or not, but one thing the past eight years taught him was that anything was possible. Memories of all the strange things that happened in Atlanta years before would forever be with him. There were so many mysteries in the world that science couldn't possibly explain so he decided to not analyze his wife but simply listen to her story. Maybe he would learn something new. Forrest pulled the blanket over his naked waist and turned to face her.

"What did Mr. Covington say?" Forrest asked. "What did he want with you?"

"He said he needed my help to save Sadie," said Sky.

"Save Sadie from who?" asked Forrest. An uneasy feeling came over him. The last time Mr. Covington wanted Sky to help Sadie did not turn out so well.

"From her first born son," Sky whispered, very aware that she sounded like a lunatic, but she truly understood that truth was always stranger than fiction.

"Khalid?" Forrest asked, one of his eyebrows lifting.

Sky crossed her arms to match her legs; her scarlet locks a curly kinky lion's mane crowning her freckled shoulders. A look of determination and fear filled her eyes. She needed Forrest to truly understand.

"Forrest, I think it's time for me to tell you about Khalid's real father."

16

"Hey Evadne!" Khalid shouted. "Evadne!" he yelled as he trotted behind her down the hall.

Evadne picked up speed. It was obvious that she heard him because every time he called her name, her feet moved faster.

"Stop!" Khalid growled. "Wait up!"

Evadne's legs froze beneath her. It felt as if her knees were magnets and the floor was metal. She fell to the floor, knees banging hard against the tiles. Confused about what happened, she tried to lift up but could not. Her books spread out across the floor framing her like tiles in a mosaic.

Khalid was at her side in a matter of seconds. He knelt down and extended his hand. Evadne looked up at him, her wild kinky hair spreading like a fan reaching beyond her shoulders. Khalid had never seen anyone so beautiful, save for the matriarchs of his family. Evadne refused his help, so he began to pick up her books.

"Are you okay?" he asked, looking back over his shoulder at her forlorn face. Her smooth onyx skin was wrinkled in embarrassment and anxiety.

"How did you do that?" Evadne asked as she slowly lifted one knee up and then the other. She stood up straight and held out her hands for her books. Khalid placed them in her arms gently as an adorable smile curled his lips. Evadne tried hard to ignore it, but there was something hypnotic about his grin. Turning away quickly, she began to walk again.

"I didn't do anything," Khalid said as he caught her pace. "What are you talking about?"

"Don't play stupid!" she snapped, turning to him like a tornado in mid spin – eyes and breath straining against her angst. "You knocked me down!"

Khalid laughed. "You're being silly Evadne. There is no way I could have made you fall. I was way down the hall," he pointed. "I was running trying to catch up with you."

Evadne looked at him sideways then let her words fall fiercely. "You got powers! That's how!" Immediately after the words left her mouth, she realized how odd they sounded but she knew what she knew and refused to back down. Evadne crossed her arms and locked eyes with the smiling boy.

"Powers?" Khalid laughed. "Like superpowers?"

"Yep!"

"Girl, you sound crazy!" Khalid howled as he laughed whole heartily. "If I did have powers, I wouldn't be in this place. I would be flying around the world like Superman or controlling people's mind like Professor X."

"I saw what you did to Mrs. Anderson," Evadne growled. "Your eyes got all funny when she looked at you and then she died."

"What?" Khalid asked mid giggle.

Evadne stepped so close to him that they could kiss. Her warm breath covered his face as she said, "You're like one of those devil kids on the scary movies."

"You cannot be serious!" he chuckled.

"I'm as serious as a heart attack!" Evadne barked, eyes wild and threatening.

"And you think I did that?" Khalid stopped laughing and his bottom lip began quivering. "You think I killed my favorite teacher?" Khalid summoned a lone tear which rolled from his right eye so slowly that it seemed to reflect every nearby light like a tiny disco ball. He let his head drop.

"I know you don't like me but I didn't think you hated me so much that you think that I could do something like that." Khalid sniffed dryly.

What looked like a camera flash caught Evadne's eye. She turned towards the light, but in an instant it was gone. A warm feeling surrounded Evadne and the smell of myrrh filled her nose. Evadne uncrossed her arms. She looked into Khalid's weeping brown eyes and her heart bled. All of her anger dissipated and turned into compassion. Seeing Khalid cry made her feel awful. No one had superpowers. How could she have believed something so dumb? He was just a little kid, and she made him cry. Evadne pushed her raven hair from her face; it looked like a storm cloud shifting, and placed her hand upon his shoulder.

"I'm sorry Khalid," Evadne mumbled. "Please don't cry."

Khalid wiped his eye and looked away from her for a moment. He exhaled and said, "It's okay." He sniffed. "I'm acting like a baby."

"No you're not," Evadne replied. "I'm the one acting like a baby. I let my imagination get the best of me." Evadne leaned to the side trying to catch his eyes. Khalid avoided hers at all cost. She was relentless until their eyes locked. Then, she extended her hand.

"Friends?" she asked.

Khalid slowly accepted her hand, feeling her skin wrap around his fingers like silken snakes. Warm currents of pleasure drifted up his arm as her grip tightened around his hand.

"Friends," he responded as he shook her hand firmly, then hesitantly letting it go.

Instantly, Evadne was filled with an icky feeling that made her stomach twirl. There was something very strange yet alluring about Khalid. Her spirit groaned against a thought of friendship with him, but her curiosity seduced her with possibilities of great adventure.

"I gotta go to class. See you later," Evadne said as she waved goodbye and walked down the hall as fast as she could with an uneasy feeling she could not shake.

Khalid watched her fade into the door of a classroom. A wicked smile curled his lips. He whispered, "Thank you father."

17

The office was uncommonly quite as Sadie sat in her large mahogany desk with her stocking covered feet resting upon a stack of manila files. Her heart rejoiced that it was a few minutes after six o'clock and she could leave for the day. It had been so busy. Who would have thought nuns could be so active? Sadie dropped her feet to the floor and picked her suit jacket up from the back of her desk chair.

It had been so difficult for her to keep focus all day. She found herself buzzing her assistant with identical requests throughout the day. Sadie dropped so many things that her hands seemed to be greased thoroughly. All day, thoughts of Khalid summoning Turiel dominated her mind. Thoughts of Turiel in her house terrified her. What if he wanted her again? What if he had some diabolical intention towards her children? There was no way that she was going to allow him to wreak havoc on her life again. If only she would have listened to her father. She could still hear him saying, "I am against you having that baby. You and I both know what could happen if you carry that thing to term." That thought made her cringe. She could never have listened to her father. There was no way in the world that she could have aborted Khalid even if she wanted to. Memories of a blinding light filling the abortion clinic and an ominous voice warning her not to harm the child filled her mind. Besides, Sadie loved Khalid and there had to be a way to save him from himself and his father.

Sadie turned out the lights and closed her office door. The building was almost completely empty.

"Goodnight Kevin," she said as she waved goodbye to the congenial security officer sitting at his desk in the lobby. He waved back as he flashed a dashing smile followed by a wink. Kevin's flirting made Sadie smirk as she walked out of the large glass doors into the warm sunshine. She found her car quickly and climbed inside, checking her mirrors before shifting gears and pulling off. Sadie turned on the radio in hopes of getting thoughts of Turiel out of her head. It didn't work. It simply provided background music for the horror movie playing in her mind.

Sadie pulled out of the parking lot and made her way through the horrendous Atlanta traffic. Cars littered the street from corner to corner. Home seemed like a destination she would never reach; but an hour later she pulled into her driveway and allowed her key to penetrate the keyhole.

"Mama!" Uriel squealed as he ran to Sadie with arms wide open. "I'm so glad you're home!"

"Aww, I missed you too baby," Sadie said as she picked her baby boy up and spun him around. "Were you a good boy for grandma?"

"Of course Mommy," Uriel grinned. He placed his hand in hers and led her to the sofa. She willingly sat down and handed him her jacket and kicked off her shoes. Uriel handed her of cool glass of sweet tea mixed with lemonade.

"You're so sweet baby," Sadie cooed as she kissed him on the cheek. "Where is everyone?"

Uriel sat beside her and picked up a book from the coffee table. He leaned back on the pillows and said, "Khalid is in the room taking a nap. Daddy is in the backyard playing basketball with Mr. Luis, and grandma went to her water aerobics class. I was sitting here reading a book so I can add it to my booklist for school. If we read twenty-five books before we leave for the summer, we can get a ticket to Six Flags, and I'm on book number eighteen!"

"Good job baby. I'm so proud of you." Sadie took a sip of her beverage and said, "What did you eat for dinner?"

"Dad made turkey burgers, coleslaw, baked beans, and sweet potato fries. He put some up for you. Want me to go get it?" Uriel asked.

"No sweetie. I'll get it a little later. How have you been? How is school going?" Sadie asked.

Uriel put his book back on the table and turned to his mother and answered, "School is fun. I won an art prize, and I made a hundred on my spelling test last Friday. Mark Mendez tried to punch me because I wouldn't give him my cookie, but he missed and I told the teacher on him. He got put in time out." Uriel smiled a snaggletooth smile. "I used self-control like you told me. I did not hit him, but told the teacher." Uriel smiled proudly.

"Very good baby. Self-control is very important. You are such a strong boy. I don't want you to hurt anyone," Sadie said as she pinched his cheeks. Her statement was serious. Uriel was extremely strong for his age. He reminded her of Bam Bam from the cartoon *The Flintstones*. The boy could lift his father's twenty-five pound barbells. When he wrestled with Khalid, Uriel could hold his own. His older brother could hardly hold him.

"How are you and Khalid getting along?" Sadie asked, "Mom said that you two were fighting last weekend. What was that about?"

"We were just playing," Uriel answered.

"Good. I ask because your brother is growing up so fast and sometimes big brothers can be a little bossy. The older kids get, the weirder kids become." She chuckled. Now was the time to fish. She needed to know if Uriel had seen the angel as well. Sadie forced another smile to her face and asked, "Has Khalid been acting a little strange lately? Have you seen anything odd?"

A shadow fell across Uriel's face. He remembered how his brother levitated in midair and his eyes completely blacked out. Khalid told Uriel to say nothing, but Uriel could never lie to his mother. His little heart started to beat fast. He opened his mouth when a voice came from behind him.

"Hi Mom," Khalid, seeming to appear out of nowhere, said as he ran over to his mother and gave her a big hug. He kept his eyes on his younger brother.

Uriel turned away in fear, and began to whisper a prayer under his breath.

Sadie kissed Khalid on his cheek. Uriel jumped up from the sofa and ran into the bedroom. Sadie watched him zoom past.

"How was school today?" Sadie asked before taking a big gulp from her glass.

A big grin appeared on Khalid's face.

"It was great!" he exclaimed. "I am going to get an award for honor roll, the math and science award, and I got perfect scores on all my advancement tests. The awards program will be Friday morning at 9am."

"I'm so proud of you!" Sadie kissed his cheek. "We'll be there!" She looked in his eyes shining with pride. Yes, she was a proud mother. What mother wouldn't be? He was so handsome, smart, and charismatic; but, he was also manipulative, selfish, and cruel at times. Sadie knew her son well. With every single accomplishment, she was filled with pride and trepidation. Her love for him was pure and unadulterated but her fear of him grew every moment of every day. What would he become? How would he benefit the world? Would he save innumerable lives with some fantastic reign of benevolent power or would he be a catalyst of suffering and destruction? If the latter was the case, could he be stopped and would she allow him to be stopped? So many questions plagued her. The optimist in her prayed that her father had been wrong about Khalid. Maybe Khalid wasn't the monster Mr. Covington assumed he was. *Khalid was just a boy. A normal boy...* Sadie laughed at the ludicrosity of that thought. Khalid was a lot of things, but normal was not one of them. He was son of Turiel: the Watcher, the fallen one, the rock of God; and that was not normal.

18

Sky, as naked as a jay bird, sat down at the kitchen table across from her husband; divided only by a plate of mini cinnamon rolls. Sky rubbed the sides of her cup, enjoying the warmth of her coffee mug. She refilled the mug with dark hot chocolate and did the same for her lover.

Forrest picked up a cinnamon roll and popped the sticky dough into his mouth. He quickly licked the icing from his thick long fingers before chasing the roll with a big gulp of cocoa.

"Mmm, that was good," he said as he reached across the table and caressed his wife's hand.

Sky immediately understood the double meaning of his statement and smiled. She took his hand and licked up a drop of icing that he missed; then, kissed the palm of his hand. The scent of her lingered on his fingers and butterflies fluttered through her belly.

"I love you," she whispered.

"And I love you Mrs. Cohen. Forever," Forrest replied freeing his hand so he could grab another cinnamon roll. "Are you going to finish telling me about Khalid's real dad?" he asked, chewing loudly.

Sky stared at the sticky crumbs on the corner of Forrest's mouth. She scooped them up with a finger and sucked up the gooey residue.

"Mmm," she purred.

"You're so gross!" Forrest laughed.

"And you love every bit of it!" Sky giggled. The kitchen light illuminated her red hair causing it to look like the burning bush.

Forrest hopped up from his chair and poured himself a glass of water. Sky watched his manhood swing as he walked back to the table. Her eyes lifted to meet his only after he sat back down.

"Do you remember all the drama surrounding Sadie's pregnancy?" she asked.

"Yeah, James was so angry. His heart was shattered into pieces. He couldn't believe that Sadie had been with someone else. I'm so happy that he found it in his heart to forgive her," responded Forrest. "They belong together."

"Forgive her for what? She did nothin' wrong!" Sky yelped. "Sadie was raped!" A tear formed in the corner of Sky's eye. She hated that she could do nothing to help her friend in her time of need. "You think she chose to be violated?" Sky cried. "Sadie was being tortured and no one could help her! Helpless and afraid, she still tried to be strong and bear that burden alone. If anything, she forgave James for not standing by her side when she needed him the most not the other way around!"

Forrest stretched his eyes in horror. He instantly remembered the night James called him and Luis over to Sadie's house. Sadie was ravished, battered, and bruised from head to toe. Her night gown was in bits and pieces and her thighs were singed and smoking. Her genitals were misshapen and grossly swollen. Forrest was repulsed by the sight of it all, and the thought of his best friend doing such a heinous crime angered him beyond limit. Forrest had wrongly assumed that James had a hand in abusing Sadie until Sadie miraculously healed right before their eyes. Forrest remembered the confusion and fear that filled him when the dark marks on her skin faded from sight and her smoking flesh ceased to make vapors. Sadie's body went from the brink of death to perfect health within seconds.

"W...w...who did it?" Forrest stammered, ashamed of himself for blocking the incident from his mind. Sadie's healing was much too illogical for his scientific mind to comprehend. Allowing himself to think about what had occurred made his soul cringe.

"Turiel," Sky swallowed hard. The act of saying his name out loud horrified her. His name felt like a spell upon her lips. Chills formed on her reddish brown arms. In any moment, she expected him to materialize before her eyes and choke her with his nauseous scent.

"Who is Turiel?" Forrest inquired with unease caused by the pimpling of his wife's flesh. It was unusual to see fear in Sky's eyes. She was the bravest and most courageous woman he had ever encountered. "Who is Turiel?" he asked again, resting his big hand on her thin arm. "Baby, talk to me."

"He is an angel."

"An angel?" Forrest stared at her with a blank expression. He tried desperately not to reveal his disbelief.

Sky recognized the skepticism in Forrest's eyes and said, "I know it sounds crazy, baby, but it is true. I was in the house with her when it appeared."

"Did you see it?" Forrest asked, one of his eyebrows rose.

"No, but I saw its blinding light coming from beneath her door and I smelled its scent," said Sky.

"Its scent? What kind of scent?" Forrest inquired. He reached for another cinnamon roll but the present conversation spoiled his appetite. Quickly, he put the roll back and waited for Sky's response.

"It smelled like incense," Sky answered. "It was strong and suffocating. Once you got a whiff of it, you would never forget it. I remember trying to get into her room to save her but the door would not bulge, and the light shining through the cracks terrified me. When I finally got inside, Sadie looked like a dead woman. She was totally unresponsive. Convulsions and vomit flowed from her mouth when she came to. Between seizures, she told me about the angel. I watched her body mend itself, but the convulsions did not cease. That's when I called 911 and we ended up in the hospital. I didn't believe her about the angel until Mr. Covington confirmed it all."

Forrest sat quietly for about five minutes. He looked at the clock on the microwave. The clock read 2:25am. The silence of the house sang an eerie song.

"I don't want to talk about this anymore." Forrest stood up and extended his hand to his wife. "Let's go to bed." His eyes were unwavering and his voice was stern. "Now."

For once in her life, Sky was speechless. Authority and tenaciousness laced Forrest's words. Sky placed her hand in his and allowed him to lead her to bed.

Knock knock. Sadie hit the door to her mother's room lightly. She waited to hear her mother's voice. Mrs. Covington was very adamant about people not entering her room without permission. Sadie remembered being put on punishment about it several times as a child. The thing that broke her habit of opening her mother's door without knocking was when she caught her mother and father doing the horizontal tango. Sadie could have sworn she went blind for a good minute. Sadie knocked again. When she heard that it was safe to enter, she twisted the doorknob and walked into Mrs. Covington's room.

Mrs. Covington's bedroom was unapologetically very lavender. A lavender lace bedspread draped her bed. Lavender curtains trimmed in white dressed her windows. A matching lavender table cloth covered a small table in the corner of the room; topped with a framed picture of Mr. Covington smiling and at the peak of his virility. A vase of fresh flowers, next to the picture of Mr. Covington, scented the room sweetly. A bench with lavender pillows sat under her window and, her walls were an egg shell white with a lavender accent wall behind the bed.

Mrs. Covington sat upon her bed, back to the headboard and ankles crossed, reading a book. She looked up at Sadie as she entered the room. Mrs. Covington secretly examined Sadie with her eyes making sure that Sadie had not gained any weight, and that she looked well rested.

"Mom," Sadie said as she walked over to her mother and kissed her on the cheek. Sadie sat down next to her.

"Yes, sweetheart," Mrs. Covington answered putting down her book.

"What are you reading?" Sadie asked, distracted by the blue fire on the book's cover.

"*This Sickness We Call Love*," Mrs. Covington answered. "It is truly an achingly beautiful book of poetry. Listen to this," said Mrs. Covington. She cleared her throat and read:

Flat Lining

I loved you
As Gilgamesh did Enkidu
I would've traveled beyond the end of the earth
Just to revive you
But...

It seems as if your pulse is still weak
Fading and nearly still...
When it comes to me
You have lost your will to live

You rather pass away to the unknown
That to dwell in our home
Where a decade has built our twin thrones

Once upon a time you would have stolen fire from the gods
Just to ignite my failing heart

If the land of shade summoned me
You would've threatened the Witch of Endor
Forced her to use her dark charms
To bring me back from Sheol into your arms

Now if I perish
I perish
If you die
you die
The passion has left us both
Passion-our life fuel- is flat lining

"That's beautiful Mom," Sadie responded. "It's heartbreaking yet shows the depths of her love. I love the imagery, the illusions to Middle Eastern and Greek mythology is amazing. I hope I never ever feel that way."

"You won't baby. Your husband loves you very much." Mrs. Covington smiled and squeezed her daughter's hand. "I'll let you read the book when I am finished."

"Please do," Sadie responded with a smile. Her mother loved lovely literature. Sadie's smiled waned. Poetry was not what was on her mind. Her first born son Khalid was.

"Mom, I'm worried about Khalid," said Sadie.

Mrs. Covington's eyes immediately intensified. She did not believe in having favorites because she truly loved both of her grandsons, but Khalid held a special place in her heart. She felt that he was hers to protect. No one had been on his side from the very beginning but her. From the moment he was conceived, Mrs. Covington embraced him. Mrs. Covington knew that in time that few would understand him and many would turn against him. No precedence was set to validate her feeling. It was simply innate, a raw instinct that compelled her to want to guard the boy with her very being. That's why she knew that she had to always be his advocate, guide, and protector. Despite his origins or his ability to be a little cruel and selfish, Mrs. Covington knew that she had to guard his life even if it meant her own. Khalid was her calling. Her soul told her that her divine purpose was to protect him. As much as she loved her late husband, she hated that Mr. Covington did not want Khalid; that he wanted to terminate the boy's life. When Sadie was pregnant with Khalid, Mr. Covington tried to talk Sadie into getting an abortion and when she could not, he later coerced her best friend Sky into putting abortion pills into Sadie's tea. Khalid was much too strong. He survived the prenatal assassination attempt. Even after Khalid was born strong, his grandfather was not swayed. Mr. Covington still felt that something needed to be done. There was no telling what Mr. Covington would have done to get rid of the boy if he had lived. Mrs. Covington damned herself for momentarily being grateful for her husband's death; however, she was thoroughly convinced that no one loved Khalid as much as she did, not even his mother.

"Worried about what?" Mrs. Covington asked; her dark and lovely face frowning. She looked like a statue carved in ebony.

Sadie looked deep into her mother's eyes, trying desperately to search them for the unbiased ability to receive her words. Sadie wanted to speak freely. She knew that her mother was always slanted when it came to Khalid but Sadie hoped that her mother would be open to hear, to truly listen, if only for a moment.

"What's going on Sadie? You're making me nervous looking at me like that. Spit it out dear!" Mrs. Covington demanded. "Your procrastination is driving me insane. I taught you to speak your mind girl!"

"I think Khalid may be dangerous," Sadie blurted out.

"Nonsense! He wouldn't hurt a fly!" Mrs. Covington shot back.

"He hurt Mrs. Anderson," Sadie said, voice getting high pitched with every syllable.

"The woman died of a heart attack Sadie." Mrs. Covington crossed her arms and waited for a response.

"He told her to die and she did," Sadie exclaimed. She immediately realized how crazy she sounded but she knew in her heart that it was true. Khalid admitted to the murder and she believed him.

"Sadie, you and I both know that he can't just will someone to die. Besides, Khalid is a good kid. He is kind to his brother. He has lots of friends, and he is an extraordinary student. If by some queer chance he had such power, he would never purposely do something so evil." Mrs. Covington put her hand on her daughter's knee and said, "Don't you think we would know if evil lived among us?"

"Mother, evil is rarely blatantly noticeable on first glance or presents itself as something utterly repulsive. If that was the case, temptation wouldn't be tempting or the forbidden attractive. If evil was always so easy to detect, so many people wouldn't willingly do things that would ultimately destroy their lives. If Khalid revealed himself as a brutal, manipulative killer without a conscious, we all would flee from him. His malevolent aura would freeze us with fright and we would shrink away from him like criminals in police lights or hostages begging for deliverance and mercy. No one wants to pet a hell hound, but we will automatically be drawn to a puppy not thinking that it may have the capacity to rip our very throats from our necks. Oh no! Khalid would never appear that way. Evil is discreet like a lurid affair in a dark hotel room. Evil creeps in when we least expect it; without warning. Mom, we have been warned time and time again. We have been warned by his conception, by Dad's death, and now by Mrs. Anderson's death!" Sadie exclaimed with tears in her eyes. "How many more do we need to see die? Must we worry ourselves crazy trying to figure out who is next?"

Mrs. Covington looked her daughter in the eye and said, "You sound like a lunatic! Maybe you have been around those nuns for too long filling your head with supernatural mumbo jumbo or maybe you have watched too many movies. I have never seen you be so dramatic!" she snapped. "You sound like you are touched in the head!" A tinge of anger entered Mrs. Covington's voice. "I know that you have been through a lot and whatever happened to you eight years ago was truly traumatic, but our child is a good child! It is insane that you think Khalid has the power to kill by will."

"He is not your child," Sadie snapped. "He is my child and my child alone."

Mrs. Covington grabbed her heart as if she was pressing a dagger deep into her chest. She fell back against the wall, moaning from heartbreak.

Sadie regretted her words for she knew how much her mother loved Khalid. This was the second time Sadie had pointed out that Khalid was solely her son. She had wounded James with that fact and now she was wounding her mother.

"I'm sorry. I didn't mean it Mom. Khalid is your grandchild but my father..." Sadie was quickly cut off.

"Carlos was speculating! He had no proof of anything. His assumptions were based on books and mythology. He wanted to sacrifice our grandson and your child on the merit of ancient gibberish written by imaginative men. He..."

Sadie's eyes narrowed and her words shot at her mother like bullets. "Don't you dare pretend to be ignorant of Khalid's birth! How short your memory has become! Do you not remember how I was violated by that...that...demon? And do not pretend that you do not believe. I know that you have seen things. Daddy told you everything! James is not Khalid's father and you know it!" Sadie bellowed. "Khalid said that thing was in our house! Has evil gotten to you too?"

Mrs. Covington turned away. She knew Khalid was the seed of Turiel; the same Turiel that killed Dr. Putina whom Mrs. Covington commissioned to summon him. Mrs. Covington saw the angel turn the professor's chest into a gaping hole. She also watched, with cowardly guilt, an innocent college student get arrested for Dr. Putina's murder. All of this was Mrs. Covington's secret; her cross to bear. The thought of the angel being under the same roof with her and her family drove her near insanity; but her pride would never allow her to admit to knowing that the supernatural was very much real.

Mrs. Covington growled at her daughter, "Don't come in my room with this foolery! It is between you and James who your baby daddy is!"

Mrs. Covington's words punched Sadie in the chest. Tangible pain spread from her shoulders to her pelvis. Sadie could hear her heart break. With tears in her eyes, she stood up and left her mother's room.

Mrs. Covington picked up her book, and tried unsuccessfully to decipher the words through tears.

When Khalid got off the school bus, he was ecstatic. His eyes smiled bigger than his mouth. Evadne wasn't turned off by him anymore and there just might be a chance that she would go to the dance with him.   Khalid ran past his grandmother and through the front door of his house. He skipped straight to his room and dropped his book bag on the floor.

"Thank you father!" he whispered.

The lights blinked. Khalid grinned.

Out of his drawer, he pulled out a pair of shorts and a T-shirt. He changed clothes quickly and folded up his school clothes. Khalid placed them in his drawer as Uriel walked into the room.

"Hey," said Uriel.

"What's up?" Khalid answered, a smile still stretching his face.

"What are you so happy about?" the younger boy asked, his voice deep for a six year old. Uriel tossed a football from hand to hand.

"I think I'm gonna have a date for the dance," Khalid bragged. He nodded his head and smirked.

Uriel shrugged his shoulders. He did not care. Girls were way off his radar.

"Wanna play?" Uriel asked.

"I thought you were afraid of me?" Khalid asked as he leaned so close to Uriel's face that their noses touched. His eyes grew dark.

Uriel backed away in caution then smiled. He said, "Not anymore. God told me that I was to fear no one because

He is my rock and salvation and His angels have charge over me."

Khalid smacked his lips and rolled his eyes. He hated when Uriel talked like that. He had no idea where Uriel learned such foolishness. Their grandmother called it crazy talk, and their parents were one step from atheist. It gave Khalid chills every time Uriel started rambling on about God.

"Whatever," Khalid mumbled. "You want to play or what?"

"Yep!" Uriel exclaimed as he skipped out of the room. Khalid followed close behind him.

As the boys made their way down the hall, their mother rushed past them in a flurry of sobs and tears.

Uriel immediately dropped his ball and pursued his mother. Khalid stared in calculated observation.

"Mommy, are you okay?" Uriel whined. The sight of his mother in tears instantly brought tears to his eyes.

"I'm fine sweetheart," Sadie lied. She bent down and kissed Uriel's cheek. She looked up and saw Khalid staring at her as emotionless as the wall behind him. They locked eyes for a moment before she turned away and fled into her bedroom; locking the door behind her.

Uriel stood before a closed door. His little heart raced, tears streaming from his eyes. He knocked twice. Sadie told him through the door to go outside and play, and assured him that she was okay. Uriel obediently turned on his heels and rejoined his waiting brother.

"I wonder what's wrong with Mom." Uriel said as he walked out of the back door into the back yard. "She seemed really upset."

"Who knows?" said Khalid. "Women are weird. She's probably having a bad hair day. We would never see Dad running through the house crying."

Khalid threw the football and Uriel caught it and tossed it back. Soon laughter filled the silence between them, and a game of catch turned into tag.

In the window above, Mrs. Covington stood staring down at her grandsons. Thoughts of her argument with Sadie dominated her mind. At that moment, she truly knew it would be her and Khalid against the world.

It was 7:45pm and James was still at the office. Usually he left around five daily but today was very busy, and honestly he didn't feel like being home. The tension in his home between him and Sadie and Sadie and her mother made home life intolerable at the moment. Everyone walked past each other with sour faces. The silence of the home was louder than anything he had ever heard. Today, James just wanted peace, and sitting in his office listening to Prince was perfect peace.

James kicked off his shoes. He knew he needed to call Sadie so she wouldn't worry, but the thought of hearing her depressing voice made his head hurt. Sadie had been in the worst mood possible for the past two weeks, and their sex life had gone the way of the dodo. James instantly felt selfish for thinking about sex or the lack there of, but he was used to having his wife every night. Now a week had passed since Sadie had her legs wrapped around his back. James sighed a sigh of frustration tinged with disappointment. Although he was annoyed by the situation, he picked up the phone and stared at it. He decided not to make things worse and called his wife. Sadie answered quickly.

"Hi sweetie," he said.

"Hi," Sadie responded in a monotone voice.

James sighed. His faint hopes of normality at home were shattered. "I just called to let you know that I'm still at the office and I'll be leaving in an hour."

"Okay," Sadie breathed. "I'll see you when you get home."

"I love you," said James.

"I love you too James," Sadie responded and hung up the phone before James could say goodbye.

James placed his office phone back on the receiver and turned up the volume on the music. He picked up a stack of invoices, and began to thumb through them when his office door swung open; startling him.

"Timoo, why are you still here? I thought you clocked out at six," James asked his new secretary. She had only been at the company for a week, and she had him more organized than he had ever been. James' office was now running like a well-oiled machine. Timoo always knew what James needed before he asked and she worked hard and fast the way he loved his assistants to work. Timoo was a dream come true. James never thought he would have anyone as good as his first assistant Princeston, but that was many years ago. Princeston owned a string of night clubs and had assistants of his own.   With Timoo, things were definitely looking up. James hoped that Timoo was on the job for the long haul because James' search for the perfect assistant had been a tumultuous one.

"I'm sorry I scared you Mr. Tucker. I did clock out at six, but I decided to stay late to finish up my work." Timoo answered shyly. "I don't like for work to pile up."   She handed him a stack of files. "I finished up all the invoices."

"Thank you Timoo," James said. "That was very nice of you. I'll make sure you get overtime on your next check."

"That won't be necessary," Timoo smiled. "I didn't ask your permission to stay; therefore, the overtime wasn't authorized."

James smiled. It was not often that he encountered truly hard working people. They were a rare breed that James felt an instant kinsmanship with. He decided that he would put the overtime on her check whether she wanted it or not. Hard work deserved reward.

"Have a seat," James offered. He noticed how she shifted from foot to foot. Her four inch heels must have been killing her.

"Would you like something to drink?" he asked as he walked over to the small refrigerator in the corner of his office.

"Sure, what do you have?" Timoo answered, a great big smile on her face. Her medium brown cheeks flushed red and her hazel eyes danced every time she looked at James.

"I have soda, apple juice, lemonade, water, sweet tea, coffee, and rum," James called out as his eyes moved over his collection of beverages. He took a mental note of how low his chocolate milk had become. Like a kid, he still loved chocolate milk and he drank it with his meals at least once a week.

"I'll take rum and coke," Timoo said. She turned in his direction and crossed her long curvy legs.

James took notice and was instantly uncomfortable. For the first time he realized how attractive Timoo was. Her skin was smooth and brown, and her eyes were amazing. Dreadlocks colored to match her skin hung below her tiny waist but stopped above her ample hips and bottom. Her large breasts strained against her button down top, and her full lips glistened with lip gloss.

James swallowed hard. *Do Me Baby* came on the radio. He looked at his watch and decided that home was where he needed to be, so he poured her drink into a plastic cup and handed it to her.

"Good work Timoo," James said, trying to avoid her eyes. Suddenly the room seemed to get warmer and a feeling of supreme discomfort snaked through him. James always had a perfect understanding of boundaries and inappropriate circumstances. He knew in his heart that Sadie would not approve of him being alone in his office drinking with a single woman because he would not approve of her spending time with another man. Indeed, Timoo was hot but no woman was hot enough to jeopardize the love of his life and his relationship with his boys. James could see how Timoo grinned, like a kid when they saw an ice cream truck, when she looked at him. It was time for Timoo to go home.

"See you tomorrow Timoo," James said. "Thanks for everything. Have a good night."

Timoo stood up, a bit confused by James' sudden push to get rid of her. She thought maybe asking for alcohol was a bad decision.

"See you tomorrow," she said nervously and left the room.

James walked behind her and closed the door; then, he went to his desk, picked up his jacket and briefcase, put on his shoes, and headed out of the door. When he got to his car, he pulled out his cell phone and called Sadie again.

"Hello," she answered; her voice still lifeless and depressing.

"I want you to know that I love you and that our family will be okay. Things will get better. Everything will work itself out, and I am willing to have an open mind about all of your concerns," James said.

Sadie began to cry. James heard her whimpering on the phone and his heart ached for her.

"Everything will be okay," he said. "I promise. Things are never as bad as they seem. We're in this together baby. I love you so much."

"Okay," she whimpered. "Thank you for trying to understand. I'm sorry I've been so negative. Things will get better. They have to, right?"

"Right," he answered.

"You coming home?" Sadie asked. "I want you here with me."

"I'm on my way baby," James said as he sped through the parking lot and hit the main street.

21

"Sky, wake up!"

Forrest shook Sky's shoulders as her arms flailed around in bed, threatening to hit him.

"Wake up!" Forrest yelled as he dodged her bony arms.

Sky opened her eyes and sat up. Sweat ran down the side of her face, her hair sticking to her face like thick red veins; her pulse pumping profusely beneath her copper colored neck.

"Are you okay?" Forrest asked as he pulled her hair back from her face, and dropped her ruby mane behind her shoulders.

Sky nodded. She reached for the glass of water that perpetually sat on her nightstand, and took a big gulp. She replaced the glass and turned to face her husband.

"Yeah," she responded, still breathing hard. "I'm good."

"What were you dreaming?" Forrest inquired. "You were going crazy in your sleep. I thought I would get a black eye before the night was over."

Sky picked up her water glass and took another swig, then replaced it and lay back on the bed. She pulled the covers up over her shoulders, and waited for Forrest to settle back in bed beside her.

"So…" Forrest coaxed. "What's going on?"

"I had the strangest dream," Sky whispered. "I saw Mrs. Covington. Not the Mrs. Covington that we know, but a vicious woman full of malevolence. Her eyes were glowing yellow. Her movements were inhuman. Her body contorted with every movement. She was so frightening that the sky opened up, and these female angels swooped down on her, picked her up, and dropped her into a giant basket. Then, they carried her away."

"Did she try to attack you?" Forrest asked.

"No," Sky responded. "But she was so abnormal. I can't explain it. She was not herself."

"Well, that hardly seemed like a nightmare. Sky, you were flailing around like a maniac," said Forrest. "You woke up dripping in sweat."

"That's the thing; it was a nightmare. Mrs. Covington had the aura of a monster. I could see the iciness in her eyes. Wickedness pulsated from her very soul. The angels were taking her away to protect the world from evil," Sky said. "She was creepy as all hell!"

"It was only a dream Sky. You and I both know that Mrs. Covington is a kind and gentle woman. There isn't an evil bone in her body."

"I know," Sky replied. "But it all seemed so real. She was so frightening to look at. It was like she was possessed or something."

"I wouldn't worry about it. It was just a dream. Let's go back to bed," Forrest insisted. He turned off the lamp and pulled his wife into a spooning position. Lightly, he kissed her cheek and whispered, "I love you."

"Love you too," Sky whispered back and closed her eyes. *Maybe Forrest is right,* she thought. She closed her eyes and allowed sleep to come.

An hour passed. Forrest's snores stirred Sky out of her sleep. Sky reached out into the darkness to find the lamp switch. It clicked under the press of her finger. The room brightened with a soft glow. She picked up her cell phone to check one of her social media pages. It was uneventful as usual so she put the phone down and picked up a book. The cover read: *The ScreamBed Chronicles: The Last Days of Playas & Other Insecure Men by Ari Meier.* Sky laughed under her breath. Forrest's choice of books tickled her sometimes, but she had heard great reviews so she decided to give it a read.

"Sky," a voice whispered.

"Yes Forrest," she answered. She looked over at him but he was still sound asleep. Sky assumed he was mumbling in his sleep and kept on reading.

"Sky," the voice called again.

Sky put the book down and climbed out of bed. She grabbed her nightgown from the floor and stepped into it; clumsily pulling it over her belly.

"Sky," the voice whispered again. It sounded like it was coming from the hallway or living room. At first she thought it may have been one of her children, but they wouldn't dare call her by her first name.

"Sky," it repeated.

Sky pulled a Louisville slugger out of her closet. She knew that she should have awakened Forrest, but a feeling deep within her told her that what she would encounter wouldn't be physical danger; however, she would rather be safe than sorry. Sky stepped out of her room into the hallway and was instantly face to face with Mr. Covington. She stopped in her tracks. Less than a foot from her, he stood completely solid.

A scream was lodged in her throat but she quickly forced it into oblivion with a hard trembling swallow. One hand grabbed her belly and the other hand grabbed her chest where her heart thundered under her palm.

What are you doing here?" Sky forced through her teeth; her knees knocking so hard that they sounded like castanets in the hands of a Spaniard.

"Tell me your dream," Mr. Covington requested suddenly fading in and out of sight. "I need to know your dream."

Sky recounted the details of her dream as clearly as she could; trying hard to pretend that she was not speaking to a spirit but to her beloved Pappa C. After her last word was spoken, he faded away from sight. Sky reentered her bedroom, put her baseball bat back into the closet, dropped her gown to the floor, and climbed into bed. This time, she decided to leave the light on.

22

The smell of cookies floated through the air; oatmeal raisin cookies to be precise. Mrs. Covington had just pulled them out of the oven with rooster shaped oven mitts. James hated those rooster shaped mitts. In fact, he hated all rooster themed kitchen items. There was nothing attractive about a big red cock printed on aprons, sugar bowls, salt and pepper shakers, or oven mitts. James shook his head at the silly mitts and walked over to the pan to grab a cookie.

"Ouch!" he yelped like a dog with a wounded paw. He waved his burning fingers in the air as if he could fling the pain off.

"Didn't you *just* see me pull those out of the oven?" Mrs. Covington questioned with her hands on her hips. She pulled off the rooster mitts and tossed them on the counter. "Are you okay? Do I need to put some butter on it?"

"No thanks Mama C. I'm okay," James mumbled as he ran water over his stinging finger. "I guess I was too excited." He laughed. "You make the best cookies in the world."

"I'll say," Mrs. Covington responded. She placed the cookies on a plate, and sat them in the middle of the kitchen table to cool.

"Boys!" Mrs. Covington yelled. "The cookies are ready!"

The boys ran into the kitchen and sat next to their father at the kitchen table. Mrs. Covington poured four glasses of almond milk, and handed each of them a saucer. The Tucker men grabbed up the warm cookies and began to gobble them up.

The phone rang and Mrs. Covington picked it up on the third ring. She considered it being too anxious to pick up on the first ring, and the risk of losing the call too high if picked up on the fourth ring. She had answering the phone appropriately down to a science.

"Hello," Mrs. Covington answered; her voice very professional in tone. She sounded more like a corporate receptionist than a grandmother. "Hello," she said again, not hearing anything on the other end of the phone.

"Hi Mama C," Sky sang through the receiver. "How are you?"

"I'm doing fine. How are you sweetheart? I hope you and that precious family of yours are doing well. I hope to see your beautiful children soon. Sadie showed me the pictures that you posted online," Mrs. Covington said in a monotone voice laced with insincerity. It was clear that Mrs. Covington still had not forgiven Sky for conspiring with Mr. Covington against her firstborn grandson. If they had succeeded, Khalid would not have been born and that very thought made Sky's deed unforgivable; but, in the meantime, Mrs. Covington would play nice for Sadie's sake.

Sky picked up on Mrs. Covington's tone. It was understandable so Sky embraced Mrs. Covington's fakeness and continued by saying, "I'm glad you're doing fine. Imma bring them down soon so they can meet the family. They can't wait to meet those gorgeous Tucker boys. Sadie is going to have a field day trying to beat the women off of the boys when they come of age," said Sky.

"Mmm hum," Mrs. Covington mumbled as she placed the receiver on the counter. The conversation had gone on long enough. "Uriel, go tell your mother..."

"Tell me what?" Sadie asked as she walked into the kitchen; her eyes revealing her wounded heart.

"Sky is on the phone," Mrs. Covington answered and took a seat next to Khalid.

Sadie desperately tried to avoid her mother's eyes. If she looked into them, anger and pain would pour from her tear ducts and screams of wounded expletives would pour from her mouth; but Sadie would never allow her mouth to utter the anger within her heart. Her respect for her mother was of the utmost reverence and love; so, she slunk over to the kitchen counter, careful not to look too emotionally unstable, and picked up the telephone. Sadie cleared her throat and said, "Hello."

"Now that's just gross!" Sky snapped.

"What?" Sadie asked. She knew Sky was referring to her throat clearing.

"You rattling yo' throat on the phone!" Sky laughed. "No body wanna hear that mess. You should've hocked and spat before you picked up the phone!"

"It was not that serious," laughed Sadie. "What's going on girl?"

"Can you talk?" Sky asked; her voice suddenly serious.

"Yes, is everything okay?" Sadie asked, her emotions gladly shifting from hurt to concern.

"I don't know. Pappa C came to me last night," said Sky.

"What do you mean, came to you?" Sadie asked, taking the cordless phone outside onto the patio. She closed the glass door behind her and asked, "Sky, what are you talking about? Daddy is dead!"

"You think I don't know that Sadie! Nevertheless, he still came to me and it wasn't the first time either!" Sky retorted uncomfortably and a little annoyed by the entire conversation.

"What are you saying Sky?" Sadie asked, pacing back and forth between her patio table and her swing bench. She could see James periodically glancing at her through the glass doors with a concerned look in his eyes. Sadie forced a smile for James and turned her attention back to Sky.

"What are you talking about?" Sadie asked.

"Your freakin' father is haunting me! That's what I'm talkin' 'bout. He came to me in the middle of the night tryin' to make me piss my panties!" Sky roared.

"You don't have to be vulgar," Sadie spat.

"Yes the hell I do!" Sky yelped. "Last night was the second time I saw him Sadie. He looked and sounded as real as you and me. It's like he's becoming more solid or something."

An eerie feeling crept up Sadie's spine. There was nothing in the world she hated more than ghost stories. Especially ghost stories told by Sky or Sky's mother. When Sky's mother was alive, she saw spirits often. Now Sky, apparently, has developed the gift. *Or is it a curse?* Sadie thought. Sky's mother, God bless her soul, was a spiritually powerful woman; a Yoruba priestess of pure Nigerian blood who spoke regularly with the ancestors and other random spirits. Mrs. Aiseosa Dawn was a renowned medium but she refused to be compensated for her gifts. If she received a message, she simply relayed it to the person it was intended for and moved on. Unlucky for her, she received a heck of a lot of messages.

Sadie shook chills away and asked, "What did he want?"

Sky answered, "The first time Pappa C visited me, he said that Khalid killed someone like Khalid killed him."

Panic seized Sadie's chest. She knew it! She always felt it in her heart that Khalid was telling her the truth about Mrs. Anderson's death. Now Sky verified Sadie's deepest fear concerning her father's death. Sadie looked through the glass door at Khalid munching on cookies. He smiled at her. Sadie wanted to throw up. She turned her back to the door.

"What am I supposed to do with this information?" Sadie screamed. "What am I supposed to do about my son? How am I supposed to live in harmony with him when I know what he is capable of? Sky, what am I supposed to do?"

"I don't know," answered Sky. "Maybe I can help. Pappa C said that I needed to help you with Khalid. Pappa C still thinks that the boy is dangerous." Sky paused. "Maybe I should have waited until I got more information. I'm sorry I told you. You know I can't hold anything!" Sky apologized, literally kicking herself for not thinking things through before she called Sadie.

"Is there anything else?" Sadie asked.

"I dreamed about your mother last night. It was a very disturbing dream. Angels threw her in a big basket and carried her off. She was...evil," Sky rambled. "She was creepy and...I don't know! Really weird. I don't understand the dream," Sky snapped in frustration. "I told Pappa C about the dream and he seemed perturbed. Sadie, do you know what it means?"

Sadie held the phone for a moment, completely speechless.

"Sadie," Sky called. "Do you know what it means?"

Sadie snapped out of her stupor and said, "No, but I will find out. Hold on. I'm going to put you on speaker," Sadie said. "Let me look it up on the internet." Sadie opened the browser on her smart phone and typed in basket dreams. "It says it represents happiness, change of seasons, and a woman that guards secrets. It could mean anything!"

"Wow, now I'm more confused than ever," Sky responded.

"Me too but I know just who to call," Sadie said.

Evadne and Khalid had become quite good friends. So much so that Zahyir became a little jealous. He was constantly annoyed by Khalid's perpetual presence. He followed Evadne around like a puppy on a leash and Zahyir was two seconds from calling the pound.

Khalid waited for Evadne in front of the school every morning, and walked her into the cafeteria where they both sat next to Zahyir. Zahyir, who had a secret crush on Evadne, was always ecstatic to see Evadne, but Khalid tagging along made Zahyir's teeth hurt. He wished Khalid would go away and play with the eight year olds. The boy was a major annoyance.

"Good morning," Evadne greeted. She smiled at Zahyir and thanked him for saving her a seat. She hung her backpack on the back of the chair and sat down.

Khalid, knowing that Zahyir purposely only saved one seat, crossed the cafeteria in search of a free chair.

While Khalid was out searching for a chair, Zahyir turned to Evadne and asked, "Why is he always around? He's annoying and he talks all the time. It's not normal for a boy his age to know so much about the news and current events. Is he trying to be an anchor man?" Zahyir shook his head. "Why is he around so much? I thought he gave you the creeps Evadne?"

"He did," Evadne answered. "But I realized how silly I was being. There was no way Khalid could have done what I thought he did."

"You're right about that. I guess," Zahyir uttered. "To think Khalid's eyes blacked out is crazy. But, I have a cousin who always claims he sees creepy stuff all the time. One time he told me he saw Slender Man," Zahyir said with such conviction that he forced goose bumps to rise up on his arms.

"Slender Man isn't real!" Evadne barked. "You need to stay off YouTube and stop believing your crazy cousin. He was just trying to scare you."

"Khalid is weird nevertheless," Zahyir uttered quickly. He wasn't sure if Slender Man was fake or not. His cousin sounded pretty convincing.

Khalid brought a chair back to the table and sat down.

"Good morning," said Khalid to Zahyir.

Zahyir pretended not to hear him and continued to talk to Evadne.

"Did you ask your mom if you could go to my birthday party?" Zahyir asked. "It's gonna be so fun. My mom rented a video game trailer and a DJ. We're gonna have pizza and hot wings. Instead of a cake, I'm gonna have a giant cookie."

"When is it?" Khalid asked.

"I didn't invite you," Zahyir snapped.

"Yes, you did," said Khalid. "You told us about it last week."

"No, I didn't," Zahyir snapped. "I told Evadne about it last week. You're just always in ear shot so you assumed that you were invited too."

Evadne shook her head and said, "Don't be mean Zahyir."

"I'm not being mean," Zahyir huffed. "I'm just saying that I didn't." He crossed his arms and looked upward.

"You didn't what?" asked a voice from behind Zahyir.

Zahyir instantly knew who the high squeaky voice belonged to and with great trepidation, he turned around.

"Hi Zahyir," Valerie waved. A big smile stretched across her face ending in blushing freckled cheeks. Her light blue eyes danced every time she saw Zahyir and her fingers involuntarily found their way to her hair and began to twirl the platinum blonde strands.

"Hi," Zahyir mumbled, irritated by the smirk on Khalid's and Evadne's face. They knew Valerie irked him.

Valerie was a fellow fifth grader who was a crossing guard who wore her sash like a pageant queen. She walked around swinging her hair like she was in a shampoo commercial. Although she was popular and pretty, she was not Zahyir's type. He liked girls with African features like Evadne. Her wild hair and dark skin was the epitome of beauty to him. Not that Valerie was ugly, he just preferred Evadne. Besides, Valerie was a complete nuisance, and he was not in the mood to have her all up in his face. She followed him around like Khalid followed Evadne. If only Valerie and Khalid would follow each other and leave him and Evadne alone, life would be grand.

"Do you have a date for the dance?" Valerie asked, tucking her hair behind her ear. She crossed her hands in front of her and waited for his response.

Zahyir turned to Evadne and asked, "You wanna go to the dance?"

Evadne froze. She looked deeply into Zahyir's eyes in an attempt to figure out if he was serious or not. Evadne would love to go to the dance with Zahyir, he was cute and funny. He was also her best friend. Evadne never thought he was interested in her that way. She thought maybe he was just asking her to get Valerie off of his back.

"I think she has a date," Valerie snapped, insulted by Khalid's disinterest in her.

"Who?" Zahyir asked. His countenance fell.

Valerie pointed to Khalid and Zahyir laughed.

"Evadne's not going to the dance with a little kid!" Zahyir exclaimed. "Khalid probably watches Sesame Street!"

Khalid looked like he had been struck by lightning. His pride swelled up like an infectious pimple and fueled the type of anger within him that leveled cities to the ground. A rage he never knew existed twisted his face without his consent.

"My bad little man, I didn't mean no harm. Don't get all puffed up," Zahyir said; patting Khalid on the back. Khalid knocked Zahyir's hand away.

"Leave Khalid alone Zahyir. You obviously upset him," Evadne said as she popped Zahyir on the arm. "Don't be a jerk!" She stuck out her bottom lip and crossed her arms. Evadne didn't like anyone to get picked on. She didn't want anyone to feel the way Mrs. Anderson used to make her feel.

"I'm sorry," Zahyir apologized to Khalid. He really didn't want to make Khalid feel bad, and Zahyir definitely didn't want Evadne to be mad with him. Zahyir just really wanted Evadne to go to the dance with him.

Zahyir turned to Valerie and said, "Val, all I was trying to say is that I was planning to go to the dance with Evadne. I didn't mean to be rude to you or Khalid." Zahyir then turned to Evadne and asked, "You're going with me, right?"

Evadne nodded her head and Valerie stomped off.

"Why did you do that girl like that? You know how much she likes you," Evadne asked with laughter between each word.

"Like what?" Zahyir answered. "I told her the truth. I want you to go with me."

"You were serious?" Evadne blushed.

"Yes," Zahyir answered, his voice trembling with humility. Thoughts of her saying no made him uneasy. He had been secretly in love with Evadne since third grade.

"If you don't wanna go with me, it's cool," Zahyir digressed. "I'm sure Khalid would love to have you as a date."

"I want to go with you," Evadne said, smiling from ear to ear. She had always liked him too.

Evadne realized that they had rudely excluded Khalid from the conversation so she turned to apologize to him, but was faced with an empty seat.

Khalid Tucker stumped through the hallway like a giant crushing forests beneath his feet. His eyes were narrow slits and his nostrils flared. His mouth twisted downward as he knocked down every student that stood between him and the doorway. When his foot hit the concrete outside, small cracks made webs beneath every footfall. Soon Khalid's path led to the grass. The emerald green blades turned ashen underneath his feet, withering and accepting instant death. Nearby animals slunk away in the opposite direction, yelping in fear and trepidation. Khalid ran into the nearby woods, tears streaming from his eyes and fists balled so tight that blood trickled from his palms. He screamed to the top of his lungs, "Father!"

Sadie sat at her desk twiddling her thumbs; her thumbnails sounded like click beetles dancing. She pushed her chair backwards and stood on her feet, and began pacing the floor in from of her gigantic office window overlooking a park dressed gloriously in greenery. The buzzing of her intercom disrupted the chaos raging in her brain causing her feet to freeze mid shuffle.

"Mrs. Tucker," a soft distinctly southern voice called through the speaker. It had the cadence of a lullaby; soothing and sweet. Sadie imagined that her secretary Emily said 'Fiddle de-de' like Scarlett O'Hara when she was working in solitude.

"Yes, Emily," Sadie answered.

"Your eleven o'clock appointment is here," replied Emily. "Would you like for me to bring him in?"

"Escort him in, in about five minutes," said Sadie.

"Okay," Emily responded and disconnected.

Sadie picked up her purse and retrieved her lipstick from its congested belly. In seconds, Sadie re-stained her lips, ran her fingers through her hair, and adjusted her dress. She searched up under her desk for her shoes and put them back on; then, she sat down and tried without success to stop twiddling her thumbs.

Sadie's appointment was with Dr. Ari Aniwodi-El always made her nervous. It was beyond her reasoning why he caused her such discomfort. He was a kind and tenderhearted gentleman with penetrating eyes and a disposition that made her feel like he knew every one of her secrets, as if he read her diary with one look in her eyes. Charismatic and attractive he was, with equally African and Native American features. Sadie was unconsciously drawn to him like all other people who had the pleasure of making his acquaintance. His aura was hypnotic. For that very reason, Sadie made a point not to travel in his social circles. His presence made her feel like a blushing fool, and her husband was not very fond of that. James couldn't stand the man. The green eyed monster came out every time James saw Sadie in the room with Dr. Aniwodi-El; but, there was no need for James to be jealous because what she felt about Ari Aniwodi-El was not desire. Sadie loved her husband dearly and desired no other but James. Besides, Ari was head over heels about his wife; although, the chemistry between Ari and Sadie was intense. Frankly Sadie found no reason to cause herself discomfort so she made a point to stay out of the good doctor's way. But in lieu of Sky's dream about Mrs. Covington and visitations from Mr. Covington, Ari was the man Sadie needed to call.

Dr. Ari Aniwodi-El was one of Mr. Covington's most prestigious colleagues. He was a minister of an alternative Christian church which integrated African culture with ancient Hebrew and Native American belief systems. Ari was a professor of Paranormal Psychology where he specialized in antiquity and dream interpretation. His interpretations of dreams were almost always accurate, and he had gained worldwide notoriety for his numinous abilities.

Sadie wasn't much of a follower of or believer in psychics, but she knew that she needed some insight on Sky's visions. There was not a better qualified person to enlighten the situation than Dr. Ari Aniwodi-El.

A light tapping sounded before Emily, with her strawberry blonde hair pulled up so tight that it gave her middle-aged face a lift, opened the door. Sadie was surprised to see that Emily had changed out of her habit into an all-black fitted suit with a white collar. Emily noticed Sadie's surprise and said, "I'm trying something different."

"I like it," said Sadie. "Very modern."

Dr. Aniwodi-El stepped from behind Emily and walked into Sadie's office with his hand extended. Sadie accepted his handshake and was pulled into his arms where he placed a soft kiss on her cheek.

"Greetings, my beautiful queen. It is so good to see you again," Ari greeted with his eyes locked on hers. He had the type of eyes that made a person feel naked when he looked at them. There was something borderline illicit in his gaze.

Flustered, Sadie pulled backwards and escorted him to a small leather couch on the far side of the office.

"It's good to see you too," said Sadie as she sat down and crossed her legs. He followed suit.

"Would you like something to drink?" she asked. All of a sudden she felt like the room was on fire. A bead of sweat formed on the top of her nose. She removed her jacket revealing firm arms and a purple silk tank top.

"Are you okay?" Ari asked. "You seem a bit nervous."

"I'm fine," Sadie responded, embarrassment all over her face. "Are you warm?"

"Not at all," said Ari smiling.

Sadie forced a smile to her face. It irked her how nervous Ari made her. She could never decipher what it was about him that made her heart beat fast, and caused her to stumble over her words. Her palms were gross and moist. She felt like she could barely catch her breath. Secretly, Sadie felt that Ari had a stolen piece of her hair hidden away in a bottle where he worked roots on her periodically. All she knew was that she needed to get on with their meeting so she could leave her office and get on with her life.

"I'll bring you some water," Emily said and walked out of the door.

"How have you been Sadie?" asked Ari. "I haven't talked to you since you and James came to one of my workshops years ago."

"I've been busy." Sadie half laughed. "But overall, things are okay. How are Latrice and the kids?"

"They are wonderful. Zahyir told me that he sees your sons at school," said Ari.

"Yes. Khalid told me that he was in a class with Zahyir," Sadie responded. "Maybe we can set up a playdate."

"Maybe." Ari laughed. "I think Zahyir is too old for playdates, but maybe James and I can take the boys out to play a game of basketball."

"Sounds like a plan," Sadie said and flashed an uneasy smile. "I'm sure they would love that," she lied.

James would never go play basketball with Ari. James would rather have his tooth pulled out with a rusty toe nail clipper.

"So what made you call me?" Ari asked, getting straight to the point.

Emily walked back into the office with two glasses of ice and two bottled waters on a tray. She sat the tray down on the coffee table in front of them and asked, "Is there anything else that you need?" She caught Ari's eye and a strange tingling swirled around in her stomach. She silently recited the Lord's Prayer and banished her tempting thoughts. After all, Emily was married to Christ, and she was not going to cheat after thirty years of celibacy.

"No Emily. Thank you," Sadie responded with a grin on her face. It was the first time she ever saw a nun blush. It was good to know that a woman's heart still beat inside of Emily's body.

Emily excused herself and went back to her desk.

"So...," Ari said as he poured water into a glass of ice. "Getting your call was quite unexpected. I was under the impression that you thought my dream interpretations were a bunch of mumbo jumbo."

"Why would you say that?" Sadie asked, surprised that he knew how she felt about his work.

"Maybe because you roll your eyes every time I interpreted a dream, and you seem bored beyond comprehension at my spiritual conferences," Dr. Aniwodi-El responded. "I'm not offended. I find you quite amusing really."

Sadie laughed. She asked, "How could you see my expression in a room full of hundreds of people?"

"I can see you anywhere." Ari smiled.

Sadie blushed.

"Seriously, what can I do for you?" Ari asked. "As much as I enjoy your company, I have a few other appointments I have to get to by the end of the day."

Sadie rubbed her palms on her skirt and took a sip of water. She felt foolish summoning a dream interpreter, but she knew that she needed to understand why Sky was having visions.

"My best friend had a dream, and I need for you to tell me what it means. Can you do that for me?" Sadie asked. "Do you have time to do that?"

"Yes I do." He laughed. "At lease I can try," Dr. Aniwodi-El said.

"Let me call my friend so she can tell you what she dreamed. I don't want to leave out any important details. It would be much better coming from her," Sadie said as she picked up her cell phone and searched for Sky's name. Her phone screen was so large that it looked like a tablet. "Also, before I call, Ari do you believe in ghosts?"

"That phone seems too big for your tiny hands," Ari said before he took another sip of water. "I do believe in ghosts. I may have seen a few."

"Really," Sadie twisted her face. She wasn't surprised at all. Ari seemed like the type that had experienced everything. She wondered if he had ever been kidnapped by aliens and charmed them so much that they dropped him back home before they reached the sky.

"Tell me about it," she requested.

Ari leaned back on the sofa and rested his ankle on his knee.

"My most recent experience happened last year. My wife's father passed away last year," said Ari.

"I'm so sorry to hear that. Please give my condolences to Latrice," Sadie replied as she rested her hand on his knee. "I know what it's like to lose a father. You know that mine died nearly a decade ago and it still hurts like it happened yesterday."

Ari placed his hand upon Sadie's, and she removed her hand quickly.

"I will tell Latrice that you sent your deepest sympathy. Seeing her distraught broke my heart in a billion pieces. She is much better these days, but last year was very difficult for our whole family. I loved her father as much as I loved my own, and the children were devastated."

"I'm glad she's better. Time heals all wounds," Sadie lied. Time still hadn't healed her heart, but she had hope that her heart would heal someday.

Perceiving the hurt behind her eyes, he said, "It will get better."

"So what happened?" Sadie asked, changing the subject. The last thing she wanted to do was get emotional about her father; especially now since she knows her son may have killed him. "With the ghost?"

"Well, one night I was at home and fell asleep on the couch. Latrice came downstairs to wake me up and to tell me to come to bed. She shook me until I was moderately conscious; then, she went upstairs into the bedroom. I lingered on the sofa for a second to break out of my trance. When I finally got up, I walked up the stairs. As I walked up the stairs, her father appeared and walked down the stairs. Then, he passed right by me. I was still a bit groggy at the time so I was not alarmed until I got into the bedroom and realized what had just happened," said Ari.

"Were you afraid?" Sadie asked.

"Not at all. If anything, I was shocked. I told Latrice about it and she told me I was dreaming," said Ari.

"And you sure you weren't?" Sadie asked.

"I wasn't dreaming about him before my wife woke me up, and I wasn't thinking of him at all that night. Why would I suddenly start dreaming of him while I was walking up the stairs?" Ari let a piece of ice fall into his mouth and began to chew.

Sadie pondered his question and had no retort. She looked back at her phone and touched Sky's picture to dial her number. It rang thrice before she picked up.

"Sky," Sadie called into the phone.

"Hey Sadie!" Sky exclaimed.

"Are you busy at the moment?' asked Sadie.

"No. What's up?" She asked.

"I'm going to put you on speaker," Sadie said and hit the speaker button. She placed the phone on the table between her and Dr. Aniwodi-El and asked, "Sky, can you hear me okay?"

"I can hear you just fine," Sky said.

"Sky, I have Dr. Ari Aniwodi-El here with me. He has the gift of interpreting dreams, and I would like for you to tell him about your dream regarding my mother."

"Okay," Sky agreed. She told Dr. Aniwodi-El about the dream regarding Mrs. Covington being taken away in a basket by winged women. When Sky finished, Dr. Aniwodi-El sat back in complete contemplation.

"What..." Sadie's words where cut short by Ari's shush.

After about five minutes, Ari turned to Sadie and asked her if she had a Holy Bible. Sadie told him that she did not have one, but he could download one on his phone within seconds. He did. After the application was successfully installed, he began to search the electronic scriptures.

"What is he doing?" Sky asked through the phone.

"I'm not sure," Sadie answered. "Let me call you back. I promise I'll tell you everything."

"Okay," said Sky, disappointment in her voice.

Sadie hung up the phone and waited for Dr. Ari Aniwodi-El to say something; anything. It seemed as if time crawled by on all fours like a sloth that fell from a tree. Finally, Ari looked up from the phone and waved from Sadie to come closer. She moved near him quickly, and looked down at his phone screen. Highlighted on the screen was Zechariah 5:5-9 which read:

> [5]Then the angel who talked with me came forward and said to me, "Look up and see what this is that is coming out." [6]I said, "What is it?" He said, "This is a basket coming out." And he said, "This is their iniquity in all the land." [7]Then a leaden cover was lifted, and there was a woman sitting in the basket! [8]And he said, "This is Wickedness." So he thrust her back into the basket, and pressed the leaden weight down on its mouth. [9]Then I looked up and saw two women coming forward. The wind was in their wings; they had wings like the wings of a stork, and they lifted up the basket between earth and sky.

Sadie looked more confused than ever. Of course she saw the similarities between the scripture and Sky's dream but she had gained absolutely no clarity.

"What does it all mean?" Sadie asked, her eyes begging for an explanation and her heart filling up with fear. The last time her life ran parallel to the Bible, she was sexually assaulted and impregnated by a fallen angel. Now what was she to expect?

Ari looked Sadie in the eye and said, "In this scenario, your mother represents wickedness or will represent wickedness in the future. I'm not talking bad. I'm talking deep primordial evil. The woman in the scriptures is so diabolical that spirits from heaven had to entrap her and remove her from the earth. I've only met your mother once, at your father's funeral, and she seemed like a very lovely lady. Has any changes occurred within her?"

"Not at all," Sadie answered sincerely. Although she had a fight with her mother recently, Mrs. Covington was always defensive and protective, especially when it came to Khalid. Sadie knew her mother loved them all. Grant it, Mrs. Covington could be brutally honest and a bit hard at times, but there was not an ounce of wickedness in her. There was no difference in Mrs. Covington that Sadie could surmise.

"Good, but keep your eyes open. Sky's dream is an omen. Don't ignore it," Ari warned.

"What about my dad?" Sadie asked.

"If he is appearing to Sky, listen to what he is saying. If he is appearing as clearly as she says, his message should be easy to understand. Borrowed time is so important for a spirit. Being cryptic would be counterproductive," answered Ari.

"Thank you so much for your time," said Sadie as she looked at the time on her cell phone. "It's getting late and I have a date with my husband."

"It was a pleasure," Ari responded. "Call me anytime if you need me." He kissed her hand, and walked toward the door. Before he exited, he turned around with a very grave look on his face and said, "Be watchful at all times." He left the office and left Sadie as confused as ever.

25

Khalid stood staring at the heavens with tears streaming down his flushed cheeks. Heavy breaths ripped through his nostrils as he growled. The grass beneath his feet dried, and turned brown with each passing of his feet. He stomped and raged, pacing back and forth.

"Father!" Khalid screamed. "You lied to me!"

A great wind knocked Khalid off of his feet. A blinding lightning bolt struck inches from him, generating clouds of dirt and debris. Khalid squealed as he scrambled away from the choking dirt cloud, his little hands grabbing the grass as if the very earth would turn sideways and drop him off.

"Respect!" a voice echoed through the air before Turiel's feet appeared out of nothingness and hit the ground in front of Khalid. Then, the angel appeared in all his glory causing the boy to fall prostrate; covering his face with quaking arms.

"Father," Khalid wailed. Dirt clung to his moist lips as he spoke with his face touching the ground. The dead grass and soil made him cough. Snot and tears watered the ground. "You promised to give her to me. Now she has chosen someone else!"

Turiel's brilliance dimmed and his countenance became easier to behold. His wings folded behind him granting him the appearance of a mortal.

"Get up!" Turiel commanded.

Khalid scrambled to his feet. Dirt and grass speckled his clothes. He wiped his face with the back of his arm leaving a shiny streak of tears, mucus, and saliva down his forearm.

"Come to me!" Turiel bellowed; his eyes golden slits.

Khalid shuffled over to him on shaking legs. He looked up into his father's face, and the angel pulled the boy close to him and folded Khalid into his arms. A feeling of euphoria filled the child as he was lifted into the air. Warmth and tingling danced across every inch of Khalid's skin. The beating of his heart lingered between life and death.

"My son, I have no power over the object of your affection. I cannot control a soul. I can only influence. If she does not choose you, I can do nothing to change that," Turiel whispered to Khalid without words.

Khalid's head spun as the wind encircled him.

"But I want her," Khalid slurred. His eyes rolled back in his head.

"Then you shall have her," Turiel echoed in Khalid's mind. "You shall have her or she shall have no one."

"Father, don't leave me," Khalid begged. "You are the only one who understands. Remain with me."

"I will never leave you nor forsake you," Turiel implanted into Khalid's thoughts.

Khalid's eyes closed and his consciousness was lost. When he came to, he was laying in his backyard beneath a pecan tree.

Mrs. Covington sat upon the small cushioned bench in front of her bedroom window, and looked out of the window into the back yard. The sky was cloudless. The trees danced in the sunlight. She allowed her eyes to admire her garden, the small pond, and her fruitful pecan tree. When her eyes moved from the top of the tree to the bottom, Mrs. Covington clasped her chest and gasped in horror. It was in the middle of the day and her grandson was lying under the tree like a corpse. Mrs. Covington opened the window and screamed his name. There was no answer. She quickly slipped her foot into a pair of clogs, flew down the stairs, and out of the door into the backyard faster than she thought her aged body could possibly move.

"Khalid," she called as she shook the unresponsive child. "Khalid," she yelled. "Wake up baby!" She fell upon her knees and shook him frantically. "Please wake up!"

Khalid opened his eyes and sat up.

"What happened?" Mrs. Covington asked, falling back on her behind. "And, what are you doing home?" Her eyes dim with confusion.

"I...I...I don't know," Khalid answered, still in a stupor.

"What do you mean you don't know? I walked you to the school bus myself! How did you get home?" Mrs. Covington barked. "Tell me what's going on here!"

"I don't know grandma," Khalid answered truthfully. "I..." Khalid looked up and then past his grandmother.

Mrs. Covington spun around to see what was behind her. Fear seized her as her eyes focused upon Turiel; the same Turiel that killed Dr. Putina before her eyes years ago; the same angel that assaulted her daughter and fathered her grandson. Mrs. Covington grabbed her grandson and crawled backwards; the roots of the tree hurting her palms, and her emerald green pantsuit getting soiled as she tried to scurry to her feet.

"What do you want?" she cried, pulling Khalid as close to her as possible.

"You," Turiel rejoined.

"Me?" Mrs. Covington asked. She wrapped her arms around Khalid, sure that death was coming.

"Yes you," Turiel said to Mrs. Covington as he tossed the boy to the side, leaving her alone with her terror.

Khalid fell backwards and watched in dismay as Turiel transformed into a cloud of light and surrounded Mrs. Covington. The cloud absorbed into her very pores as she screamed and convulsed on the ground; her legs kicking and her arms flailing. Foam dripped from her mouth and her eyes rolled back in her head. Her black skin glistened with perspiration. In seconds, the cloud was gone and Mrs. Covington keeled over.

Khalid scurried over to Mrs. Covington and shook her limp body. He squealed, "Grandma, are you okay?" Tears poured down his face. "Grandma!" he whined. Khalid checked her pulse. He couldn't find it. Her chest did not rise and fall. Her body lay completely still. Khalid let go of his grandmother, and allowed her body to rest upon the ground. He screamed into the empty air, "Father! Where are you? What did you do to my grandma?" Khalid wailed.

Mrs. Covington inhaled and started to cough. She sat up; then, slowly got to her feet. She looked deep into Khalid's eyes.

Khalid stepped backwards. His head turned sideways as he met her gaze. A look of strange recognition covered Khalid's face.

"Father?" Khalid asked; his voice trembling.

"It is I," Turiel answered through Mrs. Covington's mouth with her voice.

"What did you do with grandma?" Khalid asked; more tears began to form in his eyes. Confusion filled his mind. He saw his grandmother before him, but he knew in his heart that it was not her. Her body didn't move the same. It moved in a delayed motion with a slight tick. Her facial expressions were not her own.

"She's safe inside. I'm just using her for a while," Turiel answered. "I will do her no harm."

Mrs. Covington popped and rolled her neck, and stretched her arms and legs until her movements were smooth and near normal.

"But why?" Khalid cried, taken aback by the angel adjusting himself in Mrs. Covington's body.

"So I can be with you," Turiel answered, reaching for Khalid's hand.

Khalid looked into her eyes and accepted her hand and the two of them walked into the house.

The restaurant was swanky. Posh chandeliers dangled from the ceilings dimly lighting the dining room in a soft glow. Crisp white table cloths covered every table, and fresh fragrant flowers sat in the middle of each one. The waiters were dressed in black trousers and white shirts complete with black neckties and cufflinks. Smooth jazz played in the background as couples flirted with their eyes, and tasted food so good that it seemed to be magically produced.

James sat across from Sadie. He picked up one of her hands and kissed her palm lightly. Joy filled him to have his wife out for a romantic night. He had to call in a favor to get reservations because the restaurant was booked months in advanced. James had detailed the car of the restaurant's owner and the owner told James that if he ever needed anything, give her a call. So, James called and left her a message. When James' phone call was returned, he was granted the opportunity to wine and dine Sadie at the most exclusive restaurant in Atlanta.

Sadie had been having such a stressful time and he wanted them to unwind and get back to their old selves.

Sadie and James were close, but lately Sadie had been obsessed with thoughts of Khalid and it was driving a wedge between her and James. It was difficult for her to focus on anything. All she talked about was scenarios that repeatedly asked what if Khalid was this or that, and all of the scenarios were negative ones. James was growing quite weary of the conversations. Tonight was a night that they both promised to not talk about their family problems and just focus on themselves. Tonight was a night for love, for romance, for intimacy, and hopefully for passion.

"James, this place is beautiful. How did you ever get a reservation," Sadie inquired. Sadie knew that obtaining a reservation there was extremely difficult. A person had to be President Barack Obama to get a seat.

"Ya boy got skills," he quipped. "Nothing is too good for my baby."

Sadie blushed and raised one eyebrow. Her husband was sexy, smart, and charming, but refined he was not. At once, she became more intrigued about how he managed to get a reservation at the most high-class restaurant in Atlanta, but she would let her questions linger for a night and not let her inquisition ruin a beautiful evening.

"Thank you sweetheart. This place is amazing and so are you," Sadie said. "I'm so excited. I always wondered what this placed looked like in the inside. With their reservation schedule, I thought we would make it in on out fiftieth wedding anniversary!" Sadie laughed.

"I'm glad you like it." James smiled and said in a horrible make believe accent, "Shall we order."

Sadie laughed. "Yes!" she squealed.

When the waiter returned, they ordered the most exquisite things on the menu, and requested the finest wine available. The wine arrived quickly. The two sipped slowly.

"Mmm perfect," Sadie cooed. "Not too sweet and not too dry."

At just the perfect temperature, hot enough to eat immediately but not too hot to burn your tongue, the beautifully plated food was sat before Sadie and James. It looked so appetizing that neither of them wanted to stick their fork in it and ruin the artistry. Admiration of the food was short lived when James thrust his fork into his well-done filet mignon. Sadie tasted her golden chicken breast with a stem of buttered asparagus.

"This is delicious," Sadie exclaimed after she swallowed her first bite. "I was so afraid that this place was all hype. The food is actually very good."

"I know! Right!" James exclaimed with a mouth full of food.

Sadie turned her eyes away from him quickly so that her appetite would not be spoiled by the sight of saliva mashed food. James was an unrefined in many ways, but he was still the best man she had ever known. She took her napkin and wiped her husband's mouth; then bent over the small table to kiss him softly. James' eyes beamed. This was the first time in weeks that Sadie looked happy. He desperately missed his wife's smile. It was the most beautiful thing about her. James could be forever lost within the contours of her mouth and the sweet softness of her full lips.

"I love you," she whispered and quickly sat back down.

"I love you too," James responded with a squeezed of her hand. "I miss us bein' close like this baby."

"Me too," Sadie said, her eyes looking down at her plate. "Sorry I've been so distant. So many things have been on my mind.

"I know," said James. "But we can't let anything come between us. Baby, you and me can work anything out."

"You and I," Sadie corrected with a laugh.

James rolled his eyes and popped her thigh.

"Whateva," he grumbled. "You know what I mean."

"Yes I do." Sadie smiled. "So, how was your day?" she asked.

"It was pretty smooth. Everything was copasetic," James answered.

"I assume your new assistant is doing a good job. You haven't said much about her," said Sadie.

James took a sip of wine. He looked into his wife's eyes and smiled. He leaned back in his chair and said," Timoo is awesome. I can't even lie. She's the next best assistant I've ever had. I never thought I would ever find anyone as good as Princeston, but she anticipates my every need. All of my work is caught up. My budget is balanced, bills paid, and office organized. That chick is bad," James bragged.

"Umhum." Sadie twisted her mouth. "How does she look?" Sadie asked.

James started laughing so hard that he almost spit his wine across the table. He regained his composure and answered, "She ain't as fine as you," with a smirk on his face.

"That's a given," Sadie retorted arrogantly. "But, is she pretty?"

"Yes, she's very pretty," James answered honestly. "She's also extremely professional and qualified."

"I'm not a jealous woman James. You can have your pretty assistant as long as I am the only one you love and desire," Sadie said humbly. "I don't care how pretty she is."

James laughed again. "Yes you do!" he blurted out.

Sadie giggled.

James grabbed both of her hands and turned them palm side up. He kissed them gently and said, "I love you more than I love myself. I would never cheat on you nor leave you. You don't ever have to worry about me. Okay baby?"

"Okay," Sadie uttered. Sadie smiled. She was very secure in her relationship, but reassurance was always a nice thing to hear.

"How was your day?" asked James before he put a fork full of food into his mouth.

"It was pretty good. I implemented a hip-hop aerobics class in one of the convents and a salsa class in another one. The nuns think the classes are all the rave. You would be surprised how those sisters can shake their booties." Sadie laughed. "I also met up with Dr. Ari Aniwodi-El today to get some information about Sky's dream."

"Really?" James grumbled. His eyes narrowed into slits. He could not stand Dr. Ari Aniwodi-El. James felt that the man flirted with Sadie in front of his face. It was just plain disrespectful in James' eyes. There were a few times James considered taking Dr. Aniwodi-El outside and whooping his butt. Dr. Aniwodi-El was way too bold for James' liking. Sadie claimed that Dr. Aniwodi-El was like that with all women. She claimed that he wasn't flirting. He was just charming. *Whatever!* James thought.

"So what did he say?" James asked; his tone harsh and annoyed.

"Seriously James? Are you still jealous of Ari?" Sadie asked, putting her fork down and twisting one side of her mouth upward.

"Oh, he Ari now?" James spat.

Sadie started laughing.

"He has always been Ari. We have known each other for most of my adulthood. Did you forget that he was a friend of my father?"

"Whateva. Did he try to kiss you again?" James asked, putting his fork down and mean mugging her.

"He didn't try to kiss me the first time!" Sadie snapped. "Sometimes you can be so silly acting."

A few years ago, Sadie and James, and Ari and his wife Latrice attended a charity music festival. Ari tried to tell Sadie to move out of the way of a drunken fan who had a glass full of alcohol that was destined to drench Sadie. The music was so loud that she could not hear him, so Ari moved closer to her ear but she turned her head and they ended up lip to lip. It was simply a coincidence, but James pulled Sadie to the side and accused Ari of stealing a kiss from her. Sadie found the whole accusation foolish because for one, Ari and Latrice were madly in love and two, Ari was a gentleman and would never be disrespectful to his wife nor to Sadie; therefore, the entire accusation was absolutely ludicrous.

James twisted his mouth and took a deep breath. This was not the time to argue. They were supposed to be having a good night. He forced the frown from his face and asked, "What did the good doctor have to say?"

Sadie smirked and answered, "He said that Mom was pure evil, and that we needed to watch out for her."

"That's just plain stupid," James barked. "Your mom is freakin' awesome."

"I agree," Sadie said. "But I can't ignore all the warnings from Sky and now Ari."

"So what you plan to do?" James asked; no longer full of jealously but sincere concern. He was skeptical about Dr. Aniwodi-El's diagnosis, but it was clear that Sadie was not.

"Watch," Sadie replied. She grabbed James' hand and said, "But, tonight we won't worry about it. Tonight is about us."

27

Ari inserted his key into the keyhole of his front door. Before he could turn the knob, the door flew open and four children jumped into his arms nearly knocking him over.

Ari laughed and tumbled backwards. He kissed Aminah, Zahyir, Ru, and Aura on their foreheads, and pushed his way into the house. Each child clung to him like Velcro. He loved every bit of it. After picking up three year old Ru, he sat his messenger bag on a nearby table.

"How was your day Abba?" Aminah asked after she kissed his cheek, and plopped down on the den sofa next to Aura who was engulfed in her cell phone. "Did you have a good day at work?"

"I did," Ari answered. "I taught a few classes, had a wonderful business lunch. The food was so good."

"What did you eat?" asked Aura, looking up from her phone for a second.

"A falafel with extra cucumber sauce and a Greek salad," Ari answered.

"Mmm. Sounds good," Aura mumbled as she turned her attention back to her phone.

"What else did you do?" Aminah asked.

"I saw Mrs. Tucker today. She wanted me to interpret a dream for her," Ari responded. He sat between his daughters. He sat his third daughter upon his lap.

Aminah and Aura were sixteen year old fraternal twins, and they couldn't be more different. Aminah looked like Latrice and Aura looked like Ari. Aminah was a mama's girl, and Aura was a daddy's girl. Aminah was tall and Aura was short. Aminah was light and thin, and Aura was dark and curvy. Aminah dressed like a rebel, and Aura was conservative; but, they both were pretty, great students, and creative individuals.

"Oh, tell me about it," Aminah cooed.

"I'm out of here. Ya'll can have all the spooky talk," Aura said. She kissed her father on the forehead and said, "I'm going to my room."

Ari and Aminah watched Aura as she left the room. Aminah turned back to her father and waited for him to continue.

"Well," Ari began. "It wasn't Sadie's dream. It was her friend's dream."

"And?" Aminah asked, already becoming bored with the topic. He was taking too long to get to the juicy part of the story.

"I told her that her dream was an omen and that she should be careful," Ari answered and stood up, Ru still clinging to his hip.

Aminah turned away, picked up her cell phone and mumbled, "Okay."

"Ma! Abba is here!" Zahyir yelled through the house.

"I really wish you wouldn't yell through the house like that Zahyir," said Ari. "Next time, just go tell her."

"Sorry," Zahyir mumbled and ran over to the sofa. He picked up the video game remote and continued playing the game he was playing before his father entered the house.

Ari carried Ru on his hip up the stairs and into his bedroom. When he walked in, he found his wife asleep across the bed with a book in one hand and her phone in the other; her behind towards the door and upper thighs exposed. Her locked hair surrounded her head like black sunbeams; as if each lock was meticulously pulled straight and place in perfect juxtaposition to the nearest one until a semicircle was formed. Latrice snored quietly. Ari put Ru on the floor. He laid his body atop of his sleeping wife; careful not to put all his weight on her. Ari kissed her neck until she began to stir. Latrice turned and he slid beside her.

"Hey sweetie," Ari greeted. "I missed you today."

Latrice kissed him deeply and wrapped her legs around him and said, "I missed you too. I was so tired. I came up here to check my voicemails and fell asleep."

Ru crawled up on the bed and tried to squeeze between the cuddling couple. Ari and Latrice broke their embrace and allowed Ru to squeeze between them.

"Rest yourself. I'm going to go downstairs to my office. Do you want me to take Ru to the den?" asked Ari.

"No, she can stay up here with me. I need to wash her hair and bathe her before bed," Latrice answered and stood up. Her fitted skirt fell to her ankles.

"You're so darn gorgeous," Ari said as he let his eyes roam over her round hips and small waist. In a voice that sounded like a character in a Blaxploitation film, Ari said, "When God made you, he was just showin' off. He boasted with glee upon your creation. Anything better he would've kept for himself. What can I say, you're the perfect formation!"

"You sound like Dolemite! You're so silly," Latrice said mid giggle.

Ari chuckled, "You know it's true."

"Well, thank you." Latrice smirked. "I'll show you how grateful I am later on."

Ari smiled.

Latrice stretched and sat back down. She pulled Ru into her lap and started to untwist and take bows out of her hair. Ru squirmed and flailed until she was locked between Latrice's knees and crossed ankles. Ru stopped fighting and settled within her fleshy prison.

"How was your day?" Latrice asked her husband; her fingertips parting Ru's thick kinky hair.

Ari sat down beside Latrice, and started making faces and poking his tongue out at Ru. Ru giggled uncontrollably.

"It was interesting," Ari answered.

"How so?" Latrice asked while combing through Ru's tangles.

"I had an appointment with Sadie Tucker today. She called me to her office to interpret a dream that her friend had about Mrs. Covington. Also, Sadie's friend Sky claims that Mr. Covington has been visiting her," said Ari.

"That is interesting," Latrice replied, starting on another section of Ru's hair. "So what happened?"

"Nothing really," answered Ari. He told Latrice about the meeting with Sadie in detail. "That dream really bothers me. I'm really worried about Mrs. Covington and Sadie. I feel like something is going on with her son Khalid that she's not telling me."

"Me too," Latrice agreed. "I know it sounds awful for me to say this because children are children, but I don't like their oldest son." Latrice cringed at her own words. Guilt filled her for disliking a child, but what she felt was real. She continued, "Something is very off about that boy. I can't put my finger on it, but Zahyir senses it too. He told me that Khalid makes his skin crawl. Zahyir told me that Khalid had a crush on Evadne, and that she was freaked out by him until she suddenly had a change of heart."

"Hmm," Ari sighed. "I really don't know the child enough to make a determination. All I know is that Sadie's friend said that Mr. Covington warned that the child was dangerous. Sky's dream implies that Mrs. Covington is dangerous. I'll pray on it. Hopefully, I will gain some clarity. I'm going downstairs. I'll be back up in a couple of hours."

"Okay baby," she said as she received his kiss.

Ari headed out of the bedroom door, and went down the stairs into his office. He flipped on the light and closed the door. Stacks of paper, ink pens, and books littered his desk. Books filled shelves in every corner of the room. A shiny black laptop sat in the middle of the mess. Ari turned on a small space heater, and pointed it towards his desk. It was always very cold in his basement office no matter what time of year it was. For Ari to acknowledge the coolness of the basement, said a lot. Ari was usually hot in forty degree weather.

Ari sat down and turned on his laptop. He gathered a few nearby books, his reading glasses, and began to type on his latest research project.

"Ari," a voice called out. "Ari."

"Yes," Dr. Ari Aniwodi-El answered. He immediately stopped reading the papers in his hands, and laid them on his desk top. The voice sounded strangely familiar. His eyes scoured over the room looking for the body that the voice belonged to. "Who's there?" he asked, now standing up.

"Ari," the disembodied voice called again. "Protect my daughter."

"Who are you?" Ari asked. Chills ran down his spine. "Who are you?" he yelled into the emptiness of his office. There was no answer. He sat back down at his desk and picked up his reading glasses; his heart slamming against his ribs. He opened his Bible to Psalms 91, and began a prayer of protection.

It was late when Sadie and James came home from dinner. The kids were sound asleep. Complete silence. All the lights were off in the house. Every nightlight was turned off and every TV was black. Sadie found that very bizarre. Everyone in her household knew that she was afraid of the dark, and that there was never a time in her home when all the lights should have been out unless there was a massive blackout.

Sadie grabbed James' arm tight, afraid that the darkness would attack her. To Sadie, the darkness was an entity in and of itself. It was a thing that she could feel simultaneously crawling on every inch of her body, tempting her fear of it to come out and play.

James closed the door behind him, and guided her through the room, only causing her to bump her toe on a piece of furniture once. James flicked on the living room lamp. They both jumped at the sight of Mrs. Covington sitting on the sofa.

"Mom, what are you doing sitting in the dark?" Sadie asked, instantly worried about her mother.

Mrs. Covington wasn't a fan of the dark either. She may have been even more afraid of the dark than Sadie. Sadie was sure that she inherited the fear of the dark from her mother. Sadie could remember growing up in a house with an abnormal amount of nightlights everywhere. One room could have up to four nightlights in it. Her father said that their hallways looked like landing strips for airplanes. In each bedroom, Mrs. Covington used to have two lamps, nightlights, and a ceiling light. Darkness was not welcomed in the Covington home, and it was not welcomed in the Tucker home neither.

Mrs. Covington looked up at her daughter; her eyes unblinking. An eerie grin warped her face.

"Mom, are you okay?" Sadie asked. She rushed over to her mother and grabbed her by the hand. James followed.

Mrs. Covington sat in a catatonic state for at least five minutes as Sadie called her mother's name, squeezed her mother's hand, and waved in front of her mother's face.

"I think I need to call an ambulance," said James; pulling his cell phone out of his pocket.

Mrs. Covington blinked and smiled. She said, "I'm sorry baby. I must have been dreaming."

Sadie looked at her mother and then at James.

"Mom, have you been drinking?" Sadie asked.

Mrs. Covington didn't drink a lot but when she did, she drank until her head swam, and she was as giddy as a school girl.

"Of course not," Mrs. Covington answered. She smiled a strange smile.

"You don't seem like yourself Mama C. Are you sure everything is okay?" James asked as he sat beside her, and put the back of his hand on her forehead to check her temperature.

"I'm okay," she whispered. Her breath smelled like myrrh. James was taken aback.

"What have you been eating?" he asked.

Mrs. Covington stood up and stretched her neck. Her neck circle extended so far backwards that her head looked as if it was touching her mid-back.

The hairs on the back of James' neck stood up, so did Sadie's.

Mrs. Covington started to walk towards the stairs; her stride contrary to its normal pace; her posture slightly bent, unlike her normal straight back and high chin.

"Mom, where are you going?" Sadie called after her.

"To bed," Mrs. Covington mumbled as she disappeared into the dark hallway.

Sadie sat down next to James. They both sat in silence for a long moment.

"Now I'm getting worried," Sadie said to her husband. "It's not like Mom to act all spaced out like that." Sadie kicked her shoes off and dropped her purse in a nearby chair. She removed her jacket and propped her legs up on the coffee table. "Did you see the way she stretched?"

James nodded.

"Did you notice how she walked?" Sadie asked. "She moved differently. I can't put my finger on it, but it was definitely different."

James agreed with Sadie. Worry distorted his face. The smell of myrrh on Mrs. Covington's breath didn't make things better. He instantly decided not to tell Sadie about the smell because he knew she would become hysterical and be convinced that Sky's dream had merit.

"What if something is wrong with Mama? What if she's changing into the evil lady in Sky's dream?" Sadie whined.

"Mama C will be just fine. She just tired. Them boys probably wore her out. I wouldn't get to wound up if I were you," James said. Truth be told, he was a bit wound up himself. Mrs. Covington was behaving totally contrary to her nature. The look in her eyes was foreign, and the way she spoke and smelled made James' skin itch. He wanted so desperately to share his feelings with Sadie, but he knew in his heart that she would blow everything out of proportion and go on a witch hunt. So, James decided to keep the matter to himself. He would keep Sadie on a need to know basis and right now his wife didn't need to know what her mother's breath smelled like.

When James woke up the next morning, he awoke to the smell of absolutely nothing. He had not smelled "nothing" for breakfast in almost a decade. Ever since Mrs. Covington moved into their home, she had cooked breakfast for the family every morning except for the weekend. The family had been spoiled by the expectation of fresh fruit, pancakes, waffles, or homemade biscuits, bacon or sausage, and a beverage of choice. Now, the smell of fresh coffee was nonexistent, and the smell of turkey bacon for Sadie (real bacon for him and the boys), was a distant memory.

James grumpily climbed out of bed. He woke the boys and told them to get dressed for school. When the boys were ready, James threw on some jogging pants and a ratty T-shirt and walked them to the bus stop. When he got back to the house, he slowly climbed the stairs, still disappointed that he would not be able to eat Mrs. Covington's home cooking. James entered into his bedroom and began to get dressed for work.

"Wake up," James said as he caressed Sadie's shoulder. She stirred but did not wake. "Baby, wake up. You're gonna be late for work," said James.

Sadie rolled onto her side and opened her eyes. "What time is it?" she asked, shielding her eyes from the light.

"7:30," James responded as he pulled on his socks. He buttoned up his shirt. With every movement he grumbled, obviously irritated.

"What's wrong with you?" Sadie asked. She covered her mouth before a big yawn blew her morning breath into James' face. James backed back, thankful for the block.

"I had to give the kids money to eat breakfast at school this morning," James said with disappointment in his voice.

"Why?" Sadie asked as she threw her legs over the side of the bed and stood up. She walked into the bathroom and sat on the toilet. James followed her and stood in the doorway of the bathroom.

"I don't know," James said. He lifted and dropped his shoulders. "When I woke up, Mama C was just sittin' in the den watchin' TV."

"What?" Sadie exclaimed. "Watching TV? I can't believe that. Is she sick?" Sadie asked as she flushed the toilet and turned on the shower.

"Maybe sick in the head," James mumbled, still a little annoyed that he didn't get a good breakfast. He knew he was being selfish for feeling that way because Mrs. Covington was not obligated to fix him anything, but James was used to her good cooking and he hated the fact that he was without it this morning. He pouted about the situation, but let his selfish feelings pass as he watched Sadie undress and get into the shower. He was tempted to undress and get in behind her, but if he did, they both would be late for work. He decided against it and began to brush his teeth.

"I can't believe you said she was watching TV," said Sadie as she lathered and rinsed. "Mama hates TV! She reads her news and listens to talk radio for entertainment. What was she watching?"

James spat in the sink and washed the toothpaste out of his mouth. He wiped his mouth and answered, "I'm not sure, but it was full of naked people and killin'! It was so graphic that I had to tell the boys to close their eyes when we were walkin' out of the door. I asked her several times to turn it off, but she ignored me like I didn't say a word. When I got back in the house from the bus stop, I tried to get her attention but she stared at that TV like she was hypnotized or somethin'. I grabbed the remote from the coffee table and turned the TV off. She turned to me, hissed, and bolted up the stairs like her butt was on fire!"

Sadie stepped out of the shower and dried herself off. A fretful look was painted across her face. The behavior that James described coupled with her behavior the night they found her sitting in the dark, definitely was not her mother. Sadie dressed quickly and headed straight to her mother's room. When she arrived at the door, she twisted the knob without knocking. Instantly Sadie felt like she was causing a major violation, but she opened the door anyway.

Mrs. Covington sat motionless upon her bed, staring at the wall.

"Mom," Sadie called.

Mrs. Covington didn't respond. She sat, a shell of a woman, as if she was frozen in time.

Sadie sat down next to Mrs. Covington. She placed her hand upon her mother's knee.

"Mom, are you okay?" Sadie asked, looking into her mother's blank stare. "Speak to me Mama."

Sadie took her finger and moved a strand of her mother's hair behind her ear. Mrs. Covington's silky black hair blended seamlessly with her skin.

Mrs. Covington turned and cupped Sadie's face within her hands. She leaned forward with the intention of placing a kiss upon Sadie's forehead; but when Mrs. Covington's myrrh tinged breath drifted into Sadie's nostrils, Sadie recoiled from her mother. Sadie pounced from the bed and backed into a wall. She squawked, "Mother, what has he done to you!"

"Who?" Mrs. Covington asked as she slowly stood up and walked over to Sadie.

"You know who!" Sadie squealed. She slid sideways on the wall, then bolted across the room; almost running into her mother's side table and knocking down her father's picture. She yelped, "I know he has been here. I can smell him on you!"

Mrs. Covington cackled like a cartoon villain and said, "You're being silly." She sat back upon her bed, her eyes not leaving Sadie for one minute. "Close the door behind you when you leave. I'm tired," she commanded in a monotone voice.

"Tired of what?" Sadie balked. "You just woke up. You didn't cook breakfast, and you're still in your night gown. I have not seen you in your nightgown this late in the morning since I was four! What's going on with you? Are you okay?"

"Leave my room before you regret it," Mrs. Covington hissed through her teeth. A strange shimmer flashed across her eyes.

Sadie sprang at her mother and grabbed her by the shoulders.

"What's wrong with you?" Sadie asked, shaking her mother with hopes of shaking her back to some form of normality.

Mrs. Covington broke her daughter's grasp and pushed Sadie clear across the room and out of the door in one motion. On the hallway floor, Sadie fell with a loud thump. Before she could get to her feet, Mrs. Covington's door slammed hard in Sadie's face.

Sky, out of breath, opened the trunk of her minivan. Her three children playfully snatched her shopping bags from her and tossed them into the trunk. Sky closed the trunk and popped the locks. The children raced past her, almost knocking her off balance, to see who could get into the car first.

"Mom, tell Venus to move over!" Earth whined; trying fruitlessly to climb over her big sister. "I was here first!"

"Venus, move over so your sister can get in the van," Sky grumbled. She was way too tired to deal with their fighting today. "Jupiter, please handle your sisters for me so I can get into the car."

A wicked grin curled Jupiter's lips. He loved it when he was in charge. It was rare for him to be given power over his annoying little sisters. Now it was time for him to set them straight so he could hurry home to watch a documentary on Marcus Garvey that he had recorded the night before on the DVR.

"Venus!   You better move over now," Jupiter threatened with his eyes. He pointed to the empty seat behind Sky. "Now!" he growled; his red eyebrows pointing downward.

Venus saw her mother looking at her in the rearview mirror, and sluggishly moved to the next seat while Earth moved to the third row of the minivan.

"You better had moved," Jupiter growled as he sat down and closed the sliding door.

"Shut up!" Venus yelled. "You ain't the king of me!" she squawked with rolling eyes and crossed arms. "You can't tell me what to do. You ain't my mama or my daddy you technicolored swamp rat!"

"You don't even know what technicolored mean!" Jupiter shouted.

"The proper words to say are 'are not'. Ain't isn't a word," Earth whispered from the back seat, crossing her legs and folding her hands over her knee.

Venus spun around and yelled, "I know you ain't tryin' to correct me! I'll come back there and..."

"You won't do anything," Jupiter intervened. "Turn around and be quiet before Mama jumps on you."

Venus saw her mother's eyes burning into her through the rearview mirror, and Venus knew very well that Sky was doing a countdown in her head. Sky could only tolerate yelling and arguing for so long before she pounced; so, Venus decided it was best for her to stop while she was ahead and be quiet. She would handle Earth and Jupiter later. Venus put on her earphones and turned on her music.

"We're all buckled in Ma," Jupiter said, his voice drunk with power. He convinced himself that he tamed Venus on his own, and that his mother's deadly stare had nothing to do with Venus behaving herself.

Sky laughed under her breath and said thank you. As she turned on the ignition, Sky heard the voice of Prince singing *The Question of U*. Sky picked up her cell phone and answered, "Hello."

"Hey girl," Sadie said. "How are you?"

"Tired as hell!" Sky barked. "My kids are workin' my nerves. My stomach is getting too close to the steerin' wheel. The baby is tap dancin' in my stomach. I've been craving eggs and chocolate milk all day every day. My husband works too much. My car is low on gas. My next book is overdue, and I'm hungry!"

"You want me to call you back?" Sadie asked. "You seem like you are going through a lot at the moment. Lord knows I don't want to be the next entry on that list."

"Naw, I ain't doin' nothin'. I can talk," answered Sky when she turned on the car, and pulled out into the intersection.

Sadie sighed. Sky was always so much drama, but Sadie loved Sky to pieces. Sadie knew no better person in the world.

"So, what are you doing?" Sadie instantly hated that she asked that question. It was an opening for another tirade, and Sadie didn't have the time to have a long drawn out conversation, nor did she desire to listen to more of Sky's complaints. Sadie was at work wasting time between meetings. She simply called to hear her friend's voice.

Sky replied that she was driving.

Sadie was relieved.

"So what did that doctor dude, that you have a crush on, say?" Sky asked. She jumped in front of a car. The sound of a horn blasting filled the street. She honked back and yelled out of the car window, "This is New York! Learn how to drive," then, sped on.

"First of all, I don't have a crush on anyone, but my husband. Second of all, that dude's name is Dr. Aniwodi-El," Sadie said in the midst of laughter.

"Whatever!" Sky chuckled. "What did he say?"

"He told me to watch out for Mom," answered Sadie.

"I could've told you that!" Sky quipped. "Did he say anything else?"

"Not really," Sadie mumbled. A melancholy feeling came over her. She felt alone. James didn't truly understand or didn't want to understand her fears about Khalid. Her mother was acting extremely strange; so strange that it frightened Sadie. Dr. Aniwodi-El made her uncomfortable, and didn't seem to be privy to anything relevant to her situation. The nuns were her colleagues not her friends. She had no one to talk to, and Sky was so far away.

Sensing that something was wrong, Sky broke the silence and asked, "Are you okay Sadie?"

"I'm alright I guess," Sadie whined. "I just don't know what to do. Mom is not herself. Khalid is obsessed with this girl who doesn't want him, but that fact doesn't seem to faze him at all. I think he's a bit of a stalker. James seems oblivious to everything. Dr. Aniwodi-El didn't clarify anything. Oh Sky, I wish that you were here." Sadie sighed.

"Say no more," Sky said. "I'll talk to Forrest tonight. The kids and I will be in Atlanta next week. Maybe we'll stay for a couple of weeks. Forrest can come down the week after we arrive. His vacation time is coming up."

"Sky, I can't have you flying down here. You're pregnant, and it is so stressful here. All the drama at my house may not be healthy for the baby. Besides, your children have school. You don't..."

"I do what I want!" Sky snapped. "I'm coming down and you can't stop me. I'll call their teachers, and pick up two or three weeks of school work for the kid's. I'll make sure that they email their homework daily. They're all one grade level ahead. Trust me. They will be alright!"

"If you say so," Sadie said, smiling to herself.

"I say so," Sky answered. "Do you have a guest room for me and the kids or do I need a hotel? I refuse to stay with Forrest's parents. Now, that would be too much stress for me and the baby." Sky paused. Thoughts of last summer in the Cohen home filled her mind. Day in and out of Mrs. Cohen telling Sky how to do things properly and the importance of refining her manners drove Sky up the wall. Mr. Cohen droned on about the importance of tradition and tried to convince Sky to convert to Judaism so that his grandchildren would be Jews also. He was a kind man but very pushy. Sky couldn't wait to get back to Harlem. She continued, "I mean, The Cohens aren't horrible people, but Forrest's mom can really work my nerves. She's always lookin' at me sideways like I might steal her good china, and she's always hoverin' over me like a creep. I bet she inspired that Radiohead song.

I be tellin' Forrest that if his mama don't back up off me, Imma not so nicely tell her about herself."

"Our home has a three bedroom basement apartment. You all can stay here. There is plenty of space. I'm sure the boys would love to have you. James will be so thrilled to see Forrest," said Sadie, trying hard to hide the excitement in her voice. She knew it was selfish of her to have Sky fly down to Atlanta, but Sadie so desperately wanted her best friend to be near her.

"Great! We can't wait to see you!" Sky sang. "I need to get out of New York for a little while. Plus, I miss you so much!"

"I miss you too," Sadie paused. Her guilt got the best of her. "Sky."

"Yes," Sky answered.

"Let me pay for the plane tickets," Sadie begged. "I feel so bad that I have you all coming down here because I'm all stressed out. You're a mom-to-be and you don't need to be in this environment. At least let me buy the tickets for you and the kids. If you refuse, I will refuse to let you stay here. You will have to shack up with Mama Cohen."

"Who am I to turn down a fool and her money?" Sky quipped. "You can pay if it makes you happy."

"Thank you!" Sky yelped. "I'll get downstairs ready for you. I can't wait to tell James, Mom, and the boys. See you next week!"

"See you soon. Take care," Sky said and hung up the phone.

"Ma!" Jupiter yelled.

"What, boy?" asked Sky, looking at him in the rearview mirror.

"Where we going?" Jupiter asked. He and his sisters all leaned forward to hear.

"Atlanta," Sky answered. "We're going to start packing our bags when we get home. We're going to the ATL!"

31

"Mr. Tucker," Timoo called through James' cracked office door. She pushed her hand through the crack and peeked into the room. Her eyes lit up when she saw him. James Tucker was the most attractive man that she had seen in years. Not only was he nice looking, he was tall with an incredible body, and he owned his own business.

James looked up from his computer. He smiled.

"May I come in?" Timoo asked, her heart pounding against her blouse. She took a deep breath to calm herself.

"Of course," James answered, closing his laptop and leaning back in his chair.

Timoo opened the door and sauntered into the room, her hips swaying like arms at a concert. Her eyes danced as she walked over to James' desk, and leaned over to hand him a file; ensuring that their fingers touched when the file changed hands. Her blouse was fitted and unbuttoned just enough to tease, but buttoned up enough to still remain professional. She bit her bottom lip and smiled.

James cleared his throat and diverted his eyes from her to the file.

"How can I help you?" James asked, folding his hands together and placing them on top of his laptop.

"A new client just called and would like to hire us to be the official car detailer for a luxury car show that is scheduled for next month. He realizes that it is last minute and he is willing to pay double our normal rate if we can guarantee to have ten men on the job," Timoo said, trying to still her trembling hand. "I accepted the deal," she said quietly. "I know I didn't have the authority to do so, but it was an offer that I feel that we should not refuse. The money will be amazing and the advertising for the company will be priceless. May I sit?"

James nodded.

Timoo sat down and crossed her legs. She said, "When you hired me as an assistant, you told me that I would have slight managerial authority. Today, I exercised that authority."

James smiled. There was nothing more attractive than a beautiful woman with an incredible business mind. He admired her gumption.

Timoo continued, "I hope that I didn't overstep my boundaries. The client needed an answer immediately and you were on the phone when I buzzed you. I also shot you an email, which you didn't respond to. The client seemed to be in a hurry. I did not want to risk losing such a huge business opportunity," Timoo said. "I printed out a copy of the contract. All you have to do is review it and sign. I think our detailers would love to be at the car show. The client has included lunch and show tickets for the workers. It is a great networking opportunity for everyone."

James looked through the file that she had handed him. The contract was sound; and all the papers were in order. James already had in mind which workers he would send. He also thought it was a good idea to send Timoo as the representative for his company. James looked up at Timoo and extended his hand. She accepted it, and he shook her hand firmly.

"Good job Timoo. I'm impressed. Next time, consult me first. If I ain't answerin' you when you call, come into my office or call my cell phone," James said. "Although this is an excellent opportunity, I always need to offer final approval. Okay?"

"Okay," Timoo replied with a heavy heart, knowing she should have consulted him first, but she wanted so desperately to impress him. James' approval meant everything.

"Would you like to be the project manager over this project?" James asked.

Timoo's smile was so big that it disfigured her face.

"Yes!" she exclaimed; she clapped her hands together lightly like a child waiting on the circus to start.

"Great. Maybe we should discuss it over dinner," James suggested, his perfect white teeth flashing. "I know this wonderful restaurant that I know you would love."

"I would love to," Timoo said. "Where and what time?"

"Blue Unicorn Restaurant at 7:30pm. Is that convenient for you?" James asked.

"Quite. See you tonight," Timoo answered as she stood up and sauntered out of the room.

James watched her walk out of the door. He imagined music playing *boom chi chi boom* every time her hips rolled.

That woman is trouble, he thought to himself as he opened his laptop and continued working.

32

Sadie felt exultant inside. Sky was coming to Atlanta. It had been so long since she had seen her best friend. They had so much catching up to do. Sadie couldn't wait to call James and tell him, so she picked up her office phone and dialed James at work. He answered after the second ring.

"Hello," James said.

"Hey baby!" Sadie squealed.

"You sound happy," said James, closing his laptop.

"I am!" Sadie replied. "Sky is coming to Atlanta!"

"That's great! Is Forrest coming too?" James asked. He was so happy that Sky and Sadie were getting close again. Now his friendship with Forrest wouldn't have to be so secretive. Ever since a schism was made between Sky and Sadie, Forrest and James felt they had to speak sparingly without the knowledge of their wives. James didn't even feel comfortable telling Sadie about seeing Forrest on his last business trip because he did not want to be bombarded with a flurry of questions that would eventually rehash the events that caused the long silence between Sadie and Sky in the first place.

"When are they coming?" James asked.

"Sky is coming next week. Forrest is coming a week after that. I told them that they could stay in the basement. Is that okay with you?"

James laughed and answered, "Of course it is okay. Besides, you already told them they could. It ain't like you gone call back and say never mind."

"You're right!" Sadie giggled. "I can't wait until next week. I really miss Sky. I can't believe we let so much time pass. We ought to be ashamed."

"I know you do. I miss Forrest. Them coming will be good for all of us," James said.

"I'm so happy!" Sadie rejoiced. "That's all I wanted to tell you. I love you baby," Sadie said getting ready to hang up the phone but continued instead, "Oh yeah, what do you want me to make for dinner tonight?

"Don't cook," said James. "I have a dinner meeting tonight with Timoo. I would like for you to join us. I'm thinking about making her an assistant manager. She has a great business mind. I want to know what you think of her."

"What time?" Sadie asked. She didn't feel like eating out but she knew if it was important to James, it was important to her.

"Seven at Blue Unicorn," James replied. "I told her 7:30pm because I want us to get there early so we can talk for a bit."

"Okay, see you after work baby. I love you," Sadie cooed.

"Love you too. Bye baby," said James and hung up the phone.

As soon as Sadie put the phone on the hook, her secretary Emily buzzed in.

"Yes," Sadie answered.

"Dr. Aniwodi-El is on the line. Shall I transfer the call?" Emily asked, her southern belle accent making Sadie smile.

"Of course," Sadie said.

"Sadie?" Ari asked through the phone.

"Yes Ari," Sadie answered. "How are you?"

"I'm okay. How are you?" asked Ari.

"I'm actually feeling pretty good," replied Sadie. "Today has been a good day."

"Glad to hear that." Ari paused, trying to figure out what exactly he needed to ask first.

"Is everything okay?" asked Sadie.

"I'm not sure. I think your father came to visit me," he answered.

Sadie's smile turned upside down. She was hoping for one day without spooks or spoils. Now, her hopes were shattered.

"Why do you say that?" Sadie asked; kicking her shoes off under her desk, and rubbing her temples. She predicted a headache would be coming on soon.

Ari answered, "When I was in my office, a voice told me to watch over its daughter. Grant it, I didn't see anyone, but the voice was loud and clear. It also sounded a heck of a lot like your father.   In light of Dr. Covington appearing to Sky, I assume he was talking to me about you." Ari paused and took a deep breath.   There were clear traces of apprehension in his voice. He said, "Sadie, I feel like you are not telling me everything I need to know about your situation. I know it is not my business to pry into your personal life, but when spirits began to invade my personal sanctuary, I think I need to know what I may be dealing with."

Sadie held the phone in silence. She didn't know how much she needed to tell him. Did she need to tell him about Turiel? Did she need to tell him about her mother? Rehashing so many painful memories made Sadie anxious. What if she told him everything and he didn't believe her?

"Are you there?" Dr. Ari Aniwodi-El asked.

"I'm here," Sadie replied.

"You have to tell me something," Ari replied. "If you want me to continue to help you, I need to know what's going on. Be upfront with me. I will always be upfront with you."

"What do you need to know?" Sadie asked, her voice shaking.

"Dr. Covington's first warning to Sky was about your son. Tell me about your son. Tell me about Khalid," Ari requested. "I feel that he is at the root of all this."

"Khalid is a special boy," Sadie's voice shook uncontrollably. "H...h...his father..."

"James?" Ari asked.

"No," said Sadie. "James is not Khalid's father."

"Does James know this?" Ari asked in shock. He felt like he was sitting in the audience of a trashy talk show waiting for paternity test results.

"Yes," Sadie answered.

"Okay," Ari replied. He exhaled. "Does Khalid's father have anything to do with all this?"

"Yes," Sadie replied, then fell silent again.

Impatiently, Ari said, "Sadie, I know this may be difficult for you, but I really need you to talk to me. I have a class starting soon. As much as I would love to sit here and coax information out of you, I don't have that kind of time. Please forgive my impatience."

"Khalid's father is Turiel, an angel; a watcher to be specific. My son is a..."

"Nephilim," Ari and Sadie said in unison.

Ari almost dropped the phone. The information he had just obtained was more than he ever bargained for.

33

"Grandma!" Uriel called through the house. "Grandma!" he called again. He walked through the kitchen and den looking for her. Mrs. Covington was nowhere to be found. Uriel bumped into Khalid in the hallway and asked, "Mom just called. She and Dad are going out to dinner tonight. She wanted me to tell grandma that they will be late. Have you seen grandma?"

"She's in her room," Khalid responded. "Do you want me to tell her?"

"No. I want to talk to her. She's been acting weird lately. It seems like she doesn't want to be next to me," Uriel pouted.

"Don't be silly. She's been tired," said Khalid.

"But, she's not too tired to talk to you," Uriel whined. "She's always talking to you. She doesn't read books or play with me anymore."

"She only talks to me because I'm older. Some things you just don't understand," said Khalid.

"Like what?" Uriel asked.

"Like not knowing when to stop asking questions," snapped Khalid as he dashed past Uriel into the kitchen to fix a snack.

Uriel tried hard not to be hurt, but he could not help it. His grandmother was avoiding him. Even when she picked them up from the bus stop, she walked and talked with Khalid but ignored Uriel. Uriel could hear them whispering to one another late at night. He saw them take long walks together, engaged in deep conversation. The two shared so many secrets. Secrets that Uriel wanted to know.

Uriel shambled to his grandmother's room; the sound of his dragging feet echoing through the hall. When he got to his grandmother's room, he was surprised that her door was ajar. It was rare that Mrs. Covington's bedroom door was left open. Uriel knocked on the door. He received no response. The door was cracked, so he pushed it open and walked in.

"Grandma," Uriel called. He didn't see her. He peered into her bathroom. It was empty as well. Uriel began to pick up clothes from his grandmother's floor. It was unusual for her room to be so messy. She was an extremely meticulous woman. Usually a person could eat off of her floor; now, her carpet was speckled with all manner of things. Her bed was unmade. Books littered the side of her bed. Papers were pulled out of her drawer. Dead flowers sat in a vase next to his grandfather's picture. Dirty dishes were on her nightstand. The thing that disturbed Uriel the most were the pictures of Sadie that were sprawled across Mrs. Covington's bed. There were so many pictures.

Uriel was getting ready to back out of the room when a shadow whizzed past him. He spun around, no one was there. Chill bumps popped up on his arms. A shadow moved again; this time above his head. Uriel looked up and saw his grandmother hovering in the corner of the wall with her face pressed into the corner. She spoke in a language that Uriel did not understand.

"Grandma!" he screamed.

Mrs. Covington dropped to the floor; landing on her back. Her head turned toward Uriel; then, her shoulders, her waist, her thighs followed by her knees and feet twisted as if she was a Rubik's Cube turning piece by piece. The sound of her bones cracking made Uriel queasy.

Tears poured from Uriel's eyes. The boy grabbed his crotch in hopes of stopping urine from coming. He whispered a prayer asking God to give him strength. Uriel opened his mouth to scream but he involuntarily stepped backwards and put up his hand. He yelled, "Come out of her!"

Mrs. Covington started convulsing. I bright light began to pour out of her mouth.

Uriel started wailing so loud that Khalid ran into the room.

"What are you doing?" Khalid screamed.

Uriel pointed both of his hands towards his grandmother and started to pray for her deliverance. He asked for the Holy Spirit to give him power to help her in the name of Jesus. He asked for God's mercy and guidance.

The light continued to pour from Mrs. Covington's mouth like a glowing river.

Uriel yelled, "Come out of…"

Khalid pushed Uriel to the floor and drug him out of the room by his feet; too fast for Uriel to react. Khalid slammed the door and locked it.

"Father, are you okay?" Khalid asked, holding his grandmother's head in his hands.

The light went back into Mrs. Covington's mouth and the old woman sat up. The angel within Mrs. Covington propelled her to nod her head. Turiel replied through her mouth in his voice, "That child is powerful. God is with him. Keep him away from me!"

Blue Unicorn was an eclectic little bistro hidden in the corner of a shopping plaza. Dream catchers, crystals, waitresses dressed like gypsies wearing giant hoop earrings, headscarves, half tops and ruffled skirts, tables with crystal balls in the center of them, candle burning chandeliers, and sofas covered in lush pillows added to the charm of the Blue Unicorn Restaurant. Its dim lighting and bohemian atmosphere was ideal for intimate dates, and those who simply loved to be surrounded by exotic delights.

James was the first to arrive. He was escorted to his table by a beautiful, green eyed, red haired waitress whose scarlet lips matched her hair. Her name tag read *Esmeralda*. She looked like a gypsy he saw on a cartoon once. She turned a switch beneath the table, and the crystal ball in the center of the table revealed a drink menu.

"Would you like a drink while you wait?" the waitress asked with a very heavy eastern European accent.

"Sure. Bring me a glass of water with lemon and a glass of red wine," said James.

"Coming right up," she said as she bowed and shimmied over to the bar; her shiny red hair reflecting the candle flames.

Moments later, Sadie came through the door. She wore a silk orange blouse that accented her slender waist perfectly, and giant orange feathers for earrings. Her silver hair was slicked back away from her face revealing its youth. Orange lipstick colored her full lips. Dark liner brought out her wide eyes. James thought she looked exquisite. If he was a single man, he would want her to be his all over again. She was still the most beautiful woman he had ever encountered. James waved. Sadie saw him immediately and made her way to the table. Before she could sit down, Esmeralda was back with James' drinks.

"What lovely jewelry you're wearing!" Esmeralda complemented Sadie. Esmeralda looked at James and asked, "Your woman? Yes?"

"Yes," he responded with a smirk on his face.

"Striking!" Esmeralda said. "You're a lucky man."

"Thank you," he replied; looking at Sadie in agreement.

"Would you like something to drink Miss?" the waitress asked Sadie.

"Yes," Sadie answered, flattered by the compliment from the waitress. "I'll have what he is having."

Esmeralda disappeared in a flurry of scarves and tassels.

"She looks like a vampire," Sadie whispered. "When she looks you in the eye, it feels like she's casting a spell. I think she is trying to compel us." Sadie laughed.

Esmeralda returned with Sadie's wine and water.

James laughed in agreement. It was true. Esmeralda looked like the queen of the damned. Every time she smiled, James looked for fangs. Every time she looked at them, James expected to become hypnotized.

"May I take your order," Esmeralda asked. She touched the crystal ball in the center of the table, and the drink menu turned into a dinner menu.

"Not yet," James responded. "We're still waitin' on another person."

"Okay. I'll be back soon," she bowed and walked away, the sound of bells rang as she walked.

"I love this place," said Sadie. "We should come here more often."

"I do too. I decided to meet here because Timoo ain't from Atlanta and she always lookin' for cool places to go. It don't get no cooler than this," said James.

"True," agreed Sadie as she took a sip of wine.

The two drank and engaged in small talk until James looked towards the door. His eyes stretched open like he saw a ghost. He put his wine glass down, and shook his head in slow motion. *Nooooooooooo!* James screamed in his mind.

Standing in the doorway of the restaurant was Timoo wearing the shortest, tightest, most revealing dress he had ever seen on a woman. Timoo's cleavage looked like two bowling balls glued onto her chest. Her skirt was so short that it could double as a shirt. Every curve, contour, dimple, and crease of her body was amplified by her tiny brown dress. The dress color blended so well with Timoo's skin that James had to look twice to make sure she was wearing clothes. James almost fell out of his chair. How could he possibly introduce this woman to his wife?

Timoo spotted him and almost sprinted to the table. Her speed came to a halt when she noticed Sadie sitting beside James. Timoo recognized Sadie from the pictures on James' desk at work. Timoo's heart plummeted. She thought to herself, *How could I have been so foolish to assume he was asking me out on a date?* Suddenly, Timoo felt naked. She pulled at the hem of her dress and pulled up her top. When she arrived at the table, she extended her hand to Sadie and said, "It is so nice to meet you Mrs. Tucker. James talks so much about you."

Sadie accepted Timoo's hand, smiled, then turned and looked straight at James. Sadie's eyes were so intense that James thought she was seconds away from vamping out.

James took a big gulp of wine, and waved for the waitress to come give him a refill.

Esmeralda sauntered over with her wine jug and began to pour. With a confused look on her face, she asked Timoo for her drink order. Timoo ordered a double gin and tonic and drank it before the glass could hit the table.

"It's nice to meet you Timoo," Sadie lied. "James told me that you have been a valuable asset to his company."

"I try," Timoo responded; her voice trembling; embarrassment written all over her face. She ordered another drink to take the edge off.

James tried to avoid looking at Timoo. He turned to Sadie and said, "She closed a very lucrative business deal for me. I appreciate a worker who can think quickly and make good decisions."

"I'm sure you do," Sadie responded, her voice dripping in sarcasm. "I'm sure her decision to dress so conservatively this evening is a great representation of her thinking ability."

James' mouth fell open.

Timoo put her drink down and took a deep breath. It was time for her to woman up and take responsibility for her poor judgment. She turned to Sadie and began to apologize.

"Mrs. Tucker, I'm so very sorry that I came here so improperly dressed," said Timoo. "I was under the impression that James was asking me on a dinner date. I should have known that he was a happily married man, and that he had no intention of discussing anything but business with me. Please accept my sincerest apologies for disrespecting my employment position, and you as his wife."

Sadie and James were pleasantly surprised by Timoo's apology. They realized that there weren't many people who would be honest and humble enough to admit when they were wrong.

"I accept your apology," Sadie said as she reached over the table and held Timoo's hand. "It takes a real woman to do what you just did. I really appreciate it."

"Thank you," Timoo said.

Sadie withdrew her hand and looked Timoo straight in the eye. The look in Sadie's eyes was fierce.

James leaned back in his chair.

Sadie said, "Make this the last time you ever hit on my husband or you will be fired so quickly that you will feel the pavement under your ass before you can blink. You knew he had a wife. There are so many pictures in his office of me that one would believe that I worked there. Be a woman of good character. Having a side chick mentality will hurt no one but you. We have enough low rate home wreckers in the world. Don't be another one of them. I trust that we understand each other?"

"Yes," Timoo answered. She wanted to crawl inside herself and die. "I truly apologize." She guzzled down another drink.

"Now that we all understand each other, let's talk business," James interjected.

35

As soon as Sky arrived home, she put up her purchases, instructed the children to pick out three weeks' worth of clothes, and picked up the phone to call Forrest at the hospital.   After about two transfers, Forrest answered the phone.

"Dr. Cohen," he said.

"Hey baby!" Sky squeaked. "How's your day going?" she asked as she rambled through her closet looking for comfortable clothes to pack.

"Busy," Forrest responded with a yawn. "I have been working nonstop. This is the first break I have had all day."

"I can imagine," Sky said. "Do you have a minute?"

"For you, of course," answered Forrest. "What's up?"

"I talked to Sadie today," Sky said. "She is going to buy plane tickets for me and the children to fly to Atlanta next week. I was thinkin', since you are goin' on vacation soon, you can join us a week after we arrive."

"So I'll be without you and the kids for a week?" Forrest asked. "Thanks for discussing this with me first."

"Forrest, you're at work all the time. It's not like you will miss us," Sky said.

"I always miss you all," said Forrest, offended by Sky's comment.

"I didn't mean it like that," Sky responded. "I should have discussed it with you first, but plans unfolded so fast. I accepted the offer because I knew you wouldn't mind."

"I'll die without you," he joked.

"You'll survive," Sky retorted. "Seriously, what do you think?"

"I think it's a great idea. I know you have been wanted to visit Sadie for a while. Where are we staying? With my parents?" Forrest asked.

"Of course not," Sky answered. "Your mother drives me insane."

"She'll be hurt Sky," Forrest said. "She would want for you and the children to stay with her and Dad."

"I will be hurt more Forrest! You know your mother doesn't like me much. She was angry enough that you didn't marry a Jew, but you had to marry a loud mouth, red boned black girl," Sky chuckled. "My nerves are too shot to ignore all of her backhanded compliments. I just don't want to be bothered. If I weren't pregnant, maybe I would consider it. My hormones are too sensitive at the moment."

"She loves you and the kids and you know it," Forrest said. "She would love to see us."

"Of course we'll see her," Sky ensured. "I just don't want to stay with her. Sadie has a full basement with three bedrooms. We can stretch out there. Plus, I have so much catchin' up to do with Sadie. Hold on a minute."

Sky heard a little too much laughter coming from the children's rooms. She walked out her room to make sure the children were packing instead of playing. They were on task.

"I'm back," Sky said.

"Okay. I'm down. It would be nice to catch up with the old crew again. I haven't hung out with James and Luis in years," said Forrest. "Make reservations for me too."

"Okay baby. Bye," agreed Sky.

"Bye. I love you, said Forrest.

"I love you too," Sky said and hung up the phone. Sky went back into her bedroom and lay across the bed. A few minutes later, Earth tapped on Sky's open door.

"Mommy," Earth called with a small voice, standing at the door with her hands crossed. She was very dainty for a six year old.

"Yes baby," Sky asked as she turned onto her side to face her youngest daughter.

Earth's dark green eyes looked into Sky's bright green eyes. A look of worry was on Earth's face.

"What is it baby?" Sky asked.

"A man was in my room," Earth said.

"What man?" Sky sat up, her heart beating fast. The pin number to her gun safe flashed in her mind. She bolted up from the bed; the safety of her children was first on her mind.

"The man you were talking to in the hallway the other night," Earth answered. "The man you called Pappa C."

Sky stopped in her tracks. A different type of fear seized her. She had no idea that Earth had the gift to see spirits. Sky wondered what else Earth had seen.

"What did he say?" Sky asked.

"He said that he was glad that we are going to Atlanta. He said that he tried to get your attention but you were too focused on Daddy, so he came to me. Pappa C knew I would see him. He says I can see everyone where he is," said Earth. "But, he told me to try not to because seeing the wrong people could scare me. He told me how to get rid of people I don't want to see by praying and blocking them out."

As Sky listened, her nerves became more and more out of whack. The thought of her daughter being like that kid in the movie *The Sixth Sense* freaked Sky out. How could Sky possibly protect Earth from spirits, haints, and haunts?

"What else did he say," Sky asked.

"He told me to stay close to Uriel because he would protect me," Earth answered. "Pappa C also told me to tell you that Mrs. Covington isn't herself. He said that she is *too real* or *too ill*. I couldn't understand what he was saying. He faded away."

"When did this happen?" Sky asked, perturbed that Mr. Covington was talking to her daughter. It was okay for him to scare Sky to death, but it was not okay for him to freak out her baby girl. "Did he frighten you?"

"He came when you were on the phone with Daddy. He was standing in my closet when I opened it. He made me jump, but I am not afraid of him because he had the nicest smile ever," Earth answered; twisting from side to side as she spoke. "He's nice like grandpa."

"You mean Grandpa Cohen?" Sky asked.

"No. Grandpa Dawn," Earth replied. "He tells me stories of Ireland sometimes before I go to sleep at night. He sounds just like a leprechaun, and he has red hair like me."

Sky dropped down into a sitting position on the bed. Sky's deceased father had been visiting Earth. Sky remembered how much her father loved his homeland of Ireland. He used to speak about the lush green hills and his ancestors without ceasing. Now he was sharing his tales with Earth. Sky's emotions shifted between envy and fear. It was evident that Earth had inherited her grandmother's gift. Sky wondered if her mother was talking to Earth as well.

Sky felt a little better that Earth was not afraid, but she was still unhappy about her father's and Mr. Covington's visit. Sky knew it was only a matter of time before unwanted spirits would start visiting Earth. Sky was happy that Mr. Covington taught Earth prayers of protection and how to banish unwanted beings. Pappa C was always forever helpful.

"Thank you for telling me baby. Go finish finding what you want to wear in Atlanta. Don't forget your sleepy clothes and your underwear," said Sky.

"Okay Mommy," Earth said and skipped out of the room.

Sky sat on the end of her bed and whispered between her teeth, "No fair Pappa C! I only want you takin' to me!"

Uriel sat on the sofa in the den with tears streaming down his face; his breath blowing out in moist puffs. Seeing his grandmother twist and turn like a bottle top, was hard for his six year old mind to wrap around. *What's wrong with her?* Uriel thought. *Why is Khalid not afraid?* Uriel thought maybe Khalid had inherited some superpower from their grandmother; a power that Uriel obviously had too since he made his grandmother vomit light. He wondered if his parents had powers too. Uriel heard the keys to the front door and bolted off of the sofa.

When the door opened, Uriel pounced.

"Mama!" he yelled and threw himself upon Sadie. She almost toppled over but James caught her before she fell.

Sadie saw Uriel's wet face and asked, "What's wrong baby? Did you and Khalid get into a fight again?"

"No," Uriel cried. "It's Grandma."

"What happened Uriel? Is she okay? Did you get a spanking?" James asked.

"No," Uriel cried.

"What's wrong?" asked Sadie.

"G...G...Grandma's got the devil in her," he wailed. "She was twisting. I prayed for her. Khalid threw me out of the room."

"What are you talking about Uriel?" Sadie asked with a frown on her face.

"Something is wrong with her. God saved me from her. He told me to put my hands up and make her well," Uriel blubbered so fast it was difficult to understand his words.

"God told you that?" Sadie questioned. She shook her head from side to side. *What's the probability of having two crazy sons?* She thought to herself.

"Yes," he answered. Uriel looked up at her with innocent eyes and asked, "Mommy, are we superheroes?"

"How you go from God talkin' to you to you bein' a superhero?" James screamed. His crossed his arms and huffed. "Don't..."

Sadie interrupted James' angry tirade before it started, and sweetly asked James to stop yelling at Uriel because something had truly upset him. She reminded James that Uriel was a very honest child and that it was not like him to make up stories. If they listened carefully, they would get to the bottom of Uriel's story.

Sadie led Uriel over to the couch and sat him beside her. She wiped his face and kissed his cheeks. She wrapped her arm around him and looked him in the eyes.

"What are you talking about sweetie?" Sadie asked. "Calm down and take your time."

"Are we superheroes?" Uriel asked.

"No. Why do you ask?" asked James as calm as he could. He was becoming more impatient by the moment.

"Because Grandma and Khalid can float, and I made Grandma throw-up light!" Uriel wailed.

"Whatchu talkin' 'bout boy?" James snapped. "What I tell you about watching so much TV? Now you got me and yo mama worried about you when you're talkin' all this nonsense!"

"I wasn't watching TV Daddy," Uriel cried. "Something is really wrong with Grandma."

Sadie nor James could disagree with that. Something was definitely wrong with Mrs. Covington. Her behavior as of late was insane.

"Calm down Uriel," Sadie soothed him by stroking his back. "I'm sure there is an explanation for what you think you saw. Where is your brother?"

"I think he's still in Grandma's room," Uriel sniffed. "Khalid pushed me out of her room when she began throwing up."

"I'll go check on them," James said, and hopped up.

"Baby, let me go with you," Sadie said. She turned to Uriel and told him to go take his bath and to get ready for bed. She assured him that everything would be alright.

Uriel obediently followed his mother's instructions and disappeared down the hallway. James and Sadie followed behind Uriel, but veered off in the direction of Mrs. Covington's room. When they arrived at her door, it was closed. Sadie knocked three times. Khalid opened the door. James and Sadie walked past him, and headed straight towards Mrs. Covington who was tucked tightly in her bed; her head peaking over the covers pulled high up around her neck. Her face looked weary. Her breathing was slow. For the first time in a long time, she looked old.

Sadie sat on the side of the bed, rubbing her mother's hair. Sadie caressed Mrs. Covington face, feeling that it was hotter than normal.

James stood next to Khalid with crossed arms and a grimace on his face.

"Mama, are you okay?" Sadie asked, still gently rubbing her mother's hair. "You don't look so good."

Mrs. Covington mumbled something under her breath; her voice weak and pitiful; her facial muscles appearing nonexistent. She opened her mouth again. This time the words *help me* slipped through in a tiny whisper.

"What is she sayin'?" James asked.

"It sounds like she said help me," responded Sadie. A tear formed in her eye. The thought of her mother taking ill frightened Sadie. She could not imagine living in a world without her mother. Sadie thought she would die after she lost her father. She knew she would die if she lost her mother. Sadie wiped the doom laced thoughts from her mind. *You will be just fine.* Sadie thought to herself. *You have to be.*

Khalid stepped forward, and removed Sadie's hand from Mrs. Covington's face. Sadie looked up at him in utter disbelief. She was flabbergasted that Khalid had the audacity to stop her from touching her mother. Khalid was growing bolder by the day as if he was the one with the authority in the Tucker home.

"She'll be just fine," Khalid said. "She's just tired. Leave her to rest."

James stepped forward to grab Khalid by the arm when Mrs. Covington sat up in the bed. Her face looked renewed and full of strength.

"Leave him alone," Mrs. Covington belched in a voice that didn't sound like her own. "I'm just fine," her voice adjusted to its normal tone.

Sadie stood up from the bed and joined hands with James. Khalid sat on the bed near his grandmother and the four of them locked eyes in a silent standoff. After a few minutes, James pulled Sadie's arm and they walked out of the room; confused about what had transpired.

37

A WEEK LATER

Hartsfield-Jackson Airport was bigger and brighter than any airport the kids had ever seen. When Sky and her children stepped off of the plane, the children ran straight to a vender to buy snacks. Sky wobbled behind them, and paid for their goodies before the quartet headed towards the train that took them to baggage claim.

Sky hoped that Sadie was already waiting for them at baggage claim because Sky wanted to hurry and get out of the airport. There were way too many people rushing and brushing past her and her children. As a resident of New York, she was used to hustle and bustle, but when she landed in Atlanta, she expected everything to slow down. Besides, Hartsfield-Jackson brought back so many awful memories. The last time Sky was there was eight years ago when she and Sadie parted. Coming to Atlanta awakened all kinds of painful regrets for Sky. She was so excited to arrive until she actually stepped foot in Georgia. Now her past demons were beginning to surface, and she wasn't ready for battle.

Earth came up behind Sky and slipped her hand into Sky's hand. Earth placed her mother's hand upon her shoulder and snuggled up next to Sky. Sky smiled. Earth looked up at Sky and smiled back. Somehow, that small sentiment made Sky feel a great bit better.

"Sky!" Sadie yelled across the baggage claim area as she sprinted towards her best friend with arms waving like crazy.

"Sadie!" Sky squealed; her face shining like the sun. She ran as fast as her condition would allow her to get to Sadie. The two embraced like school girls on a playground full of laughter and joy.

"It has been so long!" Sadie exclaimed as she ruffled Sky's fiery hair and hugged her again. "I really missed you!"

"I missed you too!" Sky replied. She turned around to ensure that her children were behind her. They were. They stood quietly observing; letting their eyes roam over every inch of Sadie.

Sadie looked at the three and gave them a big group hug. She showered them with kisses until all of them broke out in giggles.

"Oh my!" Sadie exclaimed. "You all are so much more beautiful than I imagined. She extended her hand to Jupiter and said, "You must be Jupiter. What a strong name for a powerful brother like yourself!"

Jupiter grinned from ear to ear. He adjusted his dashiki and patted his red afro.

Sadie said, "Your mother told me about your passion for Black history. That is one of my passions too. I have so many books you may want to read."

"Okay," Jupiter replied. "That's cool! Nice to meet you Aunt Sadie." He kissed Sadie's hand and said, "You are a beautiful and intelligent queen."

Sadie and Sky both started laughing.

"Thank you," Sadie smiled. "You are a handsome king!"

Jupiter looked at Sadie with valentines for eyes. He never thought his aunt would be so smart and beautiful. Sky pulled Jupiter's smitten body out of Sadie's face so Sadie could meet Venus.

"And, you must be Venus," Sadie said as she extended her hand for Venus to shake.

Venus slowly accepted it then snatched it back and put her hand on her hip.

"Look at you little diva," Sadie laughed. "You're too cute for me!"

Sadie turned to Earth who was peeking from behind her mother's leg.

"And, you must be Earth," Sadie said. "You're so beautiful."

Venus grunted at the remark. She was the one who was used to being called the beautiful one. After all, she was the one with the dark shiny hair and pretty brown skin. Earth was heavily freckled, like Sky, with clownish red hair and brownish red skin.   Earth was supposed to be the shy one, not the beautiful one.

Sadie looked over at Venus and said, "You're cute too" and winked. Venus rolled her eyes.

"Cute? Humph!" Venus grunted.

Sadie shook her head and looked up at Sky.

"She acts just like you!" Sadie said as Sky laughed and nodded her head.

"You look so much like your mother," Sadie said to Earth. "I can't believe it. You are her spitting image. And, Venus looks so much like your mother Sky."

"Don't she!" Sky agreed.   "She has mama's cheekbones, lips, and thick hair.   Venus could be a supermodel with that face."

Venus smiled big.

"Jupiter looks like a darker redder version of Forrest," Sadie said. "Girl, ya'll made some pretty babies."

"I know," Sky replied arrogantly.   "Look at they mama," she said as she turned around so Sadie could get a panoramic view.

Sadie laughed aloud and said, "Girl, shut-up! Where are your bags?"

The children grabbed their bags and Sadie grabbed Sky's bags. They made their way out of the airport and into Sadie's car. The ride home was not long at all, and before they knew it, they were pulling up in the driveway of the Tucker home.

"Sadie, your home is beautiful!" Sky exclaimed. "The yard is huge. Girl you got some acres! I can't wait to get inside!" Sky wobbled out of the car, and stood on the porch and waited.

Sadie and Sky's children grabbed the bags and headed for the front door. The door opened, and James and Uriel stepped out onto the porch.

"Hey!" James said as he grabbed Sky and hugged her tight. "Look at you. I see you and Forrest have been busy." He laughed and pointed at Sky's stomach.

"Yes we have," Sky responded. "You and Sadie have too!" Sky looked down at Uriel. "How are you little one?" she asked. "You are the spitting image of yo daddy! Sadie you didn't have any genes to contribute to this one!"

"Nice to meet you Auntie Sky," Uriel said. "It is a blessing to have you here,"

"Yes it is," Sky laughed. "Consider yourself blessed!"

"Woman, you crazy," James chuckled. "Glad ya'll got here safely. Imma get your bags. Go on in and relax preggo."

"Okay. Kids!" she turned around and yelled. "Come and meet your uncle James and your cousin Uriel." She turned back to James. "Where is Khalid?"

Khalid appeared in the doorway as if he materialized. Sky jumped.

"Nice to meet you Aunt Sky," Khalid said. "You look just like your pictures."

"Nice to meet you too," Sky's voice trembled.

"Boys, come help me with these bags," said James as he took the bags from Sadie, Venus, and Earth, and handed them to his sons. James allowed Jupiter to carry his own bag. James believed that all boys needed to be trained to be considerate gentleman.

Everyone walked into the house. The temperature was cool, and the living room extremely neat. It looked unlived in. The living room was filled with plush bright colored couches, mahogany tables, a giant flat screen TV, antique chairs, and paintings on every wall.

Mrs. Covington, sitting on the sofa with her legs crossed, blended perfectly with the room in her cobalt blue pantsuit with matching sandals.

"Mama C," Sky squealed, then ran over to hug her. "It is so good to see you!"

Mrs. Covington hugged Sky softly then pulled away quickly leaving Sky with a feeling of uneasiness.

"Meet my children," Sky said, waving for her children to come near. Jupiter and Venus shook Mrs. Covington's hand but Earth hid behind her mother's leg. "Don't you want to meet Mama C Earth?"

Mrs. Covington and Earth locked eyes. Earth shook her head no and shielded her face; still staring at Mrs. Covington between her fingers. Earth grabbed Sky's leg so tight that Earth pinched Sky's skin.

Embarrassed, Sky pulled Earth away from behind and asked, "Why don't you want to meet Mama C?"

Earth wiggled out of Sky's grasp then grabbed her hand and pulled her mother away from the couch where Mrs. Covington sat.

"I'm sorry Mama C. Earth is very shy and a little tired," Sky apologized. "I'm sure she'll be ready to meet you later."

Mrs. Covington nodded, unblinking and locked eye to eye with Earth.

"Follow me," Sadie said and led them downstairs into the basement apartment. "There is enough room down here for everyone. Jupiter can have his own room. Venus and Earth can share a room, and there is a master bedroom down here for you and Forrest. There is a dresser and queen sized bed in each room. Sadly, there is only one bathroom down here," said Sadie as she showed them each room. James put their luggage in their rooms and went back upstairs.

"You want to go into the back yard and play with us?" Khalid asked Jupiter.

"Sure," he answered and followed them out of the back door.

"I'm going outside too," Venus declared.

"Me too," said Earth.

"Hold on a minute Earth," said Sky. "I want to talk to you for a second."

Venus ran out of the door, and Sadie sat down on the sofa, looking intently at Sky and Earth.

"Why didn't you want to talk to Mama C?" Sky asked, taking a seat beside Sadie.

"Because there was someone behind her face," Earth answered, and ran outside to play with her new play cousins.

Sadie tossed and turned all night trying to understand what Earth meant by saying that there was someone behind Mrs. Covington's face. Finally, when morning came, Sadie crawled out of bed and decided to forgo her usual Sunday routine of eating cereal and doing a crossword puzzle, and try to get some answers. Sadie decided to invite Dr. Ari Aniwodi-El and Sky to lunch. Maybe the three of them could put their heads together and figure some things out. Times like this, she missed her father. Mr. Covington always knew what to do, and if he did not, he found out quickly.

"Good mornin'," James yawned. "Why you up so early?"

"It's 10am sweetie. It's not early," Sadie replied while putting a gown and robe on her nude body.

"Come back to bed," he begged; his hand stretched out like he was in need of help. "I need you next to me; under me; on top of me!

Sadie walked over and kissed James on the mouth. She rubbed his bald head, and stood up again.

"I can't," she said. "I have stuff to do." Sadie put on her slippers and went to the bathroom to brush her teeth.

"Like what?" James asked, pulling the covers off, sitting up in bed exposing himself.

Sadie answered after brushing her teeth, "I have to talk to Sky to see if she is up to having lunch today. If she is, I have to call Ari to see if he is free to join us."

"Lunch for what?" James asked in a high pitched tone.

"I want Sky to meet Ari and talk to him in-depth about her dream and her visits from Daddy," Sadie said. She walked over to James and continued. "Sky said that Daddy even visited Earth. Can you believe that?"

James sat in silence for a moment. He wanted to issue a rebuttal but he knew in his heart that Sadie would not rest until she was assured that the angel was not trying to come back into her or their child's life. If Ari could provide help, James was willing to swallow his negative feelings for Ari and allow him to aid Sadie. Sadie sat down next to James and said, "I smelled myrrh on Mama the other day."

"I did too," James admitted.

Sadie's face dropped. She asked, "When? Why didn't you tell me?"

"I smelled it the night we came home and found Mama C sitting in the dark. It was on her breath," James said.

Fear grabbed hold to Sadie like a rapist in an alley. She tried to break free but its grasp got tighter and tighter.

"I didn't tell you because I didn't want you to worry," James said. He rubbed her back trying hard to ease her tensions. "I'm sorry baby. I should have told you."

Sadie leaned into James's chest and tried to steady her breathing. The thought of Turiel defiling her mother, like he had defiled her, made Sadie cringe. She knew that her mother would never admit to being harassed by the celestial stalker because her pride was too great. Mrs. Covington would never admit that the supernatural was real, even if it meant her life. She was an exceedingly stubborn woman.

"Do you think it is doing something to Mom?" Sadie asked. Imaginings of the angel's lips and hands upon her mother swirled around in Sadie's brain. Memories of his white hot kisses and ethereal penetration stirred feelings of passion and despair. Sadie did not want her and her mother to share the same experience. Sadie's unholy defiling was enough.

"No," James lied. "We would know. Try not to worry and go make your calls. I'm sure you guys will figure everything out." James kissed her cheek and lay back in the bed. He pulled up the covers and cursed his cowardice.

"Thank you for coming over on such short notice," Sadie said to Dr. Ari Aniwodi-El as she let him and his family into her front door. "Great seeing you Latrice." Sadie greeted her with a kiss; then, waved to all of the Aniwodi-El clan. "The children are all outside in the back yard. James has some hotdogs and burgers on the grill," she said to the children. "Go straight through the house and you will see the back door."

The Aniwodi-El children followed Sadie's directions and disappeared into the back of the house. The smell of grilled food guided them directly into the back yard.

Sadie turned to Latrice and said, "How have you been? It's been such a long time since I have seen you. You are even lovelier than I remember. Your hair has gotten so long! The last time I saw you, you were just locking it up."

"Thank you. You look wonderful yourself. Everything is great. I decided to leave the law firm last year and open up my own practice," Latrice responded. "So far, so good. I really enjoy the freedom. All the long hours are over. Since God has blessed me with so much financial prosperity, I am able to do a lot of pro bono cases. I have hopes of saving lots of young men from the penal system, and eradicating the world of social injustice."

"Congratulations. That is absolutely wonderful," Sadie said. "You have a lot of work ahead of you. These days it seems that injustice reigns supreme. I wish you much success."

Sadie turned to Ari and said, "Ari, I really want you to meet my best friend Sky. She is the one you spoke to on the phone in my office that day. Do you remember?" Of course Sadie knew Ari remembered. She resorted to asking silly questions to mask her nervousness around Dr.

Aniwodi-El. Sadie wondered if Latrice noticed it. Sadie dreaded the thought of Latrice thinking that there were some ill intentions. Latrice seemed happy and relaxed so Sadie decided not to stress over her self-induced anxiety.

"Of course I remember," he responded; following Sadie through the house into the dining room. "I've been eager to meet her. I filled Latrice in on everything. She finds it all quite interesting to say the least."

The green dining room table with six different color chairs, was set simply with clear, square glass plates and matching glasses. Purple napkins with happy face napkin holders sat next to the plates. The table cloth had happy faces on it also.

Before Sadie and the Aniwodi-El's could sit down, Sky walked into the room; red hair teased out so far that her hair seemed to touch the walls and ceiling. She wobbled over to Latrice and Ari, shook their hands, and introduced herself. They all sat down. Sky sat in the chair closest to Sadie.

"So do you guys want to eat first?" Sadie asked. "There is plenty of food ready and James is grilling more. We don't cook pork, but there are plenty of beef, chicken, turkey, and veggies. Mom made a boat load of side dishes. I'm sure everyone will find something they like."

"Do you want to eat baby?" Ari asked his wife. She told him that she could wait. He said to Sadie, "We can start talking and eat a bit later."

"Well, Imma get me a turkey burger. I'll be right back. I got two to feed," Sky quipped and left the table.

"What's up?" James walked into the room and shook Ari and Latrice's hand. James tried hard to look pleasant. "Ya'll doin' alright?"

The couple nodded.

"Okay cool," James uttered and walked out of the room.

Sky came back with a plate full of food and sat down.

"Okay, I'm ready," she said, getting ready to put a fork full of potato salad in her mouth.

"I don't know where to start," Sadie said honestly. "I..." her words trailed off at the sight of Mrs. Covington stepping into the room.

"Don't mind me," said Mrs. Covington as she pulled up a seat. "I just want to sit where the grown folks are."

Latrice grabbed Ari's hand tightly. Sweat started to trickle down her brow. Her body trembled. She leaned over and whispered into Ari's ear, "Do you see her face?"

"What do you mean?" Ari whispered back, fazed by his wife's reaction. He didn't see anything strange. Mrs. Covington looked like she always did, well put together and classy. Everything appeared perfect from her shoes to her clip-on earrings.

"There is a face beneath her face," Latrice whispered, attempting not to scream her head off. She blinked twice; making sure that what she was seeing was not her imagination. Mrs. Covington's face looked like a transparent mask over another translucent face.

"No. I can't see that," Ari admitted, but he took his wife's word for it. Latrice was an extremely honest person. She would never make up a thing like that.

"Are you okay?" Sadie asked Latrice.

"Yes. I'm okay," Latrice lied; her voice shaking so hard that it faded in and out with every syllable. "Where's the kitchen? I think I need something to drink."

Sadie pointed to the kitchen. Latrice left quickly.

"Mom, this is Dr. Aniwodi-El. He was one of Dad's colleagues," Sadie said. "They used to work together in Miami."

"I remember. Carlos was very fond of you. He loved your passion for your work," said Mrs. Covington. She shook his hand and asked, "What brings you here Dr. Aniwodi-El?"

"Sadie and Sky asked me to come over to help them interpret dreams and visions. It seems that Sky has been experiencing quite a lot of them lately. Have you had any interesting dreams?"

Mrs. Covington rolled her eyes and stood up.

"None that I wish to share, but nice to see you again. I think it is best for me to leave you all to this conversation," she said and walked out of the room. When Mrs. Covington was out of sight, Latrice, who was hiding in the next room, walked back in.

"What did you see Latrice?" Sadie asked as soon as Latrice sat down.

Sky leaned forward so she wouldn't miss a word.

Latrice felt instantly uncomfortable. Although her husband was used to working with preternatural elements, she was not. Witnessing such things unnerved her. Home is where she wanted to be, but she understood the importance to her husband and his friends, so she sat quietly and prayed that she would not see anything else unsettling.

"What did you see?" Sky asked impatiently.

"I don't know. It looked like she had a face under her face," Latrice said. "I know that doesn't make sense, but…"

"My daughter saw the same thing yesterday," said Sky. She turned to Ari. "What does it mean? Does it have anything to do with my dream?"

"I don't know," Ari confessed. "But it is ironic that two people have seen a double face on Mrs. Covington. I had a dream last night. I dreamt that Mrs. Covington was androgynous. As she spoke, her face and voice switched from male to female and vice versa. She was a walking paradox. She had dark light, and was both heathen and holy. I'm unsure of the meaning."

"How is this helping?" Sky asked exasperated. "Aren't you supposed to be the dream king?"

"Sky, calm down. Don't be rude," Sadie said. "He's doing the best he can."

"I'm sorry," Sky apologized. "I'm just so tired of guessing."

"We all are Sky. Do you think you are the only one who is tired? I dare you! Imagine how I feel! I am beyond tired!" Sadie harped. "My oldest son is hell spawn, and my youngest son thinks God has given him superpowers. My dead father is visiting my best friend, and my mother is reported to have two faces; literally!"

Zahyir and his siblings walked into the backyard where they found Sky's children, Khalid, and Uriel playing on a swing set. The yard was large and full of empty space save for a large pecan tree, a tiny pond, and a small garden on the far side of the yard.

"What's up Khalid?" Zahyir said as he lazily waved his hand; making it clear that he was asking only out of good home training not out of genuine interest.

Khalid looked up at Zahyir and twisted his mouth. Khalid nodded hello, and continued doing what he was doing.

Zahyir walked over to Uriel and gave him a high five. Uriel grinned from ear to ear. Zahyir introduced himself to Sky's children. Jupiter was happy to meet him. He was always happy to meet new people. Venus seemed indifferent. Earth said hello and picked up Ru, put her in a baby swing, and started to push her. Venus migrated to Aminah and Aura because she loved to be in the presence of teenagers. Inside Venus felt like she was a teen although she was only seven. The twins welcomed her with open arms.

Uriel, Khalid, and Jupiter started a game of catch.

"You wanna play?" Uriel asked Zahyir.

Khalid smacked his lips, and shot his brother a malicious glance.

"Throw me the ball," Zahyir asked Jupiter. Jupiter obliged. Zahyir threw it to Uriel.

Uriel asked, "Zahyir, are you the one who took Khalid's girlfriend?"

Jupiter started laughing. Zahyir smiled and replied, "Evadne was never Khalid's girlfriend. She would never go out with a little kid."

"Oh," Uriel responded and threw the ball to Khalid. Khalid threw the ball so hard to Zahyir that it hit Zahyir's arm and bruised it immediately. Zahyir winced in pain as he fell to the ground.

"My bad," Khalid said with a smirk on his face. "I thought you were ready. Who knew that a little kid could throw so hard?"

Zahyir jumped up and ran up to Khalid's face. He belted, "You hit me with that ball on purpose Poindexter!" He pointed his finger in Khalid's face and said, "You lucky I don't beat up little kids! I should slap the taste out of your mouth anyway!"

Khalid's face went blank. He backed up and ran into Zahyir full speed, pushing him to the ground. Zahyir hit his head, hard, drawing blood instantly. Khalid stood over Zahyir and tried to kick him but Zahyir caught his leg and pulled him down.

"Stop it!" Uriel begged as he tried to pull the two boys off of each other as they rolled around on the ground. "Stop it I said!" Uriel yelled. He reached down and grabbed Khalid by the arm. With very little effort, Uriel tossed Khalid to the side. Uriel then helped Zahyir up, and apologized for his brother's behavior.

Khalid got up from the ground, his face red as a traffic light, his mouth pulled downward, and his eyes darker than night. He punched Uriel in the face, bloodying his nose. Uriel took the punch and shook it off. He wiped the blood on the back of his arm and backed up.

"I don't want to fight..." Uriel tried to say before Khalid slapped him across the face.

Khalid threw another punch. Uriel caught Khalid's fist mid swing. Uriel squeezed Khalid's hand until he crumpled to his knees. Khalid's eyes blacked out, and Uriel felt a sharp burning pain in his chest. It felt like fire trapped within his rib cage. Uriel stumbled backwards, one of his hands grasping his bosom and the other still clinching

Khalid's fist. He screamed out, "God help me!" and the pain subsided then completely left Uriel's body, and the pain grabbed hold to Khalid. All of the kids watched in a great stupor as Khalid fell unconscious; his limp body hanging from Uriel's hand. Uriel let his brother fall to the ground.

Earth ran into the house to get the adults. She came out with the first person she ran into, Mrs. Covington. Mrs. Covington rushed past the on looking crowd of children and pushed Uriel to the side. She glared at him and screeched, "What have you done?"

Uriel said nothing. He ran into the house weeping and gnashing his teeth.

Mrs. Covington picked Khalid up in one swoop, as if he weighed ten pounds, and carried him into the house. The children looked at one another and ran into the house to tell their parents what had transpired.

"Thank you for coming over," Sadie said to Ari and Latrice. "I wish things didn't have to end so abruptly."

"I'm sorry that the boys got into a fight. Khalid is ashamed of his behavior and will be reprimanded," apologized James.

"Boys will be boys," Ari answered. "I'm sorry too. Zahyir will be punished as well."

"It was a pleasure meeting you both," Sky said. "Hopefully I'll get to see you again before I leave."

"I'm sure of it," Ari responded.

"Thank you for having us Sadie," Latrice said, not liking her husband's commitment to another meeting. She hugged Sadie and James and waved goodbye. The Aniwodi-Els climbed into their car and drove away.

Sadie closed the door and turned to James and Sky.

"We have to find out what went down. I'm going to call the kids," Sadie said. She walked out of the room, gathered all the children and her mother. She brought them into the living room and instructed them to find whatever seat they fancied. Sky's children, except for Venus, sat near Uriel, intentionally keeping their distance from Khalid.

"Who started the fight?" James asked; his eyes wide.

Khalid raised his hand.

James said, "Tell me what happened, Khalid."

"Zahyir made me mad and I hit him with the ball," Khalid confessed.

"What did he do?" asked Sadie.

"He said Evadne would never go out with me because I'm a little kid," Khalid confessed. "He was being mean on purpose. Zahyir never liked me! I wanted to show him that this little kid could crush him!" Khalid growled.

Mrs. Covington interjected, "The cretin got what he deserved."

"Mom!" Sadie said. "How can you say that? It's not okay for Khalid to hit someone because he is angry."

Mrs. Covington grunted and crossed her arms.

"How did you get in the fight Uriel?" James asked.

"I was trying to break them up. Khalid was going to really hurt him. Khalid's eyes turned black," Uriel said.

"Like a monster," Earth whispered. "His eyes looked like monster's eyes. I saw them."

"No such thing happened," Venus spat. "That's silly."

James felt silly for asking but he asked Jupiter, "Did you see Khalid's eyes change?"

"I couldn't see his face," Jupiter answered. "Even if I could, I don't think it's possible for eyes to turn all black. Sorry Uriel, I didn't see that."

James looked at everyone and shook his head. Things were more confusing now than they were before the children recounted the details of the backyard rumbles. James didn't know what to believe so he dismissed them all and himself.

Mrs. Covington went into her bedroom. Sky and Sadie was left sitting on the sofa in taciturnity.

Uriel entered his bedroom. His brother was not there. Uriel felt horrible about the fight with his brother. Khalid was his best friend, and Uriel desperately wanted to makeup. He did not want Khalid to think that the other children were more important than their relationship, so Uriel was very disappointed to see that Khalid was not sitting in their room. Uriel instantly knew where Khalid had to be.

As of late, Khalid was always with his grandmother. They seemed inseparable. It was rare to see one without the other. Khalid hardly played with Uriel anymore because Khalid and Mrs. Covington spent so much time together.

The thought of going to Mrs. Covington's room unnerved Uriel, but he knew that was where he had to go if he wanted to make amends with his brother. The last time he was in Mrs. Covington's room, his grandmother was levitating, twisting her body in inhuman ways, and vomiting light. Uriel didn't know much, but he knew that was not normal. Since that time, he avoided going near his grandmother and her room. He was no longer envious of Khalid's relationship with her because Uriel wanted no dealings with her at the moment. He loved her dearly but he was convinced that his grandmother was not herself.

Uriel walked slowly down the hallway towards his grandmother's bedroom; dragging his feet on the floor so slowly one would think the floor was made of wet sand and he was struggling to lift his legs. Despite his slowness, her closed door appeared before him in moments. The dark wooden door symbolized the gateway to perdition in Uriel's mind. He imagined his grandmother on the other side of the door gnashing her teeth and curling clawed fingers as Khalid's blackened eyes swirled in fiendish fury.

"While I walk through the shadow of death, I will fear no evil for you are with me. Your rod and staff comfort me," Uriel repeated over and over again to himself. With a quaking fist and palpitating heart, he knocked on his grandmother's door.

Khalid opened the door, his face scowling.

"What do you want?" he hissed.

"I came to apologize," answered Uriel. His eyes began to tear up. "I don't want you to be mad at me."

Khalid walked away from the doorway and sat on the bed next to his grandmother.

"You may come in," Mrs. Covington said, her voice strange and wavering, unlike her natural vocal rhythm. She waved her hand inviting him to come forward. A strange expression was on her face, both sinister and sweet.

Uriel tilted his head to the side as he looked into his grandmother's eyes. For a second, he thought that they shifted to a golden color but as he continued to look, he realized that he must have been mistaken. Her eyes were as brown as usual.

"Come sit next to me," Mrs. Covington said and patted the bed beside her.

Uriel was hesitant. Every fiber of his being issued him warning, but he wanted so desperately to be back in his grandmother's arms again, so he walked over to her and sat down. Her body was like a space heater. Uriel could feel her warmth floating towards him in periodic gusts of heat. She placed her arms around his shoulders and said, "What did you want to say to your brother?" Her breath smelled of myrrh.

Uriel winced under her hot arm. He tried to move away from her but he was locked within her grasp. Mrs. Covington's grip was so tight that Uriel thought his shoulder blades might crack.

"You're hurting me Grandma," Uriel cried. "You're holding me too tight."

Khalid sat on the other side of her watching silently with a grin on his face.

"I'll let you go soon enough," Mrs. Covington said, her voice becoming more masculine by the moment. Her grip became tighter. Her eyes looked like brown speckled with gold leaf.

Uriel instantaneously became aware of the shift, and struggled to free himself. He pulled away, flailed, and fought to no avail, she held him close and tight.

"Apologize to Khalid," Mrs. Covington commanded.

Uriel began to cry. Mrs. Covington struck him across the face and lifted him off the ground.

"Apologize!" she roared in a voice that sounded like many waves crashing upon the seashore; the smell of myrrh rushing from her mouth causing Uriel to cough uncontrollably.

Uriel started to pray but Mrs. Covington wrapped her hand around his throat and choked the words from his mouth.

"No!" Khalid yelled as he grabbed his grandmother's hand, forcing her to let Uriel's neck loose.

Mrs. Covington slapped Uriel again and bellowed, "Apologize!"

"I'm so sorry," Uriel wailed so loudly that his voice echoed through the house. Tears streamed from his eyes. His cheeks were slightly swollen from her attacks.

"If you ever attack him again, I will destroy you!" Turiel's voice thundered from Mrs. Covington's mouth. She dropped the boy to the floor.

Uriel hit the floor hard. He climbed to his knees and pointed at his grandmother. He screamed, "Come out!"

Mrs. Covington's mouth was forced open by tangible light. It was beginning to shoot out of her mouth when Sadie rushed into the room. The smell of myrrh assaulted her senses before she could open her mouth to speak.

The light went back into Mrs. Covington's mouth before Sadie could see it.

"Silence!" Turiel yelled through Mrs. Covington at mewling Uriel, and knocked him to the ground with a backhand slap.

The unmistakable sound of Turiel's voice sent shivers down Sadie's spine.

"Get your hands off of my son!" Sadie shrieked. She pushed her mother to the floor and pulled Uriel to his feet. She grabbed Khalid's hand and shoved both boys out of the room. Sadie yelled, "Run to your room!" Khalid didn't move. Sadie roared, "Now!"

Khalid ran behind his brother who was quickly disappearing down the hall.

Sadie turned to her mother, who was lying helplessly on the floor; the smell of myrrh pulsating from her body; tears of confusion in her eyes.

"Demon! Leave my mother be!" Sadie screamed; looking around the room for the angel. She saw no sign of him anywhere. *What did he do to her?* She thought to herself. Sadie grabbed her mother's hand.

"Are you okay?" Sadie asked.

Her mother's face shifted from frightened to fiend. Mrs. Covington's eyes shifted from brown to gold then back to brown. Sickening recognition seized Sadie. At that very moment she realized that the demon was not violating her mother, he was her mother!

James stood outside in the front yard to take in the fresh air. He needed to be outside of his house at the moment or he would lose his mind. For the first time in his life, he understood what it felt like to walk the thin line between sanity and insanity. Walls seemed to be closing in on him. He had no control over anything. Feeling totally helpless, James punched the air until he was too tired to take another swing.

The day had been long, and he was very relieved that it was coming to a close. His family was in total chaos. Thoughts of his sons in battle in front of a house full of guests made James extremely annoyed and totally embarrassed. Knowing that Ari saw James' family as a unit of utter discord, made him sick.

James took a few deep breaths and calmed himself. He pushed away his unpleasant thoughts and reveled in the facts that all the fighting had subsided, the children were in bed, Sky was relaxing in the basement, and Sadie and Mrs. Covington was busying themselves in the house. The peace and quiet of the front yard helped to put his soul at ease. If he had the nerve, he would grab his keys and drive his car until the gas ran out, but he knew his momentary disappearance would probably anger his wife; so he resolved to stand in the middle of the yard and stare at the stars twinkling in the sky.

Looking at the stars always calmed James. He remembered lying back on a blanket in his backyard with his friend Rayna when he was a teenager. They would steal away and watch the stars for hours. Under the stars he talked about his hopes and dreams and his fears. James got his first kiss and became a man under the stars. His heart was broken for the first time under the stars. Now he felt he might cry under the very stars that have witnessed so many milestones in his life.

James said down on the grass and looked up. He inhaled deeply then exhaled. The stars told him that everything would be okay. James laid back and became lost in the constellations.

"James, he's back!" Sadie wailed; sprinting out of the front door, her body trembling uncontrollably. She fell upon his chest like she was shot in the back.

"Who back?" James asked; distraught that his peace was disturbed. He bit his bottom lip and sighed, but looking down at his frantic wife, he was moved with compassion. He held her close; stroking her hair as she wept.

"Let's go to the porch to sit down," he suggested as he walked her over to the swing on their front porch. He didn't want the stars to see his wife so frantic. They sat down and James watched Sadie weep as if her heart was being pulled through her eyes with spiked hooks.

"Who back?" James asked again. A tear started to form in his eye. Her pain became his although he had no idea what caused the aching. "Talk to me baby. Seein' you like this finna make me go crazy!"

Sadie wailed, "Turiel is back! He's in Mama!"

"What?" James asked, not understanding what Sadie was saying. "Whatchu mean?"

"I don't know," Sadie admitted through heavy sobs. "I...I...I heard his voice when M...M...Mom was speaking."

Sadie stopped talking, and took a few deep breaths. As calmly as she could, she said, "I smelled him on her. I felt his presence in her room. I could not see him, but I knew he was there."

Sadie looked at James, silently pleading with him to make everything better. Her desperate stare made James uncomfortable, so he pushed her head upon his chest and held her tight. *What can I possibly do?* He thought to himself. The helpless feelings he felt when he first found out about Turiel came back magnified by a hundred. James prayed that Sadie was mistaken.

"I'm sure that things ain't what they seem. Yo mama will be fine. The commotion of the day may have brought back old fears and memories," James said trying to assure her.

Sadie rested silently on James' chest knowing in her heart that she would not get the empathy that she was thirsty for. James would never understand, nor would he ever truly try.

"How was your weekend?" Evadne asked as she sat down next to Zahyir at the lunch table. Before he could answer, Evadne said, "I had a pretty good weekend. It was my dad's weekend. He took me shopping and to the movies on Saturday. Yesterday, I went to church with my mom and step-dad. We all went to lunch afterwards and then to a play. I had so much fun. How about you?"

"It was crazy," Zahyir answered.

He looked up at her. He liked her hair. It was pinned up on the sides like a wild Mohawk. She reminded him of a Roman soldier.

"How so?" she asked before taking a sip of chocolate milk. Pizza, corn, and chocolate milk were a favorite school lunch. She couldn't eat it fast enough.

Zahyir looked up from his lunch just in time to see Khalid passing by the table. Zahyir grimaced. Zahyir considered sticking his foot out, but Evadne would think that would be mean. What Evadne thought meant everything to Zahyir.

"Hi Khalid," Evadne said with the biggest smile she could muster. "How are you?"

"Hi," Khalid responded and kept walking. He didn't even look at her.

"You think he's still mad about the dance?" Evadne asked Zahyir.

"You think I care what that little jerk is mad at?" Zahyir snapped. "Yesterday he hit me."

"What?" Evadne asked. "How did you see him yesterday?"

"My dad and his mom know each other. My family went over to his house for a cookout," said Zahyir. He started getting angry all over again.

"So, what happened?" Evadne asked. She reached across the table and touched Zahyir's hand. It immediately calmed him. He half smiled.

"We were playing with the football in the back yard and he hit me with it," said Zahyir; his brows furrowed. Anger began to seep in again.

"Maybe it was a mistake," Evadne said.

"It wasn't a mistake. He hit me so hard I thought he broke something! We got into a fight and his little brother broke it up," Zahyir snapped.

"Isn't his little brother in the first grade?" Evadne laughed.

"That little dude is strong!" Zahyir chuckled. His anger subsided. The thought of a little kid coming to his aid to get another little kid off of him was indeed funny.

Evadne laughed; happy that Zahyir had lightened up.

"Are you ready for the dance?" Evadne asked; a big grin on her face. She was so excited. She had the perfect outfit and the perfect date.

"Of course," Zahyir smiled back. "What color are we wearing?"

"I'm wearing purple. I don't know what you're wearing," Evadne said. "This ain't prom." She laughed.

"I didn't know," Zahyir said a little embarrassed. "I thought we were supposed to match."

"I'm sorry," Evadne said. "I didn't mean it like that."

"I know," said Zahyir as he bit into his burger.

Khalid walked back by the table.

"Chump," Zahyir mumbled.

Khalid spun around and sneered.

"You better keep it moving. Your little brother ain't here to save you this time," Zahyir jeered. He pushed his plate away and stood up.

"Stop it!" Evadne stood between them. "Or I'm gonna tell the lunch monitor."

Khalid walked away with deadly eyes locked on Zahyir.

Zahyir sat down, eyes reflecting cold fearlessness.

Evadne knew that this was only the beginning, and this knowledge shook her to her core.

Venus sat upon the bed that she shared with her little sister; tired of sleeping in a room that was not her own. Venus was bored and ready to go back home to New York. Harlem was calling her name with all of its festivals and community events. She missed all the culture: art, music, dance, and plays. Venus missed her friends and neighbors. She missed her room and her toys. Most of all, she missed her father.

Venus pulled her onyx hair into a ponytail and walked up the stairs into the main part of the house. She was hoping not to bump into her annoying brother or any of the adults. She wanted to talk to Khalid. He intrigued her, and she felt that it was time for her to get to know him better.

Venus passed through the living room and headed towards the bedrooms. She wasn't quite sure which room belonged to the boys so she decided she would knock on them all. Venus knew it was a possibility that Khalid wouldn't be in his room anyway because he was always glued to his grandmother. Venus tapped on the first door. It was cracked so she peaked through it and saw Uriel sitting in the middle of the floor playing with his toys. She opened the door.

"Hi," Uriel smiled.

"Hey," Venus responded.

"You wanna play?" Uriel asked, holding up an action figure in offering.

She rolled her eyes and placed her hands on her hips. Stupid questions irked her.

"No," she responded. "Where yo brotha at?"

Uriel's smile turned upside down. He answered, "He's probably in Grandma's room."

"Where is that?" Venus asked.

"Down the hall, and to the right. Mom and Dad's room is the one at the end of the hallway," Uriel said, volunteering unnecessary information. "You want me to go get him?" He silently prayed that she would say no, but he was afraid for her. He didn't want his grandmother to hit Venus like she hit him.

"No. I'll go," Venus said as she spun on her heals and made her way down the hall. Seconds later, she tapped on Mrs. Covington's bedroom door. Khalid answered it.

"What's up?" he asked, confused to why she was knocking on his grandmother's door.

"Whatchu doin'?" Venus asked, flashing a brilliant smile. She crossed her arms and leaned against the door post.

Khalid smiled. He liked her instantly. Her confidence was intoxicating. She reminded him of himself.

"Chillin' with my grandma," he answered.   He stepped out of the room and closed the door behind him. He grabbed her by the hand, led Venus down the hall, down the stairs, and out of the front door. They sat on the porch swing.

"Why you chill with yo grandma so much? That's weird," Venus spat.

"My grandma is cool. She understands me. How old are you?" Khalid asked. Venus looked five and talked fifteen.

"Seven? How old are you?" she asked with a neck roll.

Khalid laughed aloud. Venus had so much attitude.

"I'm eight," said Khalid.

"Just like my stupid brother. I hope I don't get stupid at eight," Venus said, crossing her legs. She pulled at her knee high socks. It was getting too hot outside to wear them. She pushed them down to her ankles, pulled them off, and let her bare feet feel the warmth of the porch floor.

"So what do ya'll do for fun?" Venus asked. "I'm bored to death."

"Play, go to the movies, and stuff," Khalid pushed off with his feet so the swing would swing.

"Oh," Venus fiddled with her fingernails. "So tell me, why you and that boy got to fightin'?"

"You have horrible English," Khalid said.

"So does your daddy but you don't hear me complaining about him. Don't get it twisted. I know how to speak correct English. I just don't see the point of doing it all the time. Now, answer me," Venus demanded.

Khalid started laughing again. It was true that James didn't speak correctly a lot of the time, but Khalid couldn't believe that Venus had the nerve to say it.

"Are you always so pushy?" Khalid asked.

"Yep," Venus answered. "You gone tell me why you started that fight?"

"He knew I wanted to ask this girl to the dance and he asked her before I did," Khalid confessed.

"So you got mad at him because you were too slow? Please!" Venus said as she smacked her lips. She sat Indian style, her long brown legs looking like pretzels.

Khalid laughed again. He liked her. She had pizzazz.

"He also embarrassed me in front of her," Khalid said, smirking. Before now he never noticed how pretty Venus was. Technically, she was more than pretty. Venus was beautiful.

"So, ask someone else," Venus barked. "Get over it."

"She's the prettiest girl in school," Khalid confessed. He leaned back on the swing and swooned. The very idea of Evadne made his stomach flip. "She's the best. I only like the best."

"I bet she don't look better than me," Venus said as a matter of fact. She looked Khalid dead in the eye and dared him to disagree.

Khalid laughed aloud. He looked Venus up and down. Prettier than Evadne, he didn't know about that, but he acknowledged that Venus was just as pretty. Both girls had a lot of beautiful hair. Venus' hair was very wavy, almost curly. Evadne's hair was wild and kinky. One girl was the color of the purest dark honey and the other girl the color of the deepest ebony. Both girls were exquisite to behold.

Evadne was definitely more humble. Humility tipped the beauty scale towards Evadne, but Khalid had to admit that Venus' confidence was quite incredible. He saw them as a true tie.

"Do you want to go to the dance with me?" Khalid asked Venus.

"Sure, I don't have nothing else to do," she replied and stood up. "I'm gonna go tell my mom to take me shopping for a dress."

"Okay," Khalid said as he smiled and watched her walk away.

When Venus walked into the basement apartment, she found her mother and siblings huddled together on the couch watching TV. It looked like they were watching the Christian singing vegetables that Venus abhorred. She understood why Earth liked it, but Venus couldn't understand why Jupiter still liked it; and, there he was bouncing from side to side to their silly songs about God and treating people well. Venus popped her lips and crossed her arms. Her family turned around when they heard her smacking lips.

"Where have you been sweetie?" Sky asked with Earth sitting under her armpit.

Jupiter and Earth turned back to the TV.

"Outside talking to Khalid," Venus answered her mother. She walked over to the sofa and sat down on the arm.

Sky's eyes looked worried. She asked, "What about?"

"Stuff," Venus mumbled.

"What kind of stuff?" Sky asked.

"School, that boy he got to fighting with, and his school dance," Venus answered.

"He's weird," Earth said, looking at her sister.

"You're weird," Venus snapped.

Earth turned back towards the TV with a pout.

"I don't like him," said Jupiter. "He started that fight with Zahyir, and he tried to fight his little brother. I think he's mean."

"He's cool to me," Venus said. "Khalid was mad at Zahyir for embarrassing him at school. I would have hit Zahyir too!"

"You would hit anyone," Earth whispered.

"Shut up before I hit you!" Venus barked.

"Don't tell your little sister to shut up," Sky intervened. "And I wish you would hit her. I will tear your tail up!"

Venus rolled her eyes and asked, "Mom, will you take me to get a dress? I want to go to the dance with Khalid," her voice surprisingly pleasant and charming.

"I wouldn't go anywhere with him if I were you," Jupiter warned.

"You're not me!" snapped Venus and shot him a vicious glare. She turned to her mother and grabbed her hand. "Mom, pleeeease. I really want to go. I want to get out of the house. Pretty please on my knees with sugar and spice and everything nice." She kissed her mother's hand.

Sky smirked. Venus was as charming when she wanted to be.

"Please," Venus begged.

Sky kept in mind that Khalid was still a child and her best friend's son. Sadie and James would be at the dance with them.

"Okay," Sky hesitantly answered.

"Thank you Mom!" Venus squealed and went back up stairs.

Sky watched as Venus skipped happily up the stairs. Sky hoped that letting her child accompany Khalid to the dance would not prove disastrous.

"I just don't get it," James said as he dribbled the basketball. "You come over here every weekend to get your butt handed to you."

He dribbled past him and dunked the ball.

"Twenty-one!" James yelled with his hands up in the air.

"Luck!" Luis belched. "I let you win." He waved James away. "A man shouldn't be humiliated at his own house. You should be thanking me for my mercy."

"Shut up!" James laughed. Luis laughed too.

"You up for another game?" a voice asked from behind them.

Luis and James spun around and saw Forrest standing on the back porch of James' home.

"Forrest!" Luis yelled. He walked over to Forrest and gave him a handshake and a hug.

"When did you get here?" James asked as he hugged Forrest.

"Just now. I walked in the house about fifteen minutes ago. I dropped my bags downstairs and came up to beat the both of you for old time sake," Forrest quipped.

"You ain't never beat me a day in yo' life," Luis retorted in his heavy New York Puerto Rican accent.

"I can beat you every day of yo' life," James joked.

Forrest started laughing. He said, "It's good to see you both. I missed you guys."

"And there he goes wit' all that sensitive crap," Luis barked. "I'm out of tissues so don't start cryin'. Don't be tryin' to hug me neither."

"Shut up!" Forrest said, laughing.

"Ya'll hungry?" James asked as he led them through the sliding glass doors into the kitchen.

"Starvin'," answered Luis.

"I can eat," said Forrest.

Forrest and Luis sat at the kitchen table and watched James make them sandwiches. James brought the food along with cold beers to the table, and sat down next to Luis.

"So, what's been goin' on with you?" Luis asked Forrest with a mouth full of food.

"Working. Working. Working. That's all I do," Forrest answered, and then took a swig of beer.

"You been puttin' in overtime. Your wife is 'bout to pop another bebe' out again," Luis said.

Forrest laughed.

"He ain't lyin'!" James agreed with Luis. "Forrest be strokin'!" James pumped his hips back and forth, moving his hand in a slapping motion.

"Ya'll dudes dumb as hell," Forrest exclaimed. He laughed hard, and started on his food.

"Tell him what you've been up to Luis," James said, putting Luis on the spot.

Forrest looked at Luis and raised his eyebrow.

"Why you trynna do me like that?" Luis asked James.

James started laughing.

"What's up with you?" Forrest asked Luis.

"I lost my job and had to move in wit' this chick," Luis answered in annoyance. "I just found a new job that pays $15,000 more than my last one so I can get my own crib again."

"You mean a woman?" Forrest corrected.

"I meant exactly what I said," Luis snapped.

"Forrest man, Luis is in love. He ain't goin' nowhere. She ain't gone let him and he don't wanna go. I think he's gonna give up his playa's card," James said getting to the point of it all.

"Neva!" Luis barked. "I'm chillin'. She's a good friend."

"A good friend he bought a three karat diamond ring for," James said.

Forrest laughed as he ate.

"She had my back when I fell on hard times. The ring was a thank you gift," Luis said, avoiding the eyes of his cronies. "She's ride or die."

"It's okay to admit that you're in love Luis," Forrest said, smirking. "I love my wife. James loves his wife."

"Get outta here with all that," Luis huffed. "Enough about me. James, what's goin' on in yo house? Yo mother-in-law been acting loopy as a mofo."

"You right man," James admitted. "I don't know what's goin' on in this house. Sadie is convinced that Khalid is the devil." James scoffed. "She thinks he has the power to kill people by will. She thinks her mama is bein' harassed by the ang..." James stopped midsentence.   He felt uncomfortable telling them about the angel.

Forrest observed James hesitation and said, "Sky told me everything about how Khalid was born."

James felt anger and relief; emotional liberation and humiliation. In his heart, he knew that his friends were aware that Khalid was different and of the mystery surrounded his birth; but James wondered who else knew that Khalid was not his biological son.

"It's okay Jay," Luis said. "We yo boys." Luis placed his hand on James' shoulder and squeezed.

"Thanks man," James said.

"So, what's going on?" Forrest asked, putting his beer down and leaning forward.

"Honestly, I don't know. I don't know what to believe. I don't know what to do. I feel like I can't protect my own family. My kids are fightin' like thugs in the street. Uriel thinks his grandma and brother are evil villains and he's some kind of superhero. He swears they all got powers. Check this out," James said. "Uriel told me that Khalid can levitate and that his grandma can too. Uriel said he made her vomit light," James took a deep breath and continued. "I don't know what the hell is goin' on in this house. Sometimes I want to get in my car and not look back."

"You sure that ain't got nothin' to do wit' that big booty hefa you got workin' for you?" Luis asked, raising one of his brows.

"I ain't thinkin' 'bout that woman," James huffed.

"I'm just sayin'. You ain't never thought about drivin' off into the sunset before. You knew what you were gettin' into when you married Sadie. You chose to love her anyway. Don't try to punk out now," Luis said. He picked up his beer and took a deep gulp.

"James, are you cheating on Sadie?" Forrest asked.

"Never," James said, hurt that Forrest would ask. "You know I love my wife."

"Well, get that ho out of yo office," Luis spat. "I see how she looks at you. She like a salivatin' wolf lookin' at a juicy lamb chop. She wanna swallow every bit of you!" Luis smirked. "With them big ole lips, I bet she can." He laughed then became serious again. "You can only play with temptation for so long brotha. There comes a time when you gotta man up and do the right thang. Don't throw pearls to swine."

"You're a philosopher now Lu?" Forrest laughed. "You must be really messing up if you got Luis preaching to you James!"

James chuckled quietly; then, looked away from Luis, and started to eat. Guilt seized James' heart. It was true that he was physically faithful to his wife, but Timoo's constant flirtations had been getting to him. Even after Sadie confronted Timoo about being inappropriate, the very next day, Timoo came to work dressed as sexy as ever and brought James a home cooked lunch. Since then, Timoo has been blatantly flirtatious. James felt that maybe Timoo took Sadie's warning as a challenge. Honestly, he was flattered by her assertiveness. It had been a long time since a woman treated him like he was the second coming of Jesus.

"Ya'll wanna 'nother beer?" James asked; eager to change the subject. He got up and went into the refrigerator realizing that he was one of the potential causes of the chaos brewing in his home.

Sky woke up in the middle of the night with indigestion. Her mother used to tell her that chronic indigestion, when pregnant, meant that the baby had a head full of hair. Sky imagined that the child within her belly had a supersized afro as red as a strawberry. Sky sat up slowly, careful not to wake up Forrest who was sleeping peacefully curled up in a ball like a baby. She touched his hip and smiled. Acid snaked up her chest. She stood up, pulled on her nightgown and robe, and stuck her feet into her slippers. Sky walked out of the bedroom door and made her way up the stairs into the main part of Sadie's house.

It was quiet. Sky was disappointed. She was hoping to run into Sadie in the hallway and maybe share some late night snacks. Everyone must have been asleep. Sky looked at the kitchen clock and it read 3:33am. *Why do I keep waking up in the witching hours?* She thought as she opened the refrigerator to look for some cold milk to drink. Milk always made her indigestion better, at least for a little while. Sky found what she was looking for, poured herself a tall glass of milk, and sat down at the kitchen counter.

"Sky," a voice called from behind her.

Sky spun around. The hairs on the back of her neck stood up. Mr. Covington stood before her with a grave look on his face; his brows furrowed and a glower on his face. Although she knew he was harmless, there was something about his facial expression and something about talking to one who had passed on that still set her nerves on edge. It was simply unnatural. She loved him, but every time he appeared to her, Sky could feel her spirit shoot warnings through her entire body. Sometimes Sky wondered if she should just command him to pass on to the next realm and forbid him from showing his face again, but she felt that he was there to help and Sadie needed him. Maybe Sky needed him too.

"Yes, Pappa C," Sky responded. She sat her milk on the counter and waited for him to respond. Sky looked at him from head to toe. He looked so solid that she felt that she could touch him. His eyes were bright and reflecting light. His skin looked flushed. Sky stared at his chest to see if it rose and fell with breath. It didn't.

Mr. Covington moved towards Sky. She shrunk back as he drew closer. He pulled out the chair beside her and sat down. Sky was in awe of his ability to move and behave as he did in his natural life. He touched her forearm and she jumped when his cold hand landed on her flesh. She recoiled from him; her heart beating erratically and her body quaking uncontrollably.

"Don't be afraid," Mr. Covington said. "I mean you no harm. I came to talk to you."

"H...h...how did you touch me?" Sky asked, her voice wavering with every word.

"I don't know. All I know is that I need to be here with you; to speak with you face to face," he responded. "I don't have much time. You don't have much time," he said as he looked down at Sky's swollen belly.

"What is it Pappa C?" Sky asked, still unnerved by him being so close to her. She could feel coolness drifting from his skin.

"The angel has infiltrated this house!" Mr. Covington hissed. "It talks with the boy without ceasing. The angel walks around in plain view of all," Mr. Covington said, his face becoming angrier with each word.

"But how Pappa C? No one has seen it. Sadie said she smelled Turiel near Mrs. Covington, but no one has seen it," Sky said.

"He is *in* my wife!" Mr. Covington yelped. A tear formed in the corner of his eye. "He has taken her hostage."

"What do you mean *in* your wife?" Sky asked, utterly confused.

"Turiel has possessed her. Its spirit is inside of her body. He is using my wife as a meat suit!" Mr. Covington howled so loud that Sky thought he would wake the entire house.

"How can that be?" Sky asked.

Although Sky's mother taught her a lot about the spiritual world, she did not teach Sky about possession. All of Sky's knowledge of the subject came from modern horror movies, and her personal beliefs about the true causes of insanity. Both sources confirmed that demons were absolute hell to deal with and get rid of. Sky was not looking forward to the challenge.

"Mama C's head hasn't spun around and she hasn't drawn upside down crosses all over her room." Sky said innocently. Although she knew that was the movie version of things, she thought maybe it could have some truth in it.

"This isn't TV Sky. This is real life. Forget all about the Hollywood magic. The signs of possession are subtle but very evident. A possessed person acts completely out of character. Sometimes they show unusual strength or speak in unknown languages. Sometimes they display supernatural powers like foretelling the future or using retro-cognition. They are completely taken over by the spirit possessing them."

Sky thought back over all the things that Sadie told her about her mother in the past month. Possession sure fitted the bill, especially the day Mrs. Covington attacked her grandson Uriel. That was totally out of her character. She would never ever hurt a child, especially her grandchild.

"Where is Mama C's spirit?" Sky asked.

"Ebbie is still inside of her body. Her spirit has been shoved in the backseat while Turiel has taken the wheel. She's very weak, but she is there. If you bind the spirit, she will speak," Mr. Covington said.

"What do you want me to do?" Sky asked.

"Cast it out!" Mr. Covington exclaimed.

"How?" Sky asked; her eyes searching his face for answers.

Mr. Covington began to fade. His lips moved but there was no sound. Diminishing quickly, he tried to reach out but she could not feel his touch. The coolness of his presence turned cold and he was gone.

Darkness moved upon the face of the earth. The lamentation of all who had breath rose to the heavens in disconsolate pleas. Armies marched from coast to coast wielding weapons of mass destruction. Every nation battled; uniforms dripping in the blood of the innocent. Sounds of bullets seeking fresh bodies to empty of souls and the screams of enemies doing the death dance sang a sick symphony. The sky was painted with crimson and black explosions; clouds so dense the blue of heaven was permanently masked. Fire and destruction was almost everywhere. Everywhere except a compound surrounded by legions upon legions of armed forces.

Inside the compound, the rulers of every powerful nation were prostrate before the throne of one whose soul was darker than the deepest pit of perdition. Striking to behold, he sat upon his throne with each foot on the neck of a servant. Fire and brimstone rained from his mouth. His fingers were impregnated with the power to suck life from anyone who dared to oppose him. He was the desolation of desecration; the archbishop of anarchy, the great tempter, father of lies, the devil incarnate. He was…

Ari woke up in a hard sweat; his t-shirt sticking to his chest; his breathing labored with moans of fear and despair. He sprang up, nearly knocking his wife out of bed. Luckily she slept like a dead person.

The face of the diabolical ruler in his dream looked so familiar. Ari knew that man, that demon, but Ari could not believe the name that matched the face.

A look of utter dread filled Ari's head. The man looked like a younger version of Dr. Carlos Covington.

"Professor Covington?" Ari whispered aloud, not understanding why he would dream that Sadie's father was an evil ruler.

"Yes," a voice answered in the darkness of Ari's room.

Ari jumped to his feet and asked, "Who's there?"

"Professor Covington. You called me," the voice answered.

Ari clicked on the light and Mr. Covington was standing at the foot of the bed. Ari jumped back. Urine tried to push itself out but Ari willed it back up.

"Why are you here? What are you, demon?" Ari whispered. He reached for his bible, his cross, his Star of David, his pentagram, and his ankh; then, he began to pray.

"I am no demon," Mr. Covington said; looking at all of Ari's trinkets. He shook his head and said, "You are doing way too much. God is not that complicated."

"I saw you in my dream," Ari snapped; dropping all of his religious symbols to the floor. He looked over at his sleeping wife and prayed that she would not gain consciousness during the ghastly exchange.

"It wasn't me that you saw," Mr. Covington said.

"Lies!" Ari hissed. "I cast you out in the name of..."

"Please don't cast me away!" Mr. Covington pleaded, his hands up in the air. "Your dream is not as it seems. Listen to me. Please."

Ari paused for a moment. Something in his soul told him to listen. He yielded to the Holy Spirit within him and sat down on the edge of the bed.

"Speak. You're on borrowed time," Ari threatened.

"My family needs your help. Turiel, a rogue angel, has possessed my wife. I need you to help get rid of him. Teach Sky about exorcism," Mr. Covington begged.

Ari listened to Mr. Covington but the dream kept nagging Ari. He asked, "Why were you in my dream?"

"It wasn't me! Think man! Think hard! You know that face! Dreams are not always in the present. Think of the future!" Mr. Covington exclaimed.

"The future..." Ari said to himself. He forced his mind to focus on the face in his dream.

"Help my family," Mr. Covington pleaded as he faded away.

Ari lay back in the bed next to his wife. He said a prayer asking God for understanding and protection. After his consternation subsided, he turned off the light and closed his eyes.   Moments later he popped up on the bed and whispered into the silence, "Khalid."

47

When Sadie went downstairs, she was surprised to see her mother cooking breakfast since Mrs. Covington had been on a breakfast hiatus for a while now. Plus, Sadie wasn't too amped up to be in the same room with her mother since she attacked Uriel.

Mrs. Covington was a stranger to Sadie. She did not know who she was looking at every time she came face to face with her mother. The sweet proper woman who had raised Sadie had transformed into a vicious, unpredictable hag who seemed to frighten everyone in the house except for Khalid. Sky and her family stayed out of Mrs. Covington's way, and James avoided almost everyone. Uriel was still very heartbroken about Mrs. Covington physically assaulting him. Amazingly, he found it in his heart to forgive her. He told Sadie that it was not his grandmother's fault. He said that maybe the devil made her do it. Sadie dismissed Uriel's comment as crazy talk, but was glad that he was not traumatized by Mrs. Covington's behavior. Whatever was making Mrs. Covington behave erratically, Sadie wished it would stop.

"Sit down sweetheart. I cooked you a big breakfast," Mrs. Covington sang. She turned towards the stove and began to fix Sadie's plate. Mrs. Covington turned back around to Sadie and said, "James and the boys already ate and are off to school and work. They were so surprised that I cooked. They all gave me a big hug and kiss!"

Sadie didn't believe for one minute that James gave her a big hug, but then again, food was involved. It seemed that food was always the perfect bribe for James.

Mrs. Covington continued, "You will be happy to know that Uriel and I made up." She grinned so eerily that it made her look senseless. "I apologized to him this morning. He said that he had already forgiven me." Mrs. Covington paused with a concerned look on her face. "He's sweet but I worry about what you allow him to read."

"What do you mean?" Sadie asked; a little offended because she monitored every source of media her children encountered in her home.

"He talks too much about God and spiritual matters. He sounds like a religious fanatic. If you're not careful, he may end up as being one of those people who wrestle with snakes and flog their own backs," Mrs. Covington said. "The last thing this world needs is another cult leader."

Sadie rolled her eyes and reluctantly put her briefcase down on a chair. She knew no such fate was in store for Uriel. Her son had plenty of sense and sanity. Her mother was overacting as usual when it came to spiritual matters. Sadie sat down at the kitchen counter; not taking her eyes off of her mother for one minute.

Mrs. Covington sat a plate of fried salmon patties, honey biscuits, and rice before Sadie.

Sadie twisted her mouth sideways and pushed the plate away.

"What's wrong sweetie?" Mrs. Covington asked. "You need some butter or salt?"

"I hate seafood and rice, Mom," Sadie responded.

"Since when?" Mrs. Covington asked with her arms crossed. "James and the boys loved it."

"Since birth!" Sadie said, surprised that her mother had forgotten something so integral to Sadie's sensibilities and wellbeing. Sadie had been allergic to seafood her whole life, and she never saw the purpose of eating rice. Rice was a flavorless food that no one should waste their time chewing. How could her mother forget that?

Mrs. Covington raised her eyebrows in surprise. She took the plate away and offered to fix Sadie some cereal.

"No thanks Mom," Sadie said. "Save it for the Cohens. I'm sure Sky and Forrest will love the salmon, and their children will love to eat cereal." Sadie patted the chair next to her. "Let me talk to you for a minute."

Her mother sat down. Mrs. Covington sat so close to Sadie that Sadie was forced to scoot over.

"Yes," Mrs. Covington said; a dreamy look in her eyes. She touched Sadie's cheek, and let her fingers trace Sadie's lips. Sadie backed away; her mother's touch a bit off putting. Mrs. Covington put her hand on Sadie's leg; her fingers tickling Sadie's inner knee. Sadie pushed her mother's hand off. The look in Mrs. Covington's eyes made Sadie feel dirty all over.

"What are you doing?" Sadie barked; imploding with disgust and anger.

"Showing you how much I love you," Turiel said through Mrs. Covington's mouth. The smell of myrrh sweetened her breath.

Sadie jumped up from the counter; unsure of what she had just heard. She grabbed her bag, and headed for work.

"The car show was a success!" James yelled as he picked Timoo up, spun her around, and kissed her on the cheek. He put her down on the floor and said, "It's all you girl! Thank you for doin' such a great job. You made us so much money! Wooooohoooo!" James yelled as he fist pumped in the air.

He was so ecstatic that he could hardly contain himself. Not only did his business make a huge profit from the car show deal that Timoo orchestrated, he also signed three more detailing contracts with new clients. Timoo brought him clientele that he never even considered advertising to. Her beauty and charm made men weak. She was a great asset to have on his team. James thanked God for her.

Timoo smiled. She loved to see James happy. He looked even more attractive when his gleaming white teeth were showing. Timoo hated that he was married. She felt that they would have made a perfect couple if circumstances were different. *Maybe things could be different?* She thought. *James seemed unhappy lately. He stayed late often.* Timoo didn't hear him talk to his wife on the phone as much as he used to. When Timoo asked him how his family was doing, he always changed the subject. Maybe Timoo didn't have to wait to see him next lifetime. Many people were married to the wrong people. Maybe Sadie was married to the man Timoo was meant for. After all, Timoo and James had become really close. They ate lunch together at least twice a week. He was playful with her. He always noticed her clothes and hairstyles. He complimented her often. Maybe he was interested but too noble to act on his feelings. Timoo smiled. If he was afraid, she would be bold for the both of them.

"You're welcome James, but I only got the first contract. You are responsible for the next three. No one can resist your charm," she cooed.

James laughed and did a happy dance.

"We need to celebrate," he said. "I have a bottle of champagne in da fridge. You want some?"

"Sure," Timoo giggled. She sat on the leather couch in James' office. When he turned his back to get the champagne and glasses, she unbuttoned the top three buttons on her shirt to reveal maximum cleavage. She hiked her skirt up mid-thigh, and crossed her legs. Timoo pulled the pins out of her hair and let her locks fall around her shoulders.

"Wow," James said a little too loud when he turned around. "A brother turn around and you change from Diana Prince to Wonder Woman."

Timoo giggled and reached out her hand for a champagne glass. James handed it to her, and poured them both a glass full.

"Too us!" Timoo toasted and drank the entire glass in one motion. She held out her glass for more. James filled it up.

"Too us," James held up his glass; his elation dissolving quickly. The scene in his office was beginning to convert into something that he had no intention of allowing. Thoughts of Luis' words filled his head.

"What's wrong?" Timoo asked. "Don't kill the vibe!" she giggled. She put her glass on the table and stood up. She sauntered over to James and put her arms around his neck.

"Let's stop playing games," she said. "I'm attracted to you and you're attracted to me..." She kissed the side of his face, his ear, and side of his lips.

He weakly pushed her away.

"I...I...I think I gave you the wrong impression," James stuttered. "We friends. That's all."

Timoo grabbed his hand, kissed it, and began to suck one of his fingers.

The warmth of her mouth made his manhood respond. James lazily pulled his hand away.

"If I didn't know how you look at me when you don't think I see you, I would be offended," Timoo purred. "Look James, I know you're married. I know you love your wife. I'm not asking you to abandon your family. I'm just asking you to love me too," Timoo cooed as she fell to her knees in front of James. "I can make you happy James. All you have to do is let me."

Timoo grabbed his belt buckle and tried to unfasten it. James stepped backwards, and yanked Timoo up by the arm. She dangled for a moment then recovered her footing.

"Sit down," he said firmly as he flung her on the couch. He touched his forehead with his hand and started to pace the floor. What had he gotten himself into? Luis was right. James was playing games.

Timoo sat, flustered and turned on by his aggression. She began pulling her shirt out of her skirt.

"Stop," James said.

She kept going.

"Stop!" James yelled; his fist balled and the vein in the middle of his forehead pulsating.

Timoo stopped; shocked by his facial expression.

"What's wrong?" she asked; tucking her shirt back in her skirt.

"Timoo, I like you as a person and I think that you are the best employee that I have ever had, but I'm goin' to have to let you go. Please leave my office. Gather your things, and never come back."

Timoo was crushed. She never in a million years thought James would fire her. She thought he was just playing hard to get. *What kind of hold does that woman have on him?* Timoo thought to herself as she remembered Sadie telling her that she would be fired if she was out of line again.

"I'm sorry. I thought you liked me," Timoo cried.

"I do like you Timoo. I like you as a friend and as an employee," James admitted. Guilt filled him. He knew he was wrong for flirting with her.

"I thought you liked me. Really liked me," cried Timoo.

"You thought wrong. Please leave. I'll write you a good reference," James said as he opened the door to his office. "By the way, I have a video camera in my office just in case what happened here was misinterpreted."

Timoo looked up at James and wanted to scratch his left eye out. She couldn't believe that he thought that she might try to extort him or sue him for sexual harassment. She genuinely liked James.

"I'm sorry she whispered," and walked out of his office. "Maybe next lifetime?" she asked with a look that begged James to give her hope.

James closed the door in her face, and damned himself for being so stupid.

The school dance was going to start in a few hours. When the school bus arrived, Khalid rushed past his grandmother and ran home from the bus stop so he could prepare himself for the evening. When he got into his room, he opened his closet and pulled out the new clothes his mother bought him to wear to the dance. Khalid laid the button down top and slacks across his bed. He pulled a shoebox from under his bed and pulled out his new Jordans. They matched perfectly.

Uriel walked into the room and climbed up to his bunk bed. He threw his legs over the side and let them swing as he watched his big brother prepare for his special night.

"Who are you taking to the dance?" Uriel asked. "Did Evadne agree to go with you?"

Khalid twisted his lips. He tried hard not to think about Evadne at the moment. She was his dream date but he realized that sometimes dreams did not come true. He cringed at the thought. Khalid wanted all his dreams to come true.

"I'm taking Venus," Khalid answered as he pulled socks from his sock drawer, and laid it next to the rest of his outfit.

"Cool," Uriel said. "You two are just alike."

"Who are you taking to the dance?" Khalid asked Uriel who was busy bouncing as he kicked.

"The prettiest woman in the world, Mom," Uriel said with a huge smile on his face.

"You're so lame it's sickening," Khalid laughed. "Why didn't you ask Earth? I'm sure she would like to go. She's pretty cute and you both are the same age."

"You don't think Mom will be mad?" Uriel asked innocently. "I told her that I would be her date."

"Of course not! Mom won't be mad at all. She's going to chaperone. Save her a dance," Khalid said as he moved out of the way so Uriel could jump off of the top bunk. "Besides, Dad will be her date. You better go ask Earth so her mom can get her a dress real quick."

"Okay," Uriel agreed and ran out of the room to ask for his first date.

"Hurry up or we'll be late for the dance," Sadie yelled through the hallway to her boys. "Make sure you tell Sky that we'll be leaving in a minute so make sure that the girls are ready to roll."

Sadie went back into her bedroom and put on her earrings. She asked James to zip up her fitted black dress.

He obliged.

James pulled on his dress shoes and straightened his tie as Sadie squeezed in front of him to see herself in the mirror. James caught her by the waist and spun her around. He kissed her lips and said, "I have a confession to make."

"What?" Sadie asked, reaching for her lip gloss.

"I fired Timoo today," James said.

"Why? I thought she was an excellent worker," Sadie asked, turning to look James in the eye. "What happened?"

"Sit down," James instructed.

Sadie walked over to the bed and sat.

"I fired her because she made a pass at me," James said. "She was tryin' to get at me."

"What happened?" Sadie asked, her hands dropping to her lap.

"She wanted to....you know," James mumbled.

Sadie's bottom jaw dropped.

"She tried to give it to me. I wouldn't take it. I fired her," James said as matter of fact.

Sadie's eyes narrowed. She said, "Why do I have a feeling that you are leaving out a whole lot of information?"

"I think she misinterpreted our friendship as a precursor to a romantic relationship," James said, having a difficult time looking Sadie in the face. He knew that all the time he spent with Timoo was inappropriate, and he totally understood why she may have felt that he was interested. Maybe on some level he was interested, but he knew that he would never betray Sadie. He thought what he had with Timoo had been harmless flirting. He never anticipated that things would go so far. James felt like he lost a valuable employee because of his failure to draw proper boundaries.

"Did you give her a reason to believe that you were interested James?" Sadie questioned, her eyes burning into him like a blow torch.

James bowed his head in shame. "Maybe I did," he confessed.

Sadie's heart dropped. She felt suddenly ill. She thought she would vomit. She asked, "D...d...did you cheat on me?"

"No! Never!" James said. He dropped to his knees in front of her and said, "You are the only one for me. I would never cheat on you. I flirted wit' her. I never touched her. Never said anything inappropriate. I never talked about my personal life."

"What *did* you do?" Sadie asked; a distrustful look on her face.

"We ate lunch together a few times. We joked a lot. I complimented her. She was a cool person. I liked her. Nothin' more," James said.

"And you did all that knowing that she wanted you? Even after she came to dinner dressed like a common street whore?" Sadie yelled. "What were you trying to do James?"

"I was stupid. I'm sorry," James said.

"I can't believe you!" Sadie screamed.

"Look, I didn't have to tell you but I did!" James yelled back. "I could've had that woman if I wanted to, but I didn't want to. I'm not the bad guy. I'm bein' real with you because I love you. I know I was wrong! I'm apologizin'!" James roared; regretting that he said anything. The truth was overrated.

Sadie looked at her husband and shook her head.

"Come here," she said with open arms. He leaned his head on her breasts and she wrapped her arms around him. She believed him. Her heart told her that every word he had spoken was true. James had given her no reason to distrust him.

"I love you," he said.

"I love you too," Sadie responded. "Now get dressed."

James hopped up from the floor and put on his blazer. He held out his arm. She wrapped her arm around his and they walked out of the room.

Rainbow colored streamers hung from the ceiling and trimmed the doors and windows of the elementary school cafeteria. Balloons on ribbons floated around the room simultaneously. Confetti littered the floor. The snack table was loaded with every goodie one could imagine from cookies to a chocolate fountain. A giant punch bowl filled to the rim sat in the middle of the snack table. Children ran around the dance in stylish splendor like wild animals dressed in silk.

Zahyir and Evadne stood in the corner of the room laughing at the shenanigans of the other children. Khalid and Venus stood on the opposite end of the room dancing to the latest music. Khalid always kept one eye on Evadne the entire time.

"Ooo, that's my song," Venus said as she spun around and started dancing.

Khalid looked at her and laughed. "Every song is your song," he said.

"Yep!" Venus retorted. "Let's go get something to drink."

Khalid took her hand and led her the long way around the room to the punch bowl. He wanted to pass by Evadne so he could flaunt Venus' beauty.

"Hi Khalid," Evadne said. "You look nice." She smiled. "Who's your date?"

Zahyir stood with is arms crossed and his lips twisted to the side. Every part of him wanted to punch Khalid in the mouth.

"Hi Evadne," Khalid responded, a huge smile of his face. No matter how much he wanted to hate her, he could not. Khalid adored every inch of her. He thought Evadne was the smartest and prettiest girl he had ever encountered.

"This is my friend Venus," Khalid answered. "She's visiting from New York City."

"Cool," Evadne said. "Nice to meet you Venus. I love your dress!"

Venus wore a lime green and black tutu with a black lace short sleeved top. She wore lace tights and black flats. Her long dark hair fell to her waist in deep waves.

"Thanks," Venus said. "I like your dress too."

Evadne wore a turquoise straight dress with purple ribbons for straps and a purple ribbon for a belt. Her hair was picked out in a wild afro with a purple flower in it. Khalid felt that the bright colors looked radiant against Evadne's black skin.

"Both of you look really pretty," Zahyir said.

"Thanks," the girls said in unison.

"I'm going to go get Venus some punch. Would you like some Evadne?" Khalid asked.

"Sure," said Evadne.

"Bring me some too," Zahyir said with a wicked smirk on his face.

"No," Khalid snapped and walked away.

Evadne and Zahyir started to laugh. Venus shook her head.

Khalid came back quickly with Venus' and Earth's punch. Both girls thanked him.

A popular dance song came on.

"Do you mind if I ask Evadne to dance?" Khalid asked Venus. Venus nodded her approval.

"She doesn't dance with little kids," Zahyir hissed and grabbed Evadne's hand and led her to the dance floor.

"Sorry," Evadne mouthed as she followed behind Zahyir.

Khalid's eyes narrowed. He balled his fist and started to huff and puff.

"Why do you let him get to you like that?" Venus asked, a little annoyed by Khalid's lack of attention.

"I hate him. He thinks he's better than me. She thinks he's better than me," Khalid growled.

"Forget them. Let's dance," Venus demanded. She grabbed his hand and started to move to the music.

Khalid snatched his hand away.

"Say something else to me punk!" Khalid growled as he pushed past Venus. He stood in Zahyir's face. "I bet this little kid can kick your butt!"

"Move on chump!" Zahyir waved him away.

Khalid knocked Zahyir's hand away.

Zahyir pushed Khalid and said, "I'll meet you in the hall."

Uriel spied the confrontation from across the room.

"What are you looking at?" Earth asked.

"I'll be back," Uriel said and made his way out of the door without any adults noticing. Uriel ran down the wrong hallway. He turned in the opposite direction, looking to find the angry boys and their dates, with full intentions of stopping the fight.

"Whatchu gone do now?" Zahyir roared. He ran up to Khalid and pushed him on the floor.

"Stop," Evadne yelled.

Venus stood with her arms crossed and watched. This was the most excitement she had since she arrived in Atlanta.

Before Khalid could get up, Zahyir knocked him back down.

"Lil man, I see your mouth ain't moving now," Zahyir provoked Khalid. "Get up!"

Khalid tried to get up again but was knocked back to the floor. Evadne grabbed Zahyir's arms but he shook her off and stood over Khalid.

"You're lucky I don't beat up little kids," growled Zahyir. "Next time I won't be so nice."

Khalid sat on the floor, his eyes narrowed into slits and his chest heaved. He looked at Zahyir and Khalid's eyes turned completely black.

Zahyir stepped backwards, his heart beating so hard that it hurt. He remembered Evadne telling him what happened when Mrs. Anderson died. Zahyir knew he was walking in the valley of the shadow of death.

Khalid stood up. He walked forward as Zahyir walked backwards. Soon Zahyir's back hit a locker.

Venus and Evadne were frozen with fear. They grabbed each other and damned their feet for not carrying them far away from the monster they saw before them.

"Get on your knees!" Khalid commanded.

Zahyir's body moved against his will and slid down the locker. His knees hit the floor hard; the sound of his knees hitting the floor echoed through the empty hallway. Zahyir felt a sharp pain travel through his body. His head began to swim.

"Beg for your life and I won't kill you," Khalid said, his eyes blacker than black; his face a demonic scowl.

"Stop!" Uriel yelled as he ran down the hallway. "Khalid stop!"

Khalid turned towards his brother.

Uriel stopped in his tracks. The sight of Khalid's eyes hit Uriel like a punch in the face.

Sadie stuck her head out of the cafeteria door to look for the missing children. When she saw the children, she was unable to speak or move. Something would not let her intervene. Her spirit told her to watch and observe; so she did.

"Go back inside," Khalid warned his brother.

"They have to come with me," Uriel said, walking towards his brother on shaky legs.

"Go back inside!" Khalid growled.

"Not unless they go with me," Uriel said.

Khalid pointed at his brother and Uriel's body went flying into the lockers, denting the metal doors instantly.

"Go inside!" Khalid yelled at his brother who was crumpled up on the floor.

Venus and Evadne tried to pull Zahyir up, but it was as if he was glued to the floor by the knees.

"God give your angels charge over me. Give me strength," Uriel prayed as he got to his feet. He stumbled towards his brother.

Khalid tried to toss Uriel again, but Uriel could not be moved. It was like an invisible force field made him immune to Khalid's power.

Uriel rushed to his brother and grabbed him by the hand.

"Peace be still!" Uriel yelled. A warm light passed through Uriel's hand into Khalid. Khalid let out a faint whimper and fell to the ground unconscious.

"Let's go back to the dance," Uriel instructed the others. "Khalid will be okay."

They all looked down at Khalid's sleeping body.

Uriel waved for them to come on, so they walked back towards the cafeteria where they saw Sadie standing in the doorway with a dumbfounded look on her face. She opened the door for them, letting them inside. All of them, like zombies, forever changed by what their eyes had seen.

Sadie walked down the hallway and stood over Khalid. *I could kill him right now and everything will be fine. All the madness will end.* She thought to herself as she knelt over him and considered placing her hands over his nose and mouth to steal his life. Sadie looked upon his handsome sleeping face. She could not slay him. Sadie loved Khalid too much. He was her first born son. He was the spitting image of Mr. Covington, Sadie's loving father. Her heart ached. Sadie pulled her eldest son up from the floor and shook him awake.

"Are you okay?" she asked; kissing him on his forehead as she held him in her arms.

Khalid looked into his mother's eyes and said, "I will never be okay again." He pushed away from her and ran down the hall.

It was late. Ari had been doing workshops at the university all day long and he was very ready to go home. He gathered his papers, closed his laptop, turned off his projector, and packed up all his belongings. Before Ari could turn the lights off in his classroom, he heard someone call his name. Ari spun around. He was sure that everyone had left. Ari looked up and searched the rows of chairs with his eyes. There was no one there. Ari chalked the voice up to his imagination and moved towards the light switch again.

"Ari," the voice called again.

Ari turned and Mr. Covington was sitting in the front row of the classroom.

Ari dropped his briefcase to the floor.

"What are you doing here?" Ari asked.

"We need to talk," Mr. Covington replied. "Come sit down. Bring pen and paper. I need you to take notes," he said; crossing his legs and leaning back in his chair.

Ari didn't move an inch. He looked at the specter trying to decide whether to comply or run.

"I won't bite," Mr. Covington laughed. His smile left and he said, ""I don't have a lot of time. Please come and sit. We have much to discuss."

Ari slowly walked over to Mr. Covington, observing every inch of this spirit. It was amazing how young and virile he looked. Ari sat two chairs down from Mr. Covington, careful not to get too close. Although Ari was not afraid, he was not comfortable conversing with the undead.

"What is it that you want Professor Covington? I mean Dr. Covington." Ari said, his voice wavering; his mind trying to reconcile what his eyes were seeing. To dream about spirits was one thing but to see and talk to a spirit in waking life was another.

"Please, call me Carlos," Mr. Covington said. "We've been friends for much too long for such formalities."

"Why are you here Carlos?" asked Ari. Calling his mentor by his first name felt strange. Ari felt more comfortable using Mr. Covington's formal titles.

"As you know, my daughter's house is in a state of chaos. I'm sure you know about the angel by now. Correct?" Mr. Covington asked.

"Correct," Ari answered.

"The angel is in my wife and I need you to get him out," Mr. Covington said getting to the point quickly.

"What do you mean?" Ari asked.

"Ebbie is possessed by that demon and it needs to be cast out!" Mr. Covington roared.

"And you want me to cast it out?" Ari asked, not welcoming the request. He wanted to stay as far away from that part of the spiritual realm as possible.

"No. I want you to teach Sky how to cast it out. I think that she is strong enough and spiritually balanced enough to do it," Mr. Covington said. He looked away with a disturbed look on his face.

"What's wrong?" Ari asked.

"Hopefully Sky's pregnancy won't be a hindrance. I don't want her or her baby to be harmed," he said.

"Are you sure you want her to do it?" Ari asked, concerned about Sky being put in such a position. *What if the angel tried to possess her unborn child?* Ari thought. He had heard of stranger things.

"She is the only one who is strong enough," Mr. Covington said gloomily. "Sadie and James aren't spiritually grounded. They are poisoned by their own logic. Forrest could. I guess; but I don't know how much he knows about the situation." Mr. Covington looked at Ari and said, "And you aren't willing."

Ari nodded his head in agreement. It was true. He was not willing and he did not feel guilty about not wanting to do battle with a demon. Binding spirits was not one of his gifts, and risking his personal safety or the safety of his family was not an option.

"So, how do I prepare her?" Ari asked. He picked up a pen and paper and sat ready to absorb the information Mr. Covington readied himself to offer.

"The very first thing needed in order to perform a successful exorcism is unwavering faith. The person performing the ritual has to believe that God has granted them the power to bind the spirit and drive it away. If faith is lacking, so many things can go wrong," said Mr. Covington.

"For example?" Ari asked.

"The spirit can become violent. It can jump out of one person and into another. Harm can be done to the person possessed," Mr. Covington said. "There is absolutely no room for doubting. The person in control has to be in total control."

"What does she need to help her: bibles, crosses, holy water?" Ari asked.

"She doesn't need any of that," Mr. Covington answered. "Sky simply needs faith and authority to cast the demon out. Keep in mind, when Jesus cast out demons, he never performed dramatic rituals beforehand. He simply told them to be gone and they were gone."

"It's that easy?" Ari said; his eyebrow rose.

"I never said it was easy. It is difficult just to subdue ones fear in the presence of preternatural evil. Some spirits are very strong so the exorcist must prepare by lots of prayer and fasting before they take on the challenge of banishing it. I suggest that you ask Sky to start fasting a week before the exorcism is to take place. Because she is pregnant, she is allowed to drink juices. If she was not with child, I would suggest a strict water fast for a week to tame the flesh. Tell her to pray without ceasing and let her husband take care of the children during her preparation period. She must evaluate her life and confess any personal sins to God she may be carrying in her heart. She needs to make sure that she asks for forgiveness, and she has to forgive others of any wrong doing. Tell her make sure her slate is as clean as possible. No one is perfect but she needs to be free of guilt, regrets, and anger. Tell Sky to make sure that she is in full submission to God. It is impossible to cast out demons with God's authority if one is disobedient to God's will or doubts that God is. I would hate for her to do this alone. Will you agree to be in the room with her?" Mr. Covington asked. "Having a support team makes the process easier."

Ari sat there and looked at Mr. Covington. The request he was asking was way too much. Ari was a friend of the family, but to be asked to engage in spiritual warfare was unreasonable. He wanted no part of it.

"I..." Ari began.

"Please," Mr. Covington pleaded. "I would not ask if I didn't think you were strong enough to help."

"What are the steps?" Ari asked; increasingly becoming uncomfortable with a spirit teaching him how to cast out spirits. Ari was a man of the cloth. He felt obligated to help. The Holy Spirit weighed heavily on his heart. "I will do it," he said.

"Thank you!" Mr. Covington exclaimed. "I am forever in your debt."

"What do we do?" Ari asked.

"You will be there for moral support. Sky will take the lead," Mr. Covington said. "There must not be any dissention between the two of you. Make sure you are on one accord before you enter into exorcism."

"Okay. Tell me about the process," Ari said; his heart racing. *What am I getting myself into?* He thought to himself. *Latrice will never approve.*

Mr. Covington said, "Before you start, make sure you have towels and a waste basket handy. Sometimes demons exit via the mouth so Ebbie may begin to vomit when it comes out. The process can get very messy. Also, don't get to close to her. Sometimes spirits may get violent. Most importantly, pray. You and Sky need to join hands in prayer before you enter that room. Ask for God's power and protection before you proceed. Ask God to anoint you and give you authority to cast out the angel. Be humble and sincere."

Ari nodded and waited for Mr. Covington to continue. Ari looked upon Mr. Covington's face and marveled at his lifelike appearance. He looked solid enough to touch, but Ari was afraid to touch him.

"When the exorcism begins, first Sky must bind the spirit. She can say something like:

In the name of God and with the authority of Jesus the Christ, God's messiah, I renounce all the powers of darkness enveloping or indwelling Ebbie Covington. Through the power of God, I bind all malevolent spirits inside of or surrounding Ebbie Covington and her family. By God's authority, I forbid you spirit(s) to function in any way, in the name of Jesus Christ the son of God.

Tell Sky to call the angel by its name. Bind Turiel. Then, cast the demon out. She could say something like:

In the name of Jesus the Christ through the power of Almighty God, I command all evil spirits to get out now! Turiel, get out in Jesus' name!

After the demon is cast out, it is important for Sky to annul all invitations to the angel or evil spirit(s) to reenter Ebbie, anyone in the family, or the house so that the demon will not return after it leaves. She can do this by issuing a prayer of protection like:

In the name of Jesus through the power of God, you shall not enter this woman, this family, or this home again. The power and protection of God surrounds us all. You are no longer welcome here.

After this is done, the angel should be gone and my wife should be back to herself. The experience may be draining for her so make sure she can get to a doctor as soon as possible. Also, make sure that this process is private. This will prevent the spirit from jumping from person to person. Keep the children away. They are easy marks," Mr. Covington said. He was beginning to fade.

"Is that all?" Ari asked quickly, afraid that his question may fall on deaf ears.

"That is all," Mr. Covington's voice faded to a whisper. "Prepare Sky for battle." His voice faded away.

Ari looked at the empty seat then down at his notepad. He didn't know how he would break the news to Sadie and convince her friend to perform an exorcism. He walked over to the door and picked up his briefcase. He turned out the lights and walked out of the building asking himself, *Why me?*

51

"How was the dance?" Sky asked Khalid as he walked into the kitchen. She sat on a stool at the kitchen counter eating cookies and drinking milk. It was late. She was surprised to see him up in the wee hours of the morning. Sky had become accustomed to having her late night snacks alone.

Khalid looked at her and his eyes narrowed. He did not want to talk about the dance.

"You all looked so nice when you left," Sky said, trying desperately to strike up a conversation. The look in his eyes made her uneasy. "Want some cookies?"

"Sure," Khalid said as he walked over and sat on the stool next to her.

"I made these a few minutes ago so they're still warm. They're not homemade like your grandma's but I think they're pretty good," Sky said and took another bite; the chocolate from the cookie smudging the side of her mouth. She stuck out her tongue and lapped it up.

Khalid picked up a cookie and took a bite. "Good," he said. He gobbled it up quickly.

"So, how is school?" Sky asked.

"School is school. Enough about me. Let's talk about you," Khalid said, his eyes piercing.

The hairs on the back of Sky's neck began to rise. She thought she would never feel fear from a child but the way Khalid looked at her made her blood run cold.

"Mom told me that you two have been friends for a long time," he said.

"Yes." Sky nodded.

"You also knew my granddaddy on my mom's side?" Khalid asked.

"I did," Sky forced a smile. "Pappa C was a wonderful man."

"Yeah," Khalid said. "I heard ya'll were close."

"I guess so. He was very close to your mother and I am very close to your mother so I guess that made me close to Pappa C. They were as thick as thieves," Sky said, wondering where this conversation was going.

Khalid looked down at her stomach. He asked, "How pregnant are you?"

"Almost seven months," Sky said.

"Congratulations. May I touch your tummy?" he asked.

"Sure," Sky answered reluctantly. She opened her robe revealing her thin nightgown.

Khalid placed his palm on Sky's belly. The baby inside of her started kicking like a soccer player. Her belly bulged with every kick.

"Ouch," Sky whimpered. "She likes you."

"He," Khalid corrected. "It's a boy."

Sky lifted and dropped her shoulders. She didn't know the sex. She just assumed it was a girl because she was carrying the baby so high and she had so much heart burn. Sky gently grabbed Khalid's hand and tried to remove it. His hand would not budge. The baby was kicking her so hard that she thought she would cry.

"Move your hand Khalid," Sky asked. "The baby is moving too hard."

"Was I this old when you tried to kill me in my mother's womb?" Khalid asked, pressing on Sky's stomach. Sky tried to remove his hand but he was too strong.

"Stop!" she cried.

"Did you stop when you and my coward of a grandfather tried to terminate my life?" he growled; his hand feeling like a hot iron on her belly.

Sky screamed.

"No!" Sky howled. Tears in her eyes blurred her vision. She thought she saw the boy's eyes blacken. Cramps shot through her belly. Warm liquid flowed from her womb. She looked down and saw blood on her thighs.

"Stop!" she screamed again. Sky began swinging her arms, fruitlessly striking the child.

"Did you stop?" he roared and pushed his palm into her belly.

Mrs. Covington peered into the kitchen doorway.

Sky screamed for Mrs. Covington to help but, she smiled and walked away. Mrs. Covington saw Uriel in the hallway and quickly entered her room and closed the door.

"Stop Khalid!" Uriel yelled as he ran into the kitchen.

Their bedroom was the closest to the kitchen. Sky's screams woke him from his slumber.

Khalid looked at Uriel and winced. He remembered his brother hurting him in the school hallway. Khalid removed his hand from Sky and said to Uriel, "I'm not afraid of you."

"And I'm not afraid of you," Uriel retorted. "Leave her alone!"

Khalid turned to Sky and spit in her face. It took all the self-control she could muster not to slap his face off. She held her tummy and prayed to herself that her baby was okay.

Khalid walked past Uriel, bumping his shoulder so hard that Uriel almost fell. Khalid left the kitchen and disappeared down the hall.

"Uriel, go get Forrest, and then your mother. Tell them that I need to go the hospital," she cried as she toppled over in pain.

Uriel bolted from the kitchen.

Sky wobbled out of the kitchen leaving a trail of blood.

52

"Dr. and Mrs. Cohen," Dr. Thornton said, his yellow-gray hair sticking out of his dark scalp like individual cotton balls. "I have great news." He came close to the hospital bed and smiled at Sky.

"Yes?" Forrest asked, holding Sky's hand tight. Her thin arm stuck out from under the hospital gown like a red straw.

"The baby is going to be just fine. It seems as if he was stressed for a moment but he is all better now," Dr. Thornton said with a grand smile on his wrinkled face. His white beard made him look like a black Santa Claus.

"He?" Sky asked, remembering that Khalid said that her baby was a boy. The thought of Khalid made her tremble.

"I'm sorry," Dr. Thornton said. "I didn't mean to give away the sex of the baby. I just assumed you knew. So many young couples today find out."

"That's okay," Forrest said, suddenly annoyed by the jovial doctor. "What caused the stress to the baby? Sky's stomach felt like it was boiling. She was bleeding profusely when we arrived."

"Honestly," the doctor said. "We don't know. The bleeding stopped almost immediately. Her embryonic sac and mucus plug was still intact. Mrs. Cohen has no bacterial infections. The baby doesn't seem to have any abnormalities or immunologic disorders. Her lifestyle is pretty healthy so we don't have to worry about caffeine, cigarettes, drugs, or alcohol. Dr. Cohen, we ran every test we could think of and everything came out negative."

"What about..." Forrest began but was cut off by Sky.

"Thank you Dr. Thornton. Could you give me a moment with my husband?"

"Sure," Dr. Thornton said.

"And please, send my friend Sadie in the room," Sky said.

"Will do," Dr. Thornton said. "Please let me know if there is anything I can do to help." He exited the room.

"What's wrong baby?" Forrest asked, smoothing her scarlet hair.

Sky began to cry.

"Don't cry sweetie," Forrest begged. "Everything will be alright."

Sadie walked into the room. She quickly moved to Sky's bedside, opposite of Forrest, and picked up Sky's other hand.

"Are you okay? How is the baby?" Sadie asked and kissed Sky's forehead. "James and Mama are at home with the children. Everyone is so worried about you.

"The baby is fine. I'm not," Sky cried.

"What's wrong?" Sadie asked, tears forming in her eyes. Seeing Sky cry broke Sadie's heart. "What happened?"

"Khalid happened," Sky bawled.

"What?" Sadie dropped Sky's hand and stepped back. "What do you mean?"

"He touched my stomach," Sky blubbered. "The baby started kicking. His hand got so hot. He told me that me and Pappa C tried to kill him," Sky sniveled. "Cramps came. Blood came. Uriel stopped him!"

Sadie began to weep. How could she defend her son when she knew what Sky was saying was probably true? Khalid was a demon. She saw him in action last night at the school. Sadie knew what her son was capable of.

Forrest looked utterly confused. He shook his head from side to side and said, "Sky you can't really believe that. Khalid is a child. I know what you said about his father but..."

"He did it!" Sky screeched in anger. "He tried to kill my baby."

"I'm so sorry Sky," Sadie cried. "I'm so sorry."

"Mama C saw him hurt me and just walked away," Sky wined.

"She what?" Anger flooded Sadie's face.

"Don't be angry with her Sadie. It's not her fault," Sky said through her tears.

"How can you defend her?" Sadie growled.

"She's possessed Sadie. Pappa C told me so," Sky cried. "The angel is in her. It's controlling her."

Forrest let go of his wife's hand and stood up.

"Forrest," Sky whispered.

He ignored her voice and walked out of the room. Talk of possession, angels, and ghosts was way too much. He didn't know whether to call a rabbi or a psychiatrist. All he knew was that he did not want to hear any more of Sky and Sadie's conversation. What he wanted was to find Dr. Thornton and talk more about real life reasons his unborn son's life was threatened.

Sky silently watched him leave; then, turned back to Sadie.

"Possessed? How?" Sadie asked.

"I don't know but Pappa C said she was and that's why she's been acting all crazy," Sky sniffled.

"What are we gonna do?" Sadie asked.

"We're gonna get that angel the hell outta her!" Sky snapped and grabbed Sadie's hand. "We're in this together girl!"

"I love you Sky!" Sadie cried.

Sadie looked at Sky laying in the bed fragile and weak; her hair wild and her cheeks peaky; tears flowing from her eyes and tubes hanging from her body; her unborn child just recovering from trauma, and Sky was ready to do battle. Sadie hugged her best friend. All of Sadie's life, she thought that she was an only child but blood could not have created a closer sister than Sky. There was no greater love.

The weekend had been a long one for Sadie with her children fighting at the school dance on Friday and Sky going to the hospital early Saturday morning. Sunday was uneventful but unnerving. Her household walked around in silence. Sadie had to break bread with her mother with the knowledge of her being possessed. James and Forrest spent most of the day out of the house. Sadie knew that all the supernatural unraveling of her family was getting to them. Sky rested most of the day; recuperating from Khalid's attack. The kids played divided into two groups. Uriel, Earth, and Jupiter made up one group and Khalid and Venus made up the other. Each group chose opposite corners of the house and worked tirelessly not to cross paths.

For the first time ever, Sadie was glad that it was Monday and she was back at work. The stress of her home had begun to give her neck spasms. Sadie rubbed the back of her neck and flipped through the files on her desk. Thoughts of her mother being possessed strained Sadie. It took over every moment and every thought. Sadie put the files down and grabbed her purse. She needed an ally greater than Turiel on her side. She needed The Ultimate but she didn't know how to make contact. It was time for her to take a trip to the convent.

Greenery and statues of saints and messiahs decorated the peaceful grounds of the convent. Nuns in flowing white habits, some unveiled, some in white veils, some in black veils, busied themselves in all directions. The tall brick walls of the convent looked gigantic against the bright blue sky. It reminded Sadie of a castle she once saw in a horror movie. A large gate surrounded the grounds. Sadie, a familiar face to the nuns, was welcomed inside eagerly. She walked into the front door and headed to the recreational room. Nuns were playing board games. Some were playing basketball. Some were playing a competitive dance video game. It tickled Sadie to see them flying around in their habits. Some were texting on their cell phones, and some were reading books.

Sadie looked at her wristwatch; she had forty-five minutes before the bells rang for nightly prayer, so she rushed to Sister Mary Agnes's office door and tapped lightly. The door opened and Sister Mary Agnes stepped out with her arms wide open; her pale white flesh in sharp contrast with her black veil.

"Sadie! It is such a pleasure to see you," Sister Mary Agnes said. "How are you?" Her blue eyes danced beneath blonde lashes.

"I'm doing just fine. How are you sister?" Sadie asked.

"I'm still sore from that dance aerobic teacher you hired last week," Sister Mary Agnes laughed. "My butt feels like I have been paddled!"

Sadie laughed and imagined the nun getting spanked with a giant ruler. She always imagined nuns with rulers in their pockets.

"I'm glad you're getting in shape," Sadie said. "Are you busy at the moment sister?"

"I'm never too busy for you Sadie. Come in and have a seat," Sister Mary Agnes said while stepping to the side and allowing Sadie to enter the office. Sister Mary Agnes closed the door and sat down.

Sadie sat down across from her. She had a difficult time looking Sister Mary Agnes in the face. How could Sadie possibly say what she needed to say aloud? Embarrassment and frustration blushed her honey brown cheeks.

"What's wrong honey?" Sister Mary Agnes said. She touched Sadie's knee and Sadie began to cry. "There, there, my dear. Don't cry. Talk to me."

"It's my mother," Sadie whimpered. "I think she is possessed."

Sister Mary Agnes' face went white. She hadn't heard of a case of true demon possession in twenty years. Most reports of demon possessions were cases of mental illness. Besides, even if Sadie's mother was possessed, Sister Mary Agnes could not help her because Sadie and her family were not Catholics. It takes an ordained priest with permission from the local bishop to perform the rite. Also, the alleged possessed person had to have a medical examination to ensure that mental illness was not the culprit.

"Why do you think your mother is possessed?" Sister Mary Agnes asked.

"She behaves totally out of character. Mom is cruel and violent. Sister Mary Agnes, you have met my mother before. She was one of the sweetest and most respectful people I've ever known. I don't know who she is now!" Sadie cried. Her last words haunted her. She knew exactly who her mother was. She was Turiel. "Mom attacked my youngest son. Uriel claims that he saw her levitating and her body contorting in her bedroom, and that she vomits out light. She watches trash TV. My mother abhorred trash TV! Also, she has the strength and speed of a twenty year old man!"

Sister Mary Agnes nodded in agreement that those were surly the signs of possession but the nun did not know how she could help Sadie. Everything in the Catholic Church was a process. Even if she wanted to, she could not go to Sadie's house to exorcise a demon nor could she ask a priest to do so. The bishop had to give approval for such a rite and the approval for non-Catholics for holy rites were next to nothing. Sister Mary Agnes' heart mourned for Sadie. Times like this the nun wished she was not bound by the rules of the

Church. If she had the nerve, she would grab the *Rituale Romanum* and deliver Sadie's mother.

"What can I do sister?" Sadie cried.

"Pray, then, find a local minister who can help you," Sister Mary Agnes said with tears in her eyes.

"So I have to go look for some snake oil preacher and pay him a thousand dollars to save my mother's soul?" Sadie snapped.

"No. No child," Sister Mary Agnes said, rubbing Sadie's back trying to cool her anger. "There are sincere people of God who will help you."

"But you won't?" Sadie asked, looking into the old nun's eyes pleading for mercy.

Sister Mary Agnes dropped her head and looked away. "I'm sorry." She said. "All I can offer you are prayers."

"What's wrong sweetie? You look stressed," Latrice asked as she sat on her husband's lap and wrapped her legs around him.

Ari pushed his chair back from his desk so that Latrice would have leg room. He wrapped his arms around her waist and laid his head against her chest.

"Talk to me baby," she said; lifting his head up so that they were face to face. "What's going on? You've been acting weird for the last few days."

"I have a lot on my mind. That's all." Ari sighed. He laid his head back on her chest.

"I wish you would talk to me," Latrice urged. "I hate to see you like this. I'm your helpmate baby. Let me help you."

"There's nothing you can do to help me," Ari whispered.

"Then let me try," she said, kissing his forehead.

He looked her in her eyes and said, "Professor Covington visited me the other day when I was at school. He told me that his wife was possessed, and that I need to teach Sky how to exorcise Mrs. Covington. He asked that I be there with Sky when she does it. So help!" he said sarcastically.

"What do you mean Dr. Covington visited you?" Latrice asked; her brows in surprised bows. "He's dead…"

"He was sitting in my classroom as sure and as solid as you are sitting on my lap. He told me about Mrs. Covington's condition and what to do to deliver her from evil," Ari answered.

"Were you afraid?" she asked.

"At first," Ari said, "but this was his third visit."

"Third! Why didn't you tell me?" Latrice yelped.

"What good would it have done? The first time I only heard his voice. The second time he appeared in our bedroom, and the third time was at school. I didn't want to alert you. It's not easy telling people that you've seen a ghost," said Ari.

"I'm not people. I'm your wife! Your dealings with the Tuckers have brought their brand of crazy into our home!" Latrice yelled, jumped off of his lap, and stood up. It angered her that he was being so nonchalant about everything. He was talking about ghosts and goblins and expected her to sit calmly while he was being sucked into God knows what.

"So help," Ari said again; this time with sincerity in his voice. He reached his hands out to her and she held them.

There was nothing she could say to help. She could tell him not to do it but she knew he would anyway. It was in his nature to help. Latrice hated that he was caught up in all this mess. She blamed Sadie for putting Ari in such a compromising position and Latrice was adamant about giving Sadie a piece of her mind when all this was over. Latrice sat on top of Ari's desk and crossed her legs. She asked, "What are you gonna do?"

"I guess I'm going to help get rid of the demon," Ari said in a monotone voice. Everything around him was simply draining. He regretted the moment he returned Sadie's first phone call.

"How are you going to do that?" she asked.

"I'm going to teach Sky the things Professor Covington taught me. I'm going to be there when she performs the rite. I'm going to support her and Sadie, and I'm going to pray for them without ceasing," he said standing up and walking towards Latrice. "I need you to pray for me. Pray for us all."

"When is this exorcism going to happen?" Latrice spat out the word exorcism like it was a bug in her mouth. The idea of dealing with malignant spirits was frightening to her. She wished it was a way for her to talk him out of it. *What if it possessed Ari?* She considered in her heart. *What if it followed him here?*" She thought about the potential danger to her and their children.

"I'm going to meet with Sadie and Sky tomorrow to explain things. Sky has to ready herself and go into deep meditation and fasting for at least a week, so I estimate in a week and a half, two weeks tops," he answered.

"Are you sure you want to do this? There is so much danger involved. What it that thing comes here?" Latrice asked, her eyes searching his for answers. "Please think this through."

"I have thought it through. I told Dr. Covington that I would and I am a man of my word," Ari said. "God is with us. You are the most spiritually sound woman I have ever encountered. You and the children are protected. I'm sure your prayers will ensure that. Everything will be just fine."

Latrice looked at him and turned her mouth to the side. She believed he was trying to convince himself not her.

"I don't want you to do it," Latrice said and stumped out of his home office.

Ari sat back down at his desk and continued to devise a plan of action.

55

Ari knocked three times before James opened the door. They greeted each other dryly and James escorted Ari into the backyard where Forrest, Sky, and Sadie waited at the patio table sipping ice tea. Ari pulled up a patio chair and joined them. Sadie poured him a glass of tea and he instantly started drinking. It was warm outside and Ari was mildly disappointed that their meeting was being held in the backyard and not inside the house where it was nice and cool. He should have known. Sadie was an outside person who loved warm weather. Ari on the other hand sweated in anything over seventy degrees. Ari just would have to grin and bear it. Hopefully his armpits wouldn't look like puddles soon.

"Good to see you Ari," Forrest said as he stood up and shook Ari's hand.

James sighed and sat down between Forrest and Sadie. Sadie rubbed his knee, silently asking him to behave.

"What's up?" James asked sharply. "What's so important that you had to take up time on our Saturday?"

Ari turned to Sadie and said, "Your father came to me the other day. He told me about your mother and how we can deliver her."

"Who's father?" James asked, his face twisted up.

"Sadie's," Ari replied.

"He dead!" James responded. "Get outta here wit' that!"

Forrest nodded in agreement with James. Forrest was weary of visions of Mr. Covington. All of a sudden, taking a vacation in Atlanta seemed like a big mistake.

Ari rolled his eyes upward and took another swallow of tea. He said to Sadie, "He told me how we can help your mother."

Sadie leaned forward and asked how.

"He asked me to teach Sky how to perform an exorcism," Ari replied.

"What does Sky have to do with this?" Forrest asked. "I mean no disrespect Sadie, but Sky is not in the position to help. She just came back from the hospital."

"Dr. Covington felt that she was the only one in the house spiritually stable enough to perform the rite. Let's face it, you guys aren't really godly people," Ari said taking another sip of ice tea. He fanned his *blue.math* T-shirt collar and placed the drinking glass against his forehead.

"What does that supposed to mean?" James barked. "I'm a believer in my own way. Just because I don't go to church doesn't mean I don't believe in God. You the preacher! Why didn't he ask you?"

"My intention was not to offend you James. Don't shoot the messenger," Ari retorted.

"Sky is in a delicate condition," Forrest spat. "I won't let you or a haunt put her or our unborn child in danger!"

Sky placed her hand on Forrest's back and rubbed it in a circular motion. "It's okay baby," she said.

"It's not okay!" Forrest yelled. "You will not be a part of this foolery one more day!"

"Yes I will," Sky said, her face stoic and strong. "If I am the only one strong enough to send that thing back to hell and free Mama C, I'll do it."

"Forrest is right," Sadie interrupted. "You can't put you and the baby in danger again. "It's not right."

"None of this is right!" Sky barked. "But I won't be able to live with myself if I don't try. I owe you that."

"Sky, you don't owe me anything," Sadie said, her eyes beginning to tear.

"I don't mean to break up this hallmark moment but I would like to get this over with and get back to my own life," Ari said. "My wife is livid with me. My son walks around brooding about the fight with your son. All this supernatural intervention has turned my personal peace inside out. And, it's hot out here! I don't mean to be insensitive, but we need to get down to business. There is much that I must tell you."

The women dried their eyes and prepared themselves to listen as their husbands fantasized about beating Dr. Ari Aniwodi-El six inches from death.

"What must I do," Sky asked. She touched Forrest's hand. He moved away. Sky folded her arms and gave full attention to Dr. Aniwodi-El. She would worry about Forrest later.

"First, you need to prepare yourself. Starting tomorrow, you need to fast and pray for at least a week," Ari instructed.

"Fast?" Forrest spat, his face as red as a beet. "That is out of the question to ask a pregnant woman to fast!"

"Sky," Ari called, ignoring her husband's voice. Ari didn't want to be disrespectful but he did not have the time nor the patience to pacify Forrest. "I know fasting will be difficult because of your condition so I suggest that you do a juice fast. That way you can still get key nutrients."

Sky nodded.

Forrest sneered.

"During your fast, make sure that you pray without ceasing. Ask your husband if he will watch the children for the next week. You will need all the silence and meditation time you can get," Ari said.

"Okay," Sky said.

"Take this," Ari handed her a few pieces of paper. "These are prayers and words that you can use to perform the exorcism. Get familiar with them and have complete faith in them or they will be worthless. Make sure that you free yourself of all guilt, secrets, and regrets. You do not want the demon to reveal things in your secret heart that may destroy you."

"Is that it?" Sadie asked.

"That's it," Ari answered. "The hardest thing will be keeping your mother in her room."

"Will she be hurt?" Sadie asked. "I looked up exorcism on the internet and it seemed that the people who were exorcized were in pretty bad shape. I don't want Mama to be hurt."

"Dr. Covington said that she may vomit and fill a little sick. He didn't say that she would be in danger. The internet can give a lot of misleading information. Rest assured. Your mother will be just fine. Dr. Covington said that she would need to see a doctor afterwards to ensure that there was not too much stress on her body."

Sadie unenthusiastically accepted his answer. She was not sure if she believed it, but what was the alternative at the moment? All Sadie could do was to support Sky and hope that her faith was strong enough to accomplish the goal at hand.

Sadie clandestinely damned her own stubbornness. Honestly, she had no idea why she could not reach out to the Divine. Something within her blocked her from asking for help from a God that allowed such evil to run rampant in her life. After all she had seen and experienced, she could not, would not seek God. She refused to humble herself. Like the Pharaoh in ancient Egypt, her heart was hardened.

"Sky," Forrest said. "I forbid this!" He jumped up, knocking his chair over and stormed out of the backyard.

James got up and followed behind him.

"I'm sorry to be the author of so much discord," Ari apologized.

"It's not your fault," Sadie said. "We understand that you are only here to help. In time, they will understand as well."

"I hope so," Sky sighed.

"I truly understand why Forrest is against you participating Sky. My fear is that the spirit can jump into anyone of us, even your unborn child. Are you sure you want to do this?"

Sky never thought that her baby could be affected. She rubbed her stomach and silently whispered a prayer of protection.

"Sky," Sadie called. "You don't have to do this."

"I know, but I'm going to do it anyway. God is with me. I have no doubt me and my child will be okay," Sky responded.

Ari turned to Sky and said, "I hate lying but I suggest that you go comfort your husband by speaking no more about the exorcism. Fast and pray in secret. Get them out of the house one week from today and the three of us will perform the rite."

"Okay," Sadie and Sky said in unison.

"Sadie, make sure that Sky stays focused, stress free, and prayed up. If you have vacation time, take it. You need to take care of the children while Sky is preparing herself to fight against the evil one," Ari said.

Sadie nodded.

Ari stood up and pushed his chair up to the table.

"I will see myself out. Please don't contact me this week. My wife is on edge and I will be in deep prayer asking for direction. I will see you ladies here in a week," he said. "Have a blessed night," Ari said and turned away. "I'll let myself out."

They watched him disappear inside the house.

"Are you sure you want to do this?" Sadie asked.

"No," Sky answered. "But, I'm going to do it anyway." She grabbed her friend's hand and they sat in silence engorged with fear.

Sky lifted the covers and slid into bed next to Forrest. He turned his back to her. The cold gesture startled her. There was never a time in their relationship when he was cold. Like all couples, they had spats and disagreements but they never went to bed angry and they never stopped touching.

"Forrest," Sky whispered. She wrapped her arm around him. He said nothing.

"Forrest, talk to me sweetie," she begged. She kissed his shoulders and arms. He pulled away from her.

"Don't be like that," Sky said. Her heart sank in her chest. The thought of Forrest being angry with her made her feel sick inside. "Talk to me," she begged. "Please."

"Why?" Forrest turned around. "Why should I say anything? My words hold no power with you. It doesn't matter what I say. You don't respect it."

"That's not true. I respect everything you say," Sky said.

"The hell you do! You do what you want. Damn how I feel," Forrest roared. "You're more worried about Sadie than you are about our baby."

"That's not true!" Sky yelled, hurt by Forrest's words.

"You think you owe her because of what you did a long time ago," said Forrest. He sat up. "You don't owe her anything. As far as I'm concerned, your debt was paid the minute her bad ass son put you in the hospital. What if you would've lost the baby Sky? What if you would've bled to death? Are you so dedicated to Sadie that you are willing to leave me without a wife and our children without a mother?"

Sky's eyes were stretched wide. Forrest never cussed. Never had she seen him so angry. His eyes looked dark and dangerous. His golden skin was flushed and his full lips curled against his teeth.

"What do you want me to do?" Sky asked searching his eyes. She placed her hands on the sides of his face and placed her forehead upon his. She kissed his nose. He pulled back from her, his eyes as furious as ever.

"I don't want you to get involved with anymore of their family's unnatural BS! I want us to call the airport and take the first flight out in the morning," Forrest growled. "That's what I want."

He touched her shoulder.

Sky withered under his touch. She craved to feel the warmth of his hand upon her. It made her feel as if his anger was subsiding.

"I can't leave like that," Sky said. "She's my best friend. James is your friend."

"James will understand. Trust me. He might want to leave with us!" Forrest spat.

Sky frowned at the remark. It angered her that James was getting flaky. If he left Sadie like he did when the angel first appeared eight years ago, Sky would kill him with her bare hands.

Forrest took his hand away.

"What if we just stay a little while longer? I promise you won't hear anything else about exorcism," she said.

"You promise?" Forrest asked, his eyes softening.

"I promise," Sky said as she buried her head in his chest and closed her eyes. "I love you." What Forrest didn't know would not hurt him. Dr. Aniwodi-El was right, silence was golden.

"I love you too," Forrest said as he held her close and silently thanked God that she was not going to be casting out anything but Sadie's problems.

57

Early Monday morning, Mrs. Covington was in the kitchen preparing breakfast for James and the boys when Sadie walked in wearing her bathrobe.

"Are you sick?" Mrs. Covington asked. Her left eye blinking uncontrollably and her tongue licking her lips every five seconds like a serpent smelling for food. "Why aren't you going to work?" She placed her hand on her scantily clad hip.

Mrs. Covington wore a conservative blouse but her skirt was so short that it was way above her fingertips. Red bottomed high heels were on her feet. Bright red lipstick was on her lips.

Sadie looked away from her mother in anger for she knew the angel was behind her mother's odd behavior and fashion selection.

"I'm on vacation," Sadie answered. She made herself a mug of hot Tang and sat down at the kitchen table. Moments later, Sky walked into the kitchen with her family.

"Good morning," Sadie said.

They all returned the greeting.

Earth looked at Mrs. Covington and hid behind her father's leg.

"What's wrong honey?" Forrest asked Earth as he picked her up.

"Mama C has two faces," Earth said and buried her face in her father's shoulder.

Forrest looked at Sky confused. Sky lifted and dropped her shoulders. She refused to reveal the supernatural nature of her daughter's comment. It would only anger Forrest and make him want to fly back to New York immediately.

James kissed Sadie and waved goodbye to everyone as he headed off to work.

"Did ya'll email your homework to your teachers?" Sky asked Venus and Jupiter.

"Yes," Jupiter answered as he plopped down in a chair.

Venus nodded and stood next to Khalid.   He whispered something in her ear and she laughed.   Khalid picked up his book bag and followed behind his grandmother and brother.

Mrs. Covington exited the house and walked the boys up the street. She still walked the boys to and from the bus stop daily although their parents felt uncomfortable about it. They knew that she would never harm Khalid. Khalid, although he and his brother were at odds at times, would never allow his grandmother to hurt Uriel.

"What's up for today?" Sadie asked, hoping that Sky had planned to get Forrest and the kids out of her hair so she could start her prayer and meditation.

"Forrest is taking the children to the science center and the planetarium. I'm going to stay home and relax," Sky said.

"There is bacon and eggs on the stove," Sadie told Forrest and the kids. "I know your stomach has been a little queasy so I bought juice smoothies for you Sky," Sadie said; reminding Sky of her fast.

"Your stomach is bothering you?" Forrest asked raising his eyebrow. Sky had said nothing to him about not feeling well.

"Not at the moment, but I think a light breakfast would be good for me," answered Sky.

Sadie left the kitchen and returned with her lap top. She logged on and purchased eight tickets to an amusement park for James, Forrest, and the children for Saturday. That was the best way she could think of to keep them away from the house while she, Sky, and Ari performed the exorcism. She closed her laptop and looked up at Sky.

"We should have a girl's day out on Saturday," Sadie said with one of her eyebrows raised. "I want to make sure we have a good time before you leave."

Sky agreed. She looked up at Forrest and back to Sadie. Sky really hated deceiving her husband.

"I purchased amusement park tickets for you, James, and the children," Sadie said to Forrest. "I bought an extra one for Luis so that the old crew will be back together." She smiled a crooked smile.

Forrest looked at her and Sky suspiciously.

Both women avoided his eyes. Sky fixed her children's plates. Forrest fixed his own, and sat down across from Sadie.

"Making plans a little early huh?" Forrest asked Sadie.

"Of course. I like to plan my week. Sky told me that you guys may be leaving soon, so I want to make sure Sky and I get our quality time in," Sadie said.

"I see," Forrest looked at Sky with a side eye. He had known Sadie for almost a decade and she was not a person who planned ahead for anything. She liked to see where the day took her. Something was going on.

"What are your plans for Sky?" he asked.

"Girl stuff," Sadie replied, looking at Sky for help to fan out the lie.

"We're goin' to get our feet done and goin' to the movies," Sky said.

"And dinner. You know we like to eat," Sadie said, smiling weirdly. "I'll print out the tickets for the amusement park on Friday. Luis will be excited when you tell him."

"Maybe if he didn't have to help with five children," Forrest replied as he loaded the coffee maker with instant coffee.

"He loves the kids," Sadie replied.

Sky sat quietly and listened to the exchange. She would go on with the plan behind Forrest's back but she did not want to technically lie using her words. It was best for her to keep quiet. Sky being quiet was like having a hurricane in midland America. It just wasn't natural. Forrest took note of her silence and was reassured that something was definitely going on.

Every Thursday Uriel's teacher gave the class a spelling test and every Thursday Uriel ran into the house with an A to show his mother. That A meant everything to Uriel because spelling was the only subject that he excelled in. He was an extremely intelligent child but sometimes school was a struggle for him. He received average grades with above average effort.

"Look Ma!" he squealed as he handed her his paper. "I got 100%!"

Sadie kissed him on the cheek and said, "Good job Uriel. I'm so proud of you."

"Thanks Mom!" he exclaimed and ran upstairs to change out of his school clothes. Khalid came into the room.

"I got an A on my spelling test," Uriel said as he pulled on a T-shirt.

"You always get an A in spelling," Khalid snapped. "Get an A in something else and then I'll be excited for you."

"Why're you being so mean?" Uriel whined.

"Because you think you're stronger than me!" Khalid barked.

"No I don't," Uriel said. "I'm just not afraid of you anymore because I know God is with me."

"Whatever!" Khalid growled. "What does God have to do with this?"

"Everything. God gave me to Mom and Dad so that I can help with you," said Uriel. He sat upon the top bunk with his legs swinging; his eyes wide and innocent.

"I don't know what you're talking about," Khalid admitted.

"You're special. I'm special too. I'm a superhero and you're a villain. We're like Batman and the Joker," Uriel laughed.

"Where do you get this stuff from?" Khalid laughed.

"God," Uriel said, still smiling.

Khalid's smile faded. There was nothing amusing about his brother being preordained to be his enemy. Something deep within Khalid knew that it was true. Uriel was born to be a thorn in Khalid's side. He knew their battles had only just begun.

Sky lay prostrate in the center of her bedroom with lips trembling in prayer. Red hair clung to her sweaty face as she raised her eyes in exaltation. She called upon the name of the Lord in a desperate whisper and asked for strength to cast out Turiel. Her thin freckled fingers grabbed hold of the carpet as her soul groaned. The child in her womb rumbled like fierce thunder. She ignored his aggression and kept her spirit focused on God. Tears streamed from her face as she paused from her supplications to wait for an answer. There was not one. Sky assumed that this is what Jesus must have felt like at in the garden when he asked God to remove the bitter cup of death and God said nothing. Sky banished those thoughts from her mind and kept praying.

Tomorrow she would challenge the fallen angel face to face. She confessed her sins and extended her forgiveness to all who had ever wronged her. Her stomach churned within her body, aching for food. Weak and humbled before God, Sky pulled herself to her feet and sat upon the bed softly so that she would not wake her sleeping husband. She cuddled up beside him, laying her head upon his chest.

She looked at Forrest and whispered an apology for deceiving him as he slumbered. Sky stood up and made her way into the kitchen for her midnight snack. As she walked through the house, she saw Khalid and his grandmother talking in the hallway. Fear grabbed hold of Sky.

They looked at her with darkened eyes and wretched smiles. Mrs. Covington stood behind Khalid with her hands on his shoulders like a hovering shadow.

"Up late again?" Khalid hissed.

Sky stepped backwards, her hand on her belly.

"Don't worry. I'm not going to bother you," Khalid said. "If I wanted to kill you, I would have already."

"*I know why you're here,*" Turiel said from Mrs. Covington's mouth. *She stepped from behind Khalid and slowly approached Sky.*

The sound of another voice coming from Mrs. Covington's mouth made Sky back away quickly and make a run for the basement door, but before her hand could hit the knob, Mrs. Covington appeared in front of the door. Sky stumbled backwards but kept her footing.

Turiel said, "*You don't have the power to drive me out. The might of your life-force is minute in the minutia of your pitiful existence. You laughable wretched dog! I dare you try to contend with me!*" *Turiel grabbed Sky by the neck and began to squeeze.*

"Sky!" Forrest yelled as he shook his flailing wife from her nightmare. "Sky!"

Sky opened her eyes and sat up. It was difficult for her to catch her breath. Her head swooned. She touched her throat. It was sore to the touch. The choking hands in her dream felt real. Too real.

"Are you okay?" Forrest asked.

Sky did not answer. She buried her head in her husband's chest and dreaded the coming day.

"I packed lunches for everyone," Sadie said as she put the last sandwich in a large backpack. "You all can buy drinks there. I made almond butter and jelly so you don't have to worry about the food going bad. There are apple and okra chips in the bag also."

Venus and Jupiter twisted their faces when they heard okra chips.

"What's that?" Earth asked Venus.

"It's a vegetable that tastes like snot," she answered.

"Mom, we're buying food there," Khalid said. "Right Dad?"

James nodded.

Sadie handed the backpack of sandwiches to James anyway and said, "Well, eat it in the car."

"I'll take it," Luis said. "I love your sandwiches Sadie," he cooed as he gave her a wicked smile and winked.

Sadie laughed. It always tickled her when Luis flirted.

"Don't make me put my foot in yo..." James started before Sadie put her hand over his mouth.

Everyone laughed.

"Have a good time," Mrs. Covington said pacing around in a circle like a dog chasing his tale.

Looking at her made Sadie's nerves bad. She could not wait to get her mother back to normal.

"What are you going to do Grandma?" Khalid asked.

"She's going to stay and have a girl's day with us," Sadie said before Mrs. Covington could answer.

Mrs. Covington frowned.

"I'm ready to go!" Venus snapped. She grabbed Khalid's arm and led him to the door.

"Me too," said Jupiter as he and Earth followed behind them.

"Let's roll," James said. Everyone who was going to the amusement park moved towards the door except for Uriel.

"What's wrong?" Sadie asked Uriel as he leaned against the counter.

"All of a sudden I don't feel so good," he said.

"What's wrong?" Sadie asked again, panicking because Uriel may have to stay home. She did not want him in the house when they performed the exorcism.

"I don't know," he confessed. "I just feel really bad. I want to go back to bed."

Sadie looked at Sky.

Sky took Uriel's hand and asked, "Are you sure? Maybe you'll feel better in a little while. I'm sure you don't wanna miss going to the fun park."

Uriel looked up at his mother with unwell eyes. He said, "I want to go but I can't. I don't want to mess up you and Auntie Sky's day. I promise I'll stay in the bed."

"Okay," Sadie unwillingly agreed. "Go to bed."

"We'll miss you Uriel," Earth said.

Uriel smiled faintly and left the kitchen.

"Have a great time," Sky said as she kissed her family.

Sadie kissed James and hugged Khalid.

Mrs. Covington went off to her room.

"Bye," Sadie waved as they all walked out of the door. She locked the door behind them and spun around to Sky.

"What are we going to do about Uriel?" Sadie asked.

"We have to keep him in his room," Sky said. "Ari will be here in an hour. We have to focus."

"You're right. Go downstairs and pray. I'll gather the towels and a bucket. I bought a bible and a cross. Do you think that will help?"

"It couldn't hurt," Sky said as she lifted her shoulders. "Bring them in the room when we're ready."

Ari arrived around noon. Sadie and Sky greeted him stoically, and escorted him to the dining room. They all sat down around the table like the Justice League plotting to destroy a super villain.

"How are you feeling?" Ari asked Sky. "Are you ready?"

"As ready as I will ever be," Sky answered, swallowing hard. She rubbed her belly and leaned back against her seat.

"Good. Let's join hands in prayer," Ari suggested.

The three joined hands and bowed their heads. Sadie tried hard to keep her eyes closed but was unsuccessful. Prayer was always difficult for her.

Ari prayed for protection and success. He asked that Mrs. Covington be delivered and the angel driven out of her. The prayer was short and powerful. They all said amen, and headed up to Mrs. Covington's room.

Sadie knocked on the door.

"Mom," she called.

"Come in," Mrs. Covington answered.

Sadie opened the door and slowly entered. She prayed that the nervous look on her face didn't betray her. The last thing she wanted to do was to make her mother suspicious.

Sky and Ari followed close behind. Ari locked the door behind him. Mrs. Covington raised an eyebrow when she saw him twist the lock.

"Mom, we need to talk to you," Sadie said. She sat down next to her mother on the bed. Sadie held her mother's hand, and kissed it gently. In that moment, Mrs. Covington was simply the loving and nurturing woman that reared Sadie; not a vessel for Turiel to wreak havoc on her household.

Mrs. Covington wore an intricately patterned dashiki with matching slippers. She looked at Sadie with curiosity.

Sadie rarely wore blue jeans and T-shirts; especially baggy jeans and old faded T-shirts. It was strange for Sadie to be dressed in that manner. Her friends were dressed similarly.

"About?" Mrs. Covington asked, searching Sadie's eyes for an answer.

"May I?" Ari asked Sadie. He stepped forward.

Sadie nodded.

"Mrs. Covington, Sadie came to me because she felt that you had not been yourself lately. Your daughter is worried about you," said Ari as he placed the folded towels on the table and sat the bucket upon the floor.

"Why would she come to you? You are not a part of this family," Mrs. Covington said, annoyed by an outsider interfering in family business. "There's no reason to worry," Mrs. Covington continued, watching Dr. Aniwodi-El carefully. The sight of towels and a bucket unnerved her.

"I think there is," Ari said. "Sky, come here."

Sky stood next to Ari.

Sadie kissed her mother on the cheek, and moved away from her. Sadie stood in front of the door; agitatedly fiddling with her hands, and shuffling her feet from side to side. She prayed that after all of this was over, her mother would not be angry with her. That Mrs. Covington would understand.

"What's the matter with you?" Mrs. Covington asked Sadie, quickly becoming aware that something fishy was going on.

"Are you ready?" Ari asked Sky. He squeezed her hand offering support.

Sky nodded nervously.

Sky stepped in front of Mrs. Covington and belted with her hands held high, "In the name of God Almighty, I ask for the power to bind Turiel!" The words that she was given to study quickly slipped from her memory. Sky looked to Ari for help but he seemed unaware of her predicament. She decided to go from the top of her head. Sky continued, "Jesus. I mean God. Umm, Lord. The power of the Holy Spirit, bind the angel Turiel which is indwelling Mama C."

Mrs. Covington fell backwards on the bed. Her body started to convulse, then she fell still as if dead.

Sky felt a little more confident. She stepped closer to Mrs. Covington and continued, "In the name of the only true and wise God, I command Turiel to get out!"

Mrs. Covington sprang up, the skin of her face so tight around her skull that it looked like it was tied behind her head. Her eyes were burning gold fireballs. Turiel's voice rumbled from her throat, "You have no power over me red one!"

Sky stepped back. The sight of fire burning from Mrs. Covington's eye sockets almost stopped Sky's heart. She yelled, "Lord God..."

"God does not live here. I do!" Turiel cackled from Mrs. Covington's throat.

"I command you to...to...to..." Sky stammered. Her legs threatened to give away. The baby in her womb beat against her belly with flailing fists.

"Shut-up you dog! You have no dominion over me. Your heart betrays you baby killer!" Turiel roared.

"I killed no baby!" Sky yelled into Mrs. Covington's face. Tears streamed down Sky's eyes. "I was trying to save Sadie from you!"

"Ahahahahahaha," Turiel laughed. "From me? Are you sure you didn't desire Sadie for yourself?"

Sky was taken aback by the accusation. There was nothing perverse about her love for Sadie.

"I dare you! You evil bastard!" Sky screamed, her face so red that it looked like it was going to pop off of her shoulders. "Sadie is my friend!" Sky slapped Mrs. Covington hard across the face.

Sadie closed her eyes. The sight of seeing her mother being struck pained her to the core.

"Don't talk back to him!" Ari screamed, grabbing Sky's arm. She snatched her arm away from Ari; her anger elevating by the second.

Ari warned, "He's trying to pull you in."

Sky closed her eyes and took a deep breath. Turiel's laugh echoing through the room made Sky want to kill him with her bare hands but she knew that it would not be his body that she would be harming but Mrs. Covington's.

Sky began again with a voice trembling in anger. "Lord God, please bind the evil spirit Turiel. Cast him out of Ebbie Covington!"

"That's facetious!" Turiel cackled as Mrs. Covington stood up and lumbered towards Sky. Mrs. Covington's body moved in ticking motions almost as it she was a pop locker.

"You're confidence is nonexistent." Mrs. Covington grabbed Sky's neck and squeezed.

Sadie grabbed her mother's arms, but was back slapped across the room. Sadie hit the wall so hard that she knocked a hole in the sheet rock.

Ari tried to pull Sky free. Mrs. Covington let go of Sky. She dropped to the ground clutching her throat, thankful that she did not fall forward onto her belly.

Mrs. Covington pushed Ari to the floor and stepped on his chest, her slipper pressing hard on his ribcage. He tried to twist her foot, but it was like a stone pillar; it could not be moved. She cut off his air supply. His hands fell to the side and his eyes closed.

Sadie pushed herself up off the floor; her shoulder and back in excruciating pain. She looked at Ari's body lying on the floor in a crumbled heap, then at Sky choking and gasping for breath. Sadie rushed over to her mother, as fast as her aching body could carry her. Sadie shoved Mrs. Covington upon the bed and helped Sky to her feet.

"G...G...God help us," Sky huffed holding her neck. "In the name of Jesus, I..." Sky fainted and fell limply to the floor.

"Sky," Sadie cried. She shook her friend. "Sky, please wake up!"

At that moment, Sadie wished she had read the prayers of exorcism. Maybe she could finish the rite; finish the fight. But she had not read them, nor did she have faith in the God that gave the prayers power, so again, she was trapped in a room with Turiel, helpless and easy prey.

Mrs. Covington sat upon the bed with a twisted smile on her face. Turiel's voice echoed from her mouth, "Sadie, it has always been you. My love has always been unrequited. If only you would submit to my will, our family could rule this earth."

"We have no family!" Sadie screamed. She looked up at the ceiling and wailed, "God, if you exist, get him out of here!"

Turiel laughed at Sadie. Her lack of faith seemed to make him more powerful. Mrs. Covington stood up on the bed and stretched her hands up in the air. A pale light shined from her eyes. The smell of myrrh filled the room.

Sadie recoiled from her mother. The thought of Turiel touching her with her mother's body sickened her. Sadie tried to resuscitate Sky. Sky was the only hope to cast out the demon.

A loud inhaling noise grabbed Sadie's attention. She turned to look. Ari had regained consciousness and rolled onto his side. Holding his aching chest, he crawled over to Sadie and Sky. He placed his hand on Sky's neck to make sure that she was still breathing and that her heart was still beating.

"Wake up Sky," Ari's voice cracked. Blood started to trickle from Ari's nose. He wiped it on the back of his arm, and fell back on his behind.

"Sky," Ari croaked. He pulled her head onto his lap and brushed her wild red hair from her face. "Please wake up."

Sky opened her eyes.

Mrs. Covington reached down and grabbed Sadie by the arm. Sadie struggled like a bug caught in a web. Her legs dangled in midair.

"Let me go!" Sadie screamed. She scratched her mother's face and bit down on her hand.

"It is not my flesh that you mar but your mother's. Be careful my love," Turiel cackled. Mrs. Covington showered Sadie's hand with kisses. Each kiss made Sadie's flesh fill like a hundred cockroaches was crawling all over her body. Mrs. Covington tried to kiss Sadie's mouth but Sadie punched her mother so hard that Mrs. Covington loosened her grasp. Sadie dropped to the floor and ran over to Sky.

"Sky! Please send him away!" Sadie begged.

Sky sat up and leaned against Ari.

Boom Boom Boom Mrs. Covington's door shook under the force of the knock. Everyone, including Mrs. Covington, turned towards the door.

Sadie opened the door not expecting to see Uriel on the other side.

"What's going on?" Uriel asked; his eyes taking in his mother's bruised body, his Auntie Sky sitting on the floor, and Dr. Aniwodi-El's bloody face.

"Get out of here!" Sadie yelled to her son. "You can't be here!" She tried to push him backwards but his feet were glued to the floor.

Sky turned to Mrs. Covington and screamed, "I banish you Turiel!"

Mrs. Covington flew off of the bed and hovered over Sky. Light shined through Mrs. Covington's eyes, nostrils, and mouth. Mrs. Covington lifted her foot to crush Sky's face when Uriel grabbed Mrs. Covington by the leg and pulled his grandmother to the floor. He pounced upon her chest and held her down.

"By the power of God and in the name of his messiah Yeshua- Jesus the Christ, I bind you! Speak your name demon!" Uriel commanded, his hand pressed hard against Mrs. Covington's forehead, planting her to the floor.

"Turiel," Mrs. Covington mumbled as she lay helplessly upon the floor like her body was bound by invisible ropes.

"Turiel, I cast you out of my grandmother. In the name of God I command you to leave her body and never return!" Uriel said as he stood over his grandmother.

Mrs. Covington started to gag. She retched upon the floor. Uriel stepped backwards. Vomit covered her arms and chest as it poured from her throat like a fetid fountain. As her mouth opened, bright light poured from her mouth like a liquid laser. She heaved until her chest folded in upon itself. She fell flaccid.

The light took form. Turiel materialized in his full glory, his beautiful face twisted in anger, his massive wings stretching across the room like two circus tents. He levitated above Mrs. Covington's head like the angel of death.

"Leave this house demon!" Uriel commanded, his baby face beaming with power.

Turiel screeched and was no more.

They all stared dumbfounded at the emptiness. The angel was gone. Nothing lingered. Not even his scent.

Uriel was the first to pull his eyes away and look down upon his grandmother's withered body.

"Grandma!" Uriel cried. "Grandma, are you okay?"

Mrs. Covington could barely open her eyes.

Sadie, Ari, and Sky gathered around Mrs. Covington.

"Mom, talk to me," Sadie cried. She held her mother's hand, kissing it every second.

Mrs. Covington looked off into the corner of the room. A smile curled her mouth.

"Mama!" Sadie cried. "Say something!"

Mrs. Covington lost consciousness and came to.

"Mama," Sadie cried out. "Someone call 911!"

Ari pulled his cell phone from his pocket and called.

Mrs. Covington looked into Sadie's eyes and smiled. She whispered, "I'm so sorry baby. Please forgive me." She coughed.

"Oh Mama, there is nothing to forgive. It was not your fault," Sadie wailed. "I love you so much."

"And I love you," Mrs. Covington mouthed. She looked back into the corner of the room and reached out.

Sadie looked over into the corner. There was nothing there. She turned back to her mother. Terror filled Sadie's face. Her mother looked so feeble and broken-down.

"Carlos," Mrs. Covington whispered; her eyes fixed pass Sadie. Her face returned to its natural beauty like before Turiel possessed her. Her ebony skin was smooth and radiant. Her features delicate, yet strong.

Sky and Ari looked over into the corner and saw Mr. Covington standing there as clear as day. As he walked over to his wife, she sat up and held her arms up to receive him.

Mr. Covington grabbed her hand and they embraced. They walked hand in hand into the corner of the room and disappeared.

Tears fell from Sky's and Ari's eyes as they watched the loving couple fade away.

Sadie only saw her mother's eyes go blank as she lay within Sadie's arms. Sadie nor Uriel possessed the gift of sight. All they saw was Mrs. Covington breathing her last.

"Mama!" Sadie screamed. Mrs. Covington's dead body rested within Sadie's arms. "Mama!" Sadie cried. "Wake up!"

"She's gone," Sky said as she wrapped her arms around Sadie.

Sadie's body rocked with pain. Her sobs could not be contained within the walls of the room. They echoed through the house and seeped through the cracks into the outside world.

Sadie pulled away from Sky and screamed at Ari, "You said she would be safe! You lied to me!"

Ari tried to touch Sadie's shoulder but she slapped his hand away. He said, "I'm so sorry."

Sadie wanted so badly to blame Ari for all that had happened but she knew it was not his fault. She looked down at her mother.

"Mama!" Primal groans escaped Sadie's lips as she showered her mother's lifeless face with kisses. "How can I live without you?" Sadie rocked her mother back and forth.

"Grandma's dead?" Uriel cried hysterically.

Ari escorted the boy from the room as Sadie wailed over the body of her beautiful mother. Sky held her friend as she howled until the walls vibrated under the force of her screams.

James, Forrest, and the children returned to the house around six 'o clock in the evening. The house was eerily quiet when they walked in the door.

"We're home!" James called through the house.

Forrest and his children went down into the basement to relax while Khalid ran straight to his grandmother's room to tell her about the great time that he had. When he arrived at her room, the door was wide open and empty. Her room was torn asunder and there was vomit everywhere. A horrible feeling swirled around in his stomach. There was something terribly wrong. He walked to his parent's bedroom and that door was open and that room empty as well. He went into his bedroom. Uriel was lying upon his bed crying uncontrollably.

"What's wrong?" Khalid asked.

"Sh...sh...she's gone," Uriel cried.

"Who?" Khalid asked.

Uriel's cries only became louder. Khalid left the room and ran into to the den where he found his mother, her eyes swollen shut from crying, and Sky rocking Sadie in her arms.

"What's wrong?" Khalid asked, tears began to form in his eyes. He knew whatever it was, it was bad. Very bad.

"Go get your father," Sky told Khalid.

"What's wrong? Where's grandma?" Khalid asked, his eyes darting back and forth from Sadie to Sky.

"Go get your father and my husband. Tell Forrest to leave the children downstairs," Sky said in a forceful tone, her eyes revealing her pain. "Now."

Khalid ran to get James and Forrest. Both men followed him back into the den.

"What's going on?" James asked, he pulled Sadie from Sky's arms and cradled Sadie in his own. "What's wrong baby?"

Sadie mewled like a wounded animal. She had become undone.

"Sky?" James looked at Sky with pleading eyes. Never had he seen Sadie so utterly broken.

"I think Khalid should leave the room," Sky suggested.

"Mama," Sadie cried. "Mama," she repeated like it was a curse upon her tongue.

"No! I'm not going anywhere!" Khalid snapped. "Where's grandma!"

"Sky, what happened?" Forrest asked.

"Mama C died," Sky cried.

"What? Where is she?" Forrest asked. He grabbed Sky's hand to comfort her.

"The coroner came to get her hours ago," Sky said, her voice soft and robotic. She felt dead inside.

"What did you do to her?" Khalid screamed! He charged at Sky but Forrest caught him by the arm and slung him onto a chair. Forrest looked at James and James nodded his approval.

"Come here son," James said as he reached out his hand to Khalid.

"No!" Khalid yelled.

"She had a heart attack," Sky mumbled, unfazed by Khalid's outburst.

"Lies!" Khalid cried and ran out of the den into his room. His weeping echoed through the house as he fled.

"I'm so sorry Sadie," Forrest said.

His words fell on deaf ears. Sadie's wails drowned them out. James held her and rocked her in his arms. His tears joined hers as he held her tight.

"Is there anything I can do James?" Forrest asked.

"No," James replied. "I'll take care of Sadie and the boys. You take care of Sky."

"Let's go to bed baby," Forrest told Sky.

Sky looked up at Forrest and opened her mouth to speak but fainted on the sofa.

Forrest lifted his pregnant wife up in his arms and carried her out of the room.

The church was filled with people of every creed and color. They filed down the aisle to lay their eyes on a woman they all loved and admired. Video screens flashed with pictures of Mrs. Covington's life. Happy times and fond memories filled the hearts of all who watched.

Ebbie Covington rested in her shiny mahogany casket in a champagne colored silk dress with champagne pearls. Her makeup was impeccable and so was her raven hair. She looked so peaceful that many people said she looked like she was sleeping.

Dr. Ari Aniwodi-El officiated the funeral. He spoke about her love of family and all of her accomplishments. He was careful not to use religious terms because she would not have approved. The family wanted the service to truly represent Mrs. Covington. The only reason it was being held in a church was because Ari insisted on taking care of the funeral arrangements and service free of charge.

The service was eloquent and beautiful just like Mrs. Covington. Flowers filled the entire front of the church. Every pew was filled with mourners. The music was soulful and tasteful. Everyone cried and smiled at the same time. After the service, everyone made their way to the gravesite. The funeral procession was so long that it held up traffic for an hour.

The immediate family surrounded the casket. James put his hands on his boys' shoulders and stood close to his wife. Forrest and Sky were bookends to their children. Luis and his fiancé' stood near the family as Dr. Aniwodi-El said a few last words.

Every funeral Sadie had ever attended had been on a windy day and her mother's funeral was no exception. Sadie always felt that the wind carried spirits away from the earth. She wondered which wind her mother would ride as the wind blew against the funeral tent. Sadie watched the casket being lowered into the ground. Everything seemed so unreal. Sadie was an orphan. It seemed impossible that her mother was the one resting in the shiny box that was slowly disappearing in the earth. Sadie let out a powerful whimper. James grabbed her by the shoulders and cuddled her close.

"Ashes to ashes and dust to dust, I send Ebbie Covington's body back to the earth," Dr. Aniwodi-El said. "May she rest in peace forever more."

When everyone returned home from the funeral, Khalid ran straight to his bedroom and locked the door. He did not want to take part in the repast. There were too many people that were coming and he was not in the mood to see any of them. As far as he was concerned, they all could drop dead.

Khalid tore off his suit and fell to the floor weeping. His heart felt like broken glass within his ribcage. His head felt like it was about to explode.

"Grandma..." he wailed, the carpet drinking his tears like thirsty earth. His body shook as he sobbed. He laid there for an hour before he got up, eyes black as pitch.

"Father!" he yelled to the top of his lungs. "You took her from me! Now I am alone. You promised to never forsake me!"

The room echoed his cries.

"Where are you?" Khalid yelled up to the ceiling. Nothing acknowledged his howls. His existence was privy to none but him.

"Where are you?" Khalid wept, falling onto his bed in the fetal position. His eyes turned back brown and for a moment in time he was not a Nephilim, a freak of nature, a genius, a villain, a brother, a son. He was just a little boy.

The airport was packed. Forrest and James pulled the luggage out of the trunk as Sadie helped Sky and her children get out of the car.

"I'm going to miss you so much," Sadie said as she hugged Sky tight. "Thank you so much for everything. I am so grateful to you. You have been more of a friend than I could ever deserve."

"I'm going to miss you too," Sky responded. She hugged Sadie back. "You are my sister."

"I love you so much Sky. No one in the world would have done for me what you have done. Not even my husband," Sadie whispered with a laugh. Sadly, she knew it was true. James would have never gone to battle with Turiel.

Sky laughed too. "That's what friends are for," she said. "I'll call you as soon as we touch down."

Sadie let her go and stepped backwards. She gave Jupiter a hug, then Venus, then Earth.

"I'm going to miss you guys too. I can't wait to come visit you all in New York," Sadie said. "Make sure ya'll keep in touch with the boys. They really enjoyed having you here."

Uriel nodded, agreeing that he will miss them. He hugged Earth and Venus, and shook Jupiter's hand.

Earth whispered into Uriel's ear, "Your grandpa and grandma are gone. Now you have to take care of your mama. Protect her from him." She pulled back and looked at Khalid. Earth ran behind her father's leg and hid her face.

Uriel looked at his brother then back at Earth. She nodded.

Venus and Khalid hugged and exchanged phone numbers.

Jupiter shook Khalid's hand.

Sky kissed Uriel on the cheek and gave Khalid a false smile. She could not bring herself to hug someone who tried to take the life of her unborn child.

"It's 'bout that time," James said as he extended his hand to Forrest. Forrest accepted it and pulled James in for a hug. The two men embraced and let go rather quickly.

"Thank you for your hospitality," Forrest said. "Despite everything, it was good seeing you."

"You too man. I'm sorry for all the chaos. It was out of our control. I appreciate you hanging in there," said James.

Forrest found no words to say. He was ready to go home; far far away from Atlanta and its demons.

"Get home safe. Make sure you keep in touch," James said, hoping that Forrest would. James would not fault Forrest if he did not, but James really hoped that Forrest would keep in touch. "We can't let years pass again."

"Okay," Forrest said. He smiled and turned to Sky. "You ready to go babe?"

"I am," she waddled over to him. "Come on ya'll," she called to the children. "Let's go."

The Cohen family disappeared into the busy airport as the Tucker family stood and watched.

Sadie turned to James and they mourned the departure of their friends. The Tuckers climbed back into their car and left the airport behind them.

65

"I'm really going to miss Earth and Jupiter," Uriel said as he pulled on his pajama pants and climbed up in his bed.

"I guess," Khalid replied. "Venus was the coolest. She's the one I'm going to miss."

"You liked her didn't you?" Uriel asked.

"Yeah," Khalid replied.

"Better than Evadne?" Uriel asked as he pulled his blanket up to his chest.

Khalid had to think on that. Evadne would always be the one who got away, but Venus was a pretty cool replacement.

"I guess," Khalid replied. "Venus is cool."

"She should be your girlfriend," Uriel giggled.

"Shut up and go to sleep," Khalid said as he threw a stuffed football at Uriel.

Uriel blocked the football and pulled the cover over his head.

Khalid finished putting on his pajamas and turned off the light.

"I'm glad we're friends again," Uriel said.

"We don't have to be friends. We're brothers. That's forever," Khalid said.

Uriel jumped off of the top bunk and grabbed his brother. He hugged Khalid as tight as his small arms allowed him too.

"I love you," Uriel said.

Khalid hugged Uriel back then mushed his face.

"Get off me!" Khalid laughed. "You're too soft."

Uriel laughed and climbed back up in his bed.

"Goodnight Uriel. I love you too," Khalid mumbled, unsure of what the future may hold for the two of them.

"Goodnight Khalid," Uriel responded, smiling. That was the first time he ever heard Khalid say I love you.

In the dark room, the two boys drifted off to sleep to the sound of each other's breathing. Starlight shined through the room casting a faint glow through the window. Two golden eyes shined in the corner of the room.

"Goodnight my son."

97322965R00153

Made in the USA
Columbia, SC
14 June 2018